Stronger Than Mountains

LYNN DEAN

Lynn Dean

ISBN: 1546611908
ISBN-13: 978-1546611905

FOR MAMA

Who taught me to play games with words
and wrote down my first stories,
who made me believe that I could be a writer,
and who introduced me to God.

Happy Mother's Day

I love you

IN APPRECIATION

It takes more than one person to write a book! So many people have encouraged me along the journey. There's always the fear of leaving someone out, but to all and to these I am deeply grateful:

To my husband, Tom, for his support and genuine interest and for talking through ideas.

To my daughter, Katelyn, and my son, David, who are world's greatest cheering section.

To my mom, who wrote down the first story I ever dreamed up. (*Lumpity-Bumpity Bear*, if you're interested--a rollicking tale of acorns stolen and then recovered.) She and my sister have patiently listened to each new chapter.

To Melinda Evaul, who has read and re-read chapters, offering suggestions to make them better.

To Anne Skrabanek, my information source for all things bovine.

Dr. and Mrs. J. Rush Pierce for a delightful afternoon and a great education in the lore of the Red River and Moreno valleys. Their publications (*Mountain Wildflowers of Northern New Mexico*, *Red River Mining District Gold Mines*, *Historic Buildings in Red River City*, and *The Big Ditch*) were invaluable resources.

The Mutz family who own and operate the Elizabethtown Museum at the site of the old town.

And to my first readers, who cheered me on, caught typos, and laughed in all the right places.

For the mountains shall depart, and the hills be removed;
but my kindness shall not depart from thee,
neither shall the covenant of my peace be removed,
saith the LORD that hath mercy on thee.

Isaiah 54:10

Chapter 1
Slim Pickens Ranch
Moreno Valley, New Mexico

Eyes wide, fingers rigid, Millie Pickens clutched the quilt below her chin, listening. The sound that awakened her was now lost on the other side of the boundary between sleep and consciousness. She exhaled soundlessly, her breath forming a cloud in the lean-to.

A faint pink glow tinged the frost on the windowpanes. She lay quiet, listening, drinking in the silence as her heartbeat returned to its normal rhythm. The few precious moments of peace before the late winter sunrise were almost enough to make its bitter cold worth enduring.

Zeke lay still beside her, jaw lax, mouth agape. Millie stretched her toes closer to his sleeping form, soaking in the warmth that radiated from his body. Most days he was up before the sun, but for a few weeks each year before calving season there was a blessed respite. Feathers rustled beneath her ear as she turned her head to study his profile in the pale light.

Despite the stubble he was still a handsome man, though the years had left their mark. His face had lost its boyish eagerness in exchange for a few wrinkles. The creases gave him character, but she missed the lopsided grin he always wore when they were young. One teasing glance—one wink—used to make her knees go wobbly. The twinkle in his eye explained the four young 'uns asleep in the loft . . . and the four young 'uns explained her gratitude for this moment of peace.

There should have been two more, but maybe the Lord knew she had all she could handle. The four she had would be up soon enough, clamoring for breakfast. Then their needs along with the duties of home and farm would claim pieces of her all day long until she collapsed onto the straw tick again tonight. She loved them, but mothering was like being nipped to death by tadpoles.

This one moment, though—this was hers alone.

With a snort Zeke stirred to life, shivered, and clawed for a larger share of the covers. "Laws a' mercy, it's cold in here!"

Just one moment—precious, brief . . . and over. Millie sighed. "I'll stir the fire."

She rolled to her side, but Zeke's arms pulled her back. "Come here, woman. I got a better idea for keeping us warm."

The twinkle was still there. Maybe two could share one moment . . .

The sudden unmistakable patter of water on the tin roof dampened any flame Zeke was trying to kindle. *Rain?*

Scuffling feet produced a downpour of dust through the boards of the ceiling that formed the floor of the loft above. "Jackson! Shut that window before we all freeze." Beau, their eldest, considered it his duty to keep order.

The moment definitely over, at least now she had a clue about the sound that woke her.

"Ew! Jackson! As if it ain't bad enough I got to share loft space with you . . . Ma!"

The shrill voice of her daughter shredded what remained of Millie's peace. Dixie Lee dressed like her older brothers, rode and roped—even talked like them. She'd soon be eleven, though. She'd need more privacy than a blanket hung over a rope to divide the attic. The girl needed a room of her own. Soon as the weather got fine

Millie'd talk to Zeke about building one, but when would he find the time?

"If you insist upon living in the manner of beasts, I suggest you move to the barn." Forrest, her second born, weighed in with a plea for the culture and decorum he craved.

"Don't tell me what to do!" Jackson, their third, nurtured a deep resentment that he hadn't been born first. "It's too cold to run out to the outhouse every blasted time."

"Ma!"

Another shower of dirt poured through the ceiling, and boots scraped against the rungs of the ladder before the window slammed shut.

"Ma!"

Millie groaned and shrugged out of Zeke's grasp. "The fruit of your loins . . ." She didn't even try to conceal the undertone of accusation as she shoved her feet out from beneath the warm covers. "I'll poke the fire. You draw water."

"Aw, girl, spare me time for a kiss at least. Just one." Her husband sat up in the bed and puckered.

Millie rose to oblige him with a peck.

Her stomach lurched. Frantic, she shoved him away and gulped against familiar spasms.

Zeke stretched, rubbed his shoulder, and scratched before it dawned on him that something was wrong. His forehead furrowed. "Are you sick?"

She shook her head. Not sick . . . at least, not ill.

Eyes wide, she clapped a hand over her mouth and fled barefoot into the snow.

Chapter 2
Bitter Creek
Red River Valley, New Mexico

The wind kicked up out of the west, knocking a hailstorm of pinecones onto the roof, but it was the scrabble and scrape of boots down the sloping shakes that sent Eliza Craig flying out the cabin door still clutching her dishtowel.

"Jake? You all right up there?" She wrung the towel as she craned her neck to look up, blinking against a shower of ice and pine needles.

The scraping sounds seemed to end where the roof changed pitch above the porch.

Tense seconds passed before Jake's answer filtered down with the last of the debris. "I'm fine."

Eliza glanced toward the western ridge and scowled at the darkening sky. "How much longer will you be at it, do you reckon?"

"Not much longer." A snicker drifted down, betraying his amusement at her Southern accent—an old joke between them. It always seemed worse when she was stressed or tired. Today she was both. The hammering started again. "Gotta fix these leaks before the next storm hits."

"Well don't fall off'a there." She shivered and wrapped her arms around herself to keep warm.

He laughed. "If I do, it'll be into one of those snow banks."

The snow mounded nearly to the eaves. An unusually cold winter had laid a deep base of snow in the Red River valley. The snowfalls continued well into the spring, piling several inches of powder in drifts around the cabin. She'd hoped by this late in April they'd have seen the last of it for the year. A few bright days had teased her into optimism, but the gray clouds heaping up above the mountain peaks promised more inclement weather by sunset.

Eliza sighed and walked back into the snug cabin. "Adam, have you finished your schoolwork for today?"

The boy nodded, earnest green eyes confirming the truth of his answer.

"Then maybe your Pa could use a hand to save him climbing up and down the log ends."

The thirteen-year-old shot out of his chair and was halfway out the front door before she could yell, "Coat!" He skidded to a halt, snatched a buckskin jacket off a peg, and slammed the door behind him without ever looking back.

Twelve-year-old Beth gazed up at her, eyes full of hope.

"Grammar done?"

Her face scrunched up as she assayed the papers spread out on the table in front of her. "Near enough?"

It was hard to tell if her reply was an answer or a wish. A wish, most likely, but Eliza decided to grant it. There was always tomorrow. "Here. Dice up these carrots and onions while I get the meat."

Beth brightened. During the winter the short days were bearable, but when the mountain cold lasted into spring the days became long and tedious. Even chores offered diversion.

On days like today, Eliza missed her Texas bluebonnets, and she'd gladly accept the heat, tornadoes, and torrential rains that came with them. She opened the door to the lean-to and shut it quickly behind her to stop the draft. This room was always cold, the better to keep the stores of meat Jake cured and laid up. She waited for her eyes to adjust to the dim light that filtered through the slat door, then examined the shelves. There was plenty to last them until the next hunting season and some besides to trade at Uncle Rufus' store for the other supplies they would need throughout the year. Jake would make a trip to Elizabethtown in the next valley as soon as the trail through the mountain pass was clear. Eliza selected a pound of venison and noted with satisfaction that the loss was barely noticeable. Hunting was good last fall. It would be a profitable year.

By the time she returned to the warm main room, the hammering had stopped. Through the window in the south wall she could see Jake and Adam making their way through the drifts to the barn to tend the horses, leaving a snowshoe trail behind them. Eliza set the jerked venison to simmer in a pot of hot water. Beth had finished chopping the vegetables, so she tossed those in too. With four fat potatoes baking in the coals, they sat down with their baskets of needlework to wait.

The warmth of the fire, the click of Beth's knitting needles, and the rhythmic creak of the rocking chairs lulled Eliza into contentment.

Beth's chair stopped creaking. "Mama?"

"Hmmm . . ."

"When Papa takes the meat and furs down to Uncle Rufus, do you think we could go with him?"

Eliza longed to see her Aunt Charlotte and Uncle Rufus again, and it seemed an eternity since she'd attended services in her father's church. More than fifteen years ago she'd left Texas and come to live in E-town where she'd met Jacob Craig, married him in that church, and come to live with the mountain man in this secluded valley. She'd found happiness here, but she, too, looked forward to the rare opportunities to visit. "I wish we could, sweetheart, but we can't get a wagon over the pass until late June at least."

"We could take the horses. I ride well enough." Beth's brown eyes pleaded.

Eliza understood. The children were as tired as she was—tired of the sameness, the isolation. When spring finally did come, they'd all be ready for a bit of adventure. But a trip to Elizabethtown was still several weeks off. "Papa will need the horses to pack out his furs." She hoped the sympathy in her voice would ease the blow of reality.

Beth looked as if she might cry.

"We'll all go down for the Fourth of July, for sure. Remember how much fun we had last year?"

Someone was having a bit of fun now. Shouts and whoops came from the direction of the barn. Beth wandered to the window to watch, and Eliza followed her. Knee deep in the snowy pasture, Jake and Adam pelted each other with snowballs on their way back to the cabin. Their voices echoed up the broad slopes that bordered Bitter Creek.

Then they were on the porch, stamping and slapping the snow off their coats and pants. They hung their snowshoes beside the door and came in, and a cold draft came with them. Soon enough, though, the fire warmed the room, and a fine meal warmed their stomachs.

Eliza's heart warmed as well. What more could she want, really? She had everything she needed right here.

ଛଔଓ

Jake lay awake long after the house was quiet. Eliza's breathing was soft and even beside him. He listened for a while then focused on the other night sounds.

An ember popped beneath the ashes on the hearth, followed by the sizzle of boiling pine sap. It was a cozy sound, evoking pleasant childhood memories, but he didn't indulge them now. It was the noises outside that concerned him.

He tuned his hearing to the music of Bitter Creek. During the long winter, there was no sound because there was no creek. Only in the spring when the snows began to melt did the runoff begin. The first tinkling whispers were barely audible, but years in this valley had taught him what to listen for. He'd heard their secret promise of coming warmth nearly two weeks ago. The sound grew louder each day until he could hear the rush of water beneath the blanket of ice and snow. This afternoon the crusty covering had broken through. He'd seen the water sparkling in the last slanting rays of sunshine as he walked from the barn. Now he heard the scrape of shifting shale as the water swept past with enough force to move small stones along its rocky bed. Even this, though, did not concern him. These sounds were part of the normal transition of seasons.

The sound that kept him awake was the sound of rain.

It had begun like most spring rains in these mountains—a rush of hail just before supper that slowed to a pleasant patter. At the time he experienced a sense of satisfaction as he examined the underside of the shakes he'd replaced, golden yellow against the darker nailing strips and rafters. His children's sleeping spaces in the loft stayed warm and dry. In this latest skirmish of man against nature, he'd won.

But the drumming increased steadily until, sometime after midnight, the drops began to pound, battering the roof like fists threatening retaliation for his small victory. Silently punching holes in the soft, deep snow. And beyond the pounding, above the moan of wind in the pines, Bitter Creek began to roar.

Still, he hated to wake the family if there was no danger. And so he listened.

Thunder rumbled up the valley, echoing off the steep slopes behind the cabin as rain continued to pour from the starless sky.

Just before dawn Jake slipped from under the quilts and padded across the cold board floor to the window. He peered into the darkness. There was no moon, but he didn't need moonlight to know where the barn was. He'd built it himself, with his own two hands, and the cabin too. Set them well back from the creek. The creek he could not see. The creek that sounded too close out there in the inky blackness.

And then the horses began to whinny—high, piercing squeals of fright.

It was the confirmation he needed—the proof he dreaded.

A flashflood.

Suddenly the time to act was very short.

"Eliza!" He grabbed his trousers from the bedpost and shoved his legs into them as he ran.

His wife sat bolt upright in bed, instantly awake, clutching a double handful of quilts to her throat. Her eyes were wide in the firelight.

He was already shrugging into his suspenders. "Get the children. Take them to high ground." He grabbed his boots and thrust his bare feet into them.

Eliza was moving—grabbing clothes and quilts. "Adam! Beth!" she called up the ladder. "Wake up and dress warmly." How she managed to keep the panic from her voice, he would never know.

He grabbed his coat and gun, and she stared at him.

"Where are you going?" Now she sounded scared.

"After the horses." He was glad she didn't argue.

"What would you like me to save?"

He had the door open now. The roar of the creek sounded like a stampede. "Just yourselves. I'll meet you at the mine," he shouted.

He ran to the end of the porch, wrapped his arm around the peeled pine post, and swung off into the darkness. Icy water rushed in through the seams of his boots with the first step, but he pushed past the shock of it, racing the rising water to the barn.

His fingers were almost too cold to lift the latch on the barn door. He had to set his shoulder to it, but on the second try the doors swung open.

There was no time to lead the horses out. No sense trying to ride them. The ground was far too slippery, and they were far too frightened. Best he could do for them was to let them loose to fend for themselves.

Jake splashed from stall to stall—tossing rails aside, coaxing each horse out, waving and shouting above the roaring water.

The horses reared and shied, unsure where safety lay. Poor beasts. Their eyes were wide with terror, ringed with white.

Jake continued to drive them toward the open doors, shouting until his throat rasped.

At last they seemed to understand. One by one they trotted through the opening and bolted off through the sheeting rain.

He prayed they'd make it to safety. They might not, but the same could be said for all of them. The water was up the shank of Jake's boots by the time he followed them out of the barn and into the deep gray light of morning.

An orange glow marked the cabin window. He headed for that.

Across the porch.

Through the front door.

House empty? He poked his head up the ladder. Checked the lean-to. A sick feeling gripped his gut as the dim light of the fire showed him the stacks of furs and smoked meats.

No good to a dead man.

Assured that his family was on their way to safety, Jake turned to go.

He closed the cabin door behind him. Wondered why, and just as quickly realized that he still had hopes of returning in the morning to find things just as he'd left them.

Not likely, though. The waters of Bitter Creek were already lapping at the bottom step as he left the porch.

Everything in him wanted to stay and fight. Beat back the waters. Protect what was his. But the three possessions he treasured most were on their way to the mine, and he had promised to meet them there. He might have to relinquish a partial victory to nature this time.

The path to the mine followed an old deer trail that started near the north end of the cabin. Jake found his footing on the slippery rock and started up it. He'd walked this trail so many times he knew it by heart, even in the dark. Would Eliza? He hurried his pace.

Adam was with her. That was a comfort. His son had always been quiet and dutiful, but this year he'd begun to leave childhood behind. He was taller—nearly as tall as Jake. The roundness was leaving his face. The shadow of a beard edged his jaw, and he delighted in his own strength. He'd be a help to his mother tonight.

Jake trusted him—and suddenly his heart felt swollen, and the rain seemed to have gotten into his eyes. He couldn't swallow right. He cleared his throat and scrubbed at his face to get a hold on his emotions. He had to find them, but would they hear him even if he shouted?

A scream cut through the deluge, plunging fear like a knife into his brain. The numbness that seized him had nothing to do with the cold. His heart skipped a beat then pounded to catch up as he grabbed at any branch low enough to pull himself to a higher level.

A flash of lightning showed him the scene. Eliza stood on a ledge above the rain-swollen creek, stooped and reaching. Below her, rushing water had undercut the bank. Adam and Beth balanced on a boulder—all that remained of the trail at that point. Beth grasped a sapling, but the young tree was unable to support her weight. It bowed and left her hanging precariously above the torrent.

She screamed again.

Jake lunged forward, bolting toward them.

Eliza grabbed Beth's wrists, but even from a distance he could see her slipping.

Adam wrapped a strong arm about his sister's legs and skirts, leaning toward the ledge, pushing her toward safety, absorbing her weight as she sat on his shoulder. With one final heave he launched her to higher ground . . . and fell backward into the raging flood waters.

"No!" Jake felt his heart tear through his chest. He'd lost one son. He was not about to lose another.

He had seconds to act.

Sliding down the steep embankment beside him, he barely felt the pain as his hand slid down the rough bark of a pine bough—barely noticed the freezing water as he slid his foot as far into the swollen creek as he could reach. The frigid torrent swirled around his boot.

As the sky growled and flashed with light, Jake searched the roiling water. Adam's head bobbed toward him, in and out of the tumbling waves, arms flailing.

Jake stretched out his arm and prayed.

One chance.

Adam rushed past him.

Jake clawed the air and water, groping frantically. His hand gripped something solid—something that gripped back.

He held on with all the strength that was in him then dug deep in a desperate search for more. The water fought him. Trying to tear his son away from him. He would not surrender this fight.

Adam wrested his free hand from the water. Swung it over his head in an arc to grasp his father's wrist.

With a shout like a battle cry straight from his soul, Jake heaved with the last of his strength. The tree branch ripped the flesh of his hand as he tore his son from the water.

Jake fell.

He dug in his heels, let go the branch, and pulled with both hands, dragging Adam onto the trail. Holding him. Embracing him. Feeling his cold skin and the warm breath still in him. Crying. Not caring.

He didn't care about anything except what couldn't be replaced.

Chapter 3

Rigid with cold, Eliza stirred on the edge of sleep, seeking a more comfortable position. Not possible. Pain shot through her, rousing her to awareness. Exhaustion had made her a part of the stone wall she'd propped herself against hours ago. Her head felt like a rock, heavy against Jake's shoulder, and a miner's pick pounded against her temple. With an effort she straightened her neck, rubbing the knotted muscles with an icy hand.

Thin daylight illuminated the entrance to the mine shaft. She pondered the watery light. Her thoughts, too, seemed dense and gray.

Beside her, Jake stirred, sat still for a moment, then patted her knee. The gesture was strangely reassuring. He was still beside her, and that was something.

He shrugged off the damp quilt they shared, heaved himself to his feet, and stumbled, stooping, through the opening.

A morning breeze touched the place he left vacant. Eliza shivered, and her teeth began to clatter. Odd. She wouldn't have thought she could be any colder. "How bad?"

"Come see." Jake reached a hand through the entrance.

She clutched the quilt with one hand and reached with the other to take his. He pulled her to her feet, and every joint rebelled.

Ducking the beamed header, she emerged to stand beside him. Together they surveyed the broad, rushing torrent that had been Bitter Creek. Yards out of its banks, it entirely filled the gap between the steeply sloping mountains—the hollow that had been their home.

"The house . . ."

". . . was there." Jake pointed over the foaming white surge.

Gone. Her heart felt as heavy as her body and brain.

"I'll round up the wood torches from the mine shaft and use them to start a fire. You and the children can dry things out while I hunt breakfast. After that, I'll take Adam and look downstream for—"

Something taut and brittle snapped inside her. "For what? There's nothing left." A sob cracked through her words. The meat. The furs. The house and everything in it. All gone.

"—the horses." Jake folded his arm around her, strong and comforting. "If they survived, they'll help us get down to Elizabethtown."

☜☞

They found three of their four horses sheltered together on a high ridge. No sign of Ledge, the young stallion Jake planned on breaking in for Adam, though they called for him up and down the valley for several miles. Devil take him, anyway. Jake had held great hopes that the colt would inherit his sire's steady temperament, but he was flighty and headstrong from the start. Two years of patient training had improved him very little. If Ledge ever did make it back, maybe he'd be older and wiser for his misadventures.

Of course, no sign of anything else, either. Barely a stone's throw from where their cabin had stood, Bitter Creek flowed into the Red River, whose torrents were even more fierce. Whatever was left of their belongings had been swept halfway to the Rio Grande by now. The search was useless. He'd known that before he began, but some foolish remnant of hope compelled him to try, if only so he could tell

14

Eliza he'd made the effort.

"Come on, son. We've done our best."

The quilts were dry when they returned. They folded them and used them as saddle blankets. No saddles. Eliza quirked an eyebrow at him as if to say, "Those too?" He nodded, stoic.

It wasn't that he didn't feel the loss, but all morning he'd been keenly aware that his son was watching—learning how a man faces setbacks. The loss of his year's work hit him like an unexpected kick to the gut, but there were more important things at stake. Besides, he'd already weathered the loss of friends in war, the loss of a wife and child in childbirth. What were a few logs and furs?

A coil of rope was tied to a bucket in the mine shaft. Jake untied the knot and slipped the rope from a series of pulleys, then pulled out his knife and cut lengths to fashion reins and harnesses.

The horses, still skittish, seemed more than willing to be led to safety.

He lifted Beth onto the oldest and gentlest mare then boosted Eliza onto his own favorite. Cupping his hands, he jerked his head toward Adam. "Step on up."

"What will you do, Papa?"

Jake gathered the lead lines in his hands. "I'll lead."

Beth stared at him, wide eyed. "You're going to walk the whole way to Elizabethtown?"

"We'll take it slow. Camp along the way and hunt for our food."

His daughter searched her mother's face and took her cue from Eliza's gentle smile. His wife had endured trials and losses of her own—trials that molded her into a strong, capable woman. When Beth turned again, she showed no fear—only a hint of sadness. "Papa, what about Ledge?"

"Well, sweetheart, in times of trouble it's important to stand together lest we fall apart. I guess Ledge hadn't figured that out."

Beth nodded and fixed her eyes on the road ahead. "I'm glad we're going to see Grandpa and Aunt Charlotte and Uncle Rufus after all."

At the mention of Charlotte and Rufus, Jake's heart sank. He didn't realize it showed on his face, but Eliza asked, "What's the trouble?"

"Oh, I hate to presume on their generosity, that's all." This would not be the first time Eliza's aunt and uncle had taken them in.

"Jacob Craig! I seem to remember you helped them out of a tight spot."

"Well that's a truth," he said with a huff of humor. "I guess I'm just more comfortable being the helper than the one asking."

"It's all part of standing together," Eliza replied. "It's what family does."

That gentle smile again. Lord, he loved this woman. Enduring all that had brought them together gave him confidence that no circumstance could tear them apart.

"Papa," Beth asked, "how did you help Aunt Charlotte and Uncle Rufus out of a tight spot?"

"Well, that's a long story. Come on. Let's cover a few miles while we have light, and I'll tell you along the way."

Chapter 4
Slim Pickens Ranch
Moreno Valley, New Mexico

Zeke drove his pitchfork into a trampled layer of hay and heaved the rotting, stinking mass—manure and all—over his left shoulder into the muck pile.

A sharp pain, as if the tines of the pitchfork had been driven between his ribs, caused him to suck in a breath and wince. Wheeling, he dropped the instrument, slammed a hand to his back, and groped for support. He sank onto a hard bench that ran along the log wall of his barn. His first two attempts to exhale and inhale normally stripped his breath away, but on the third try he succeeded, blowing out a thin stream of air and filling his lungs again.

It wasn't pain that caused him to break out in a cold sweat. It was fear.

He didn't have time to be laid up with a bad back, nor money, either. The doctor had already ridden out twice to check on Millie. Her morning sickness didn't last this long with the other babies. Doc said it was nothing to worry about. Left some tonic . . . and a bill. They couldn't handle any more unexpected expenses.

Zeke rubbed slow circles with his knuckles, kneading knotted muscles.

Last year was a rough one for the ranch. Shoot, last year? Last decade. Caught between rival interests in the local land war, he'd struggled to tend to his own business and keep his nose out of everyone else's. All he wanted to do was clear enough profit to pay his rents, but to whom? Lawyers and journalists wrangled over rights of ownership, arguing the international transfer of the original Mexican land grant in high-sounding terms. And of course there was the usual cadre of crooked politicians looking to cash in on both sides. The flap and squawk died down between hearings only to reignite like a wildfire with each gaveled decision.

He had no time to squabble over politics. The usual trials of land management kept him busy enough. Intermittent drought made for bad grazing. Last winter was long and hard. He'd lost several cattle in the fierce blizzards. Snow blind and wandering, they'd frozen to death. The stock that survived ate what little hay he'd managed to store up, and they'd be getting mighty thin before there was more.

With one thumb, Zeke idly fretted the edge of a hole in his work gloves.

When the spring rains came, it was too much and too late. The grass was green, but the grazing land was sodden—conditions just right for hoof and mouth disease.

As if he didn't already have troubles aplenty, there was the problem of bears. Owing to the summer's drought, they didn't get enough to eat before hibernating. Then winter struck early and stretched into spring. Now that they'd waked up the bears were hungry, coming out of the woods to find food. He lost two calves last week.

Up all day tending the ranch, and up half the night delivering calves and watching for bear, he was hurting for sleep. There'd be no rest for another month, though. The rent came due at the end of July. After this year, the land would be his . . . if he could pay the last installment. If the new owners even honored the terms of his original agreement. If not, hired enforcers were already removing settlers who couldn't—or wouldn't—pay up.

Most summers he drove his cattle to the railheads in Springer, just beyond Cimarron, but last month's storms washed out the canyon road. He could drive his cattle the long way down the Moreno valley, but he'd have to hire on hands, and that would cost money—money he didn't have. Besides, who could he trust? Most of the folks around these parts had chosen up sides in the land disputes. By showing preference for neither, he feared he'd made enemies of both.

Zeke snatched his hat from his head and used his sleeve to wipe the sweat from his brow. On top of everything else he had to do, Millie was pining to go to the Fourth of July shindig tomorrow up in E-Town. He hadn't even taken a Sunday off since March. He sure didn't have time to squander on a social nor any great desire to run into rivals, but she'd be disappointed if he didn't take her and might stage a few fireworks of her own.

His head dropped beneath the weight of his thoughts, and he slapped his Stetson idly against one bony shin.

Millie's mother had warned her he wasn't good enough, and he was proving it every blasted day.

∞)(∞

Filling her lungs, Millie clapped a hand over her mouth and pinched her nose before lifting the skillet lid. She forked the sizzling meat and turned it, replacing the cover before the odors breached her defenses. Morning sickness . . . all day long . . . was worst when the smells of cooking assailed her. She'd hoped it would pass, but the nausea raged on five, six, now seven months into her pregnancy, making her dread even the thought of food.

Still, her family had to eat. Beau and Jackson prowled the kitchen like spring bears.

"I'm starving, Ma." Beau never seemed to get full. He was just less famished after a meal than before.

"I'll have it ready in a bit." It would be much longer than that, but she was doing the best she could. Millie glanced out the window toward the barn as she reached for the flour sack. Zeke always came in hungry. She liked to have supper waiting.

"What're we having?" Jackson crowded in and raised the lid for a peek before Millie could stop him.

Steam billowed, filling the lean-to with the stench of searing flesh.

Millie grabbed the lid and slammed it back on the frying pan with a bang. "Out!" By instinct she snatched up the turning fork, wielding it like a weapon.

Her youngest son backed away, more shocked than frightened.

Beau leapt to his mother's defense. "Oaf!" He shoved his brother toward the door.

The spark of indignation blazed into an inferno of offense. Head down, Jackson rammed a shoulder into his brother's midsection.

They slammed into the can shelves. Millie dropped the flour sack as dozens of glass jars crashed to the puncheon floor—their ruined contents oozing among razor sharp shards. The bitter tang of pickled cabbage mixed with the smell of charring meat.

Beau lifted his brother by the collar, threw him through the door, and charged after him with balled fists. Chickens squawked and scattered as they scuffled in the dirt yard.

"Oh!" Millie bolted out behind them. She made it no further than the edge of the stoop before a wave of nausea seized her.

From the corner of her eye, she saw Zeke dashing across the yard, sending the poultry flying. A strong arm held her waist and a rough hand gathered her hair away from her face as she emptied her stomach. When the worst was over, Millie leaned against the wall of the lean-to, wiping her forehead with the back of her arm.

Zeke peered into the devastated kitchen, then waded into the fracas, coming up with a boy in each fist. His eyes flashed lightning that was sure to herald a good deal of thunder.

"I'll clean it up, Pa. It was my fault." Jackson owned his sins without hesitation.

Beau slanted his eyes at his brother, then straightened and set his shoulders. "It was my fault, Pa. I threw the first punch."

Zeke glared from one boy to the other, but his eyes cast accusation at Jackson.

Millie's stomach churned—and not from the nausea. Zeke's temper was fierce, but the storm was usually short-lived. Trouble was, Jackson drew his thunderbolts like a brass rod. After Zeke's hail of words melted away, she was the one left to repair the damage. She offered her youngest son a smile of compassion.

He didn't see it. Red-faced, teeth clenched, chin quivering, Jackson stared at his boots.

"Dixie Lee!" Zeke's bellow would have brought the girl running if she'd been in the next county, but the commotion had already drawn her. She peeked around the corner of the lean-to. "Help your mother."

Square jawed, Zeke turned and thrust his sons toward the barn as his daughter reached for a broom.

৯৩৪৩

Forrest wandered to the table, book in hand, and raised an eyebrow at his brother's empty chair. "Where's Jackson?"

Beau and Dixie Lee shot their brother warning glances, but it was too late.

"Where were you the last hour while everyone was working?" Zeke barked.

Forrest slid into his chair and shoved the book beneath it. With his gaze glued to his plate, he shrugged but said nothing.

Supper promised to be a sparse and silent affair.

Millie picked at her food, her insides twisting. Jackson meant no harm. She shouldn't have lashed out at him. The morning sickness was a blessing, really. It stopped abruptly before the pregnancies she lost.

"How much did we lose?" Zeke frowned.

He wasn't going to like the answer.

Millie couldn't look at him. "I burned the chicken. " Her chin began to quiver. Fried chicken was Zeke's favorite. She'd killed and plucked two extra fryers today, hoping the prospect of a picnic might incline him to take a much-needed holiday tomorrow. All for nothing.

"And the canned goods? "

"All the sauerkraut." Her memory seemed to follow the order of obnoxious odors.

Zeke harrumphed. "No loss there."

Dixie Lee stifled a snicker.

"What else?"

"A shelf of canned carrots. The last of the pole beans. My prize chow-chow relish. And I dropped the flour sack into the middle of it. I'm afraid it's ruined, too." The loss was considerable. Those stores were meant to last until harvest, and that was months away.

Zeke drew in a slow breath and blew it out between clenched teeth.

Millie hazarded a glance at her husband.

"When we go into Elizabethtown tomorrow, we'll stock up at Rufus and Charlotte's store," he said, resigning to the inevitable.

Any other day Millie would be thrilled at the prospect of a day away from the ranch. She hadn't been to E-Town for months. Hadn't seen a soul she wasn't related to since last autumn. Until this morning she'd been itching to attend the annual Fourth of July celebration in town. Now worry ate away any pleasure. She had no idea how they'd pay for such a trip. They'd have that conversation later.

As it turned out, "later" came sooner than she'd expected. Little enough of their supper remained edible, and no one lingered afterward for conversation. Dixie Lee washed up the dishes without prompting, Forrest escaped to the loft with his book, and Beau headed to the barn with a plate—presumably in search of Jackson.

Zeke's chair scraped as he stood. "I'm going out to check the cattle."

She nodded, guiltily glad he was going.

The door slammed shut behind him like an accusation. The commanding clomp of his boots on the porch was punctuated by chicken squawk when he reached the end of it.

Millie heaved to her feet with a groan and lifted her skirts to assess her feet and ankles. Badly swollen, they throbbed. She had shed her shoes as soon as the weather got warm enough, but she'd have to find some way to wedge her feet into them tomorrow. She certainly couldn't go into town barefooted.

She hobbled to her rocker. Maybe if she sat for a bit . . . got her feet up on a stool.

Sweet relief. She closed her eyes just for a moment, but guilt goaded her at the thought of indulging in idleness.

Her work basket was close to hand. Four babies had worn the hand-me-downs to tatters. This little one would need warm clothes. With a length of soft woolen yarn laced through her fingers, her wooden needles soon scraped and clicked in rhythm with the chair's rocking. Worries darted through her mind like the needles, slipping through endless loops, but unlike her knitting they produced nothing useful—only knots and quandaries until her distraction began to show up as dropped stitches. With a sigh, she set the work aside. The light was fading anyway.

"I believe I'll turn in early," she said as she entered the lean-to kitchen, but Dixie Lee had already completed her chore and slipped off like the others, leaving the washbasin upended and the dishtowel hung over a peg to dry. Millie's bare feet padded over a damp stain—all that remained of the earlier catastrophe. A stain, bad memories, and a crop of new worries.

The failing light from their bedroom window did little to disperse the chill of approaching darkness in the high valley. Surely Zeke would return soon.

Millie lit the gas lamp and turned the wick down low. She shivered as she changed into a flannel gown and slid her puffy feet between the covers, but she wasn't sure if the cold she felt came from outside or from within. The warm-hearted cowboy who'd won her heart was not the same man who shared her bed these last many months. Was it the baby? The work? The worry? She didn't know, but she'd do anything to lighten his load, to hear his laughter ringing off the walls again.

The bedsprings squeaked, rousing her though she couldn't remember falling asleep. As Zeke pulled off one boot, she laid her hand on his back, massaging the spot where his muscles always knotted. "Tell me how I can help."

The lamplight cast harsh angled shadows beneath his brows, his cheekbones, and his jaw giving him a haggard look. "Ain't anything you can do."

He placed his hand on her mounding stomach.

The baby kicked in response to its pressure.

"Maybe Rufus and Charlotte would let us open a line of credit."

"No." He withdrew his hand abruptly. Where once there was warmth and intimacy, only a cold shadow of tenderness remained. "We will not ask for charity."

"It's not charity, Zeke. We'll pay them back."

His scowl did not soften.

Millie pressed on. "Rufus is getting up in years. Maybe they could use some help. Maybe they'd let me work off the debt. I could . . ."

Zeke punched to his feet. Whipping the belt from his britches, he looped the leather double and waved it for emphasis. "No wife of mine will jeopardize her health and the health of my child working for the public."

Millie stared at him wide eyed. For a moment she'd thought he might . . . no. Zeke would never strike her. That she knew.

He tossed the belt onto the bureau. "We have money."

"But Zeke . . . the ranch rent . . ."

". . . is my worry, not yours." He stripped to his long johns and crawled into the bed they shared.

She turned the lamp stem to douse the light and rolled toward his embrace, but Zeke grabbed a fist full of covers and turned toward the wall.

"Good night, then," she said.

There was no answer.

Chapter 5
Elizabethtown, New Mexico

Beau, Forrest, and Jackson vaulted the wagon sides as soon as Zeke pulled up on the hand brake, and Dixie Lee followed her brothers over the slats, skirts flying. The long silent ride to town had united his youngsters at last, if only in their desire to abandon his presence. For six long miles Millie had sat beside him on the buckboard, stiff as a poker and quiet. No, not quiet. Silent. And that was fine with him.

Zeke climbed down, looped the driving reins over the rail that edged the boardwalk, and reached up to lift Millie down. He'd act the part of a gentleman whether he felt like one or not. He didn't look at her, though, afraid of what her face would reveal. He didn't need evidence of her disappointment, his failure to provide. Millie's tight, bulging belly beneath his hands was a tangible reminder of their troubles.

"Zeke Pickens!"

He jerked around toward the familiar voice and instantly wished he hadn't, grimacing as his back muscles twisted and grabbed.

Jacob Craig propped his broom beside the door of the mercantile and crossed the porch in two strides, hand extended.

"Jake. " Zeke stuck out his hand, shrugging to ease the soreness. "Brought the family down for the celebration, did you? "

"No, been here a while. That big rain we had back in April . . . "

Oh yes. He knew. The rain that had turned his best pastures into mud. "A goose-drowner, for sure. Washed the snow out of the pass early, did it? " From the corner of his eye, he saw Millie cup her hands to peer through the store window, then wave.

Too late it occurred to him there must have been trouble of some sort.

"The snow. Our cabin. My stock. Storm washed it all right down the Red River. Everything we owned has likely washed up in Mexico by now."

Millie whirled. "Oh, Jake! What will you do?"

Zeke huffed. Where was that sympathy and confidence when it came to him? They stood to lose their home just as surely unless he managed to scrape together this year's payment, but the offer Millie made last night—to work or ask for charity—was all the proof he needed that she had no faith in his abilities to get the job done.

Jake shrugged, but his shoulders were unbowed. "We'll do the best we can. Eliza's Uncle Rufus and Aunt Charlotte are feeling their age a bit. Say they can use the help, and the upstairs room was empty."

It galled Zeke to acknowledge that Millie had been right about Rufus needing help, so he took satisfaction in noting that her offer to work off their debt would have done no good. The job was taken. He didn't dare say that out loud, but he did raise an eyebrow in Millie's direction as if to say, "I was right."

Eliza joined them on the porch, closing the door softly before slipping her arm around her husband's waist.

"It's a bit tight dividing the space with Adam and Beth," Jake continued, "but at least we got a roof over our heads. And we traveled light." He flashed a rueful grin. "There wasn't much left to pack."

How could he joke about such loss? As Zeke looked at Jake, and at Eliza standing tall beside him, a familiar fear crept up his gullet and threatened to choke him. To hide the feeling, or perhaps to explain it, he cleared his throat suddenly and said, "You remember our children . . ." He jerked his head toward the line of youngsters fidgeting on the boardwalk.

Eliza smiled. "Of course." Her gaze rested on Millie's swelling midsection. "And another on the way, unless I miss my guess."

"'Fraid so," Zeke quipped. "If Millie don't stop popping out babies, we're gonna run out of generals to name them after."

He knew his mistake the instant the words left his mouth.

An awkward silence swallowed the conversation.

Jake's eyebrows sprang up in query.

Eliza drew in a startled breath and held it.

Millie stared at him, hurt pinching deep lines in her brow. Tears pooled like rain puddles in her blue eyes.

He'd only meant to laugh in the face of hardship. Like Jake. But it came out wrong. Not like he'd intended.

"Please excuse me." Millie's voice sounded thin and stretched— the way he felt most days. She slipped past him, ducking into the mercantile with as much haste as her girth and dignity allowed.

Eliza followed before the door had time to swing shut, leaving Zeke to face the uncomfortable stares of his children and his friend.

Jake coughed into his fist, hiding whatever he was thinking. "Adam and Beth are likely out back in the garden."

All four of the Pickens progeny took the hint and lit out around the corner of the barn with obvious relief.

Zeke stared at his boots.

"Hard times?"

He didn't want Jake's sympathy. His friend had worries enough of his own. Friends or not, Jake was likely to tell him straight up what a self-centered idiot he'd been. He had it coming. In fact, he'd welcome it. Even a pop in the mouth would hurt less than the emotions that had been beating him up inside. "You could say that."

"Anything I can help with? "

"Nothing anybody can help with."

Jake laughed softly. "You know, sometimes I wish I was a betting man. I could be rich."

"Yeah? Well, it would take some mighty big winnings afore I could break even."

"That's not what I meant, but I assure you, I know the feeling."

Shame flooded him, but Jake seemed not to notice.

"I meant, I'd bet there's help for the asking, if you'd be willing to take it."

Now humiliation piggybacked the shame that piled onto the fear. Zeke lashed back. "I've worked as long and as hard as I know how, but I just can't seem to get ahead. Shoot, I can't even catch up." Talking about his troubles made him squirm, but now that he'd started a dam cracked inside him. "I can barely feed the kids I've got, and soon there'll be another." He snatched the hat from his head and slapped it against his thigh, raising a cloud of dust. "We get not enough rain or too much. Fifteen years of my life I've poured into that land." Still clutching the hat, he mopped his brow. "I need to sell my herd to pay my lease, or I stand to lose the ranch." His voice was ragged with desperation.

"So tell me what you need."

Zeke stared. "I don't know where to begin—haven't even known what to pray for."

"Start anywhere. I'm fairly sure the Lord didn't bring me down here to play shop keeper."

Zeke accepted the mountain man's verbal nudge. "I usually sell my cattle at the railhead in Springer, but the Cimarron Canyon's torn up after this year's floods. All them loose rocks in the Palisades—it'd be dangerous for a man on foot. A herd of cattle would bog down completely." He pinched the folds of his hat and used it to point toward the south. "Been thinking Fort Union's where I'll get top dollar for my herd anyway. Lot of hungry men in the Army, and they like to eat regular. Government gets a better product at a better price if they buy beef from here in the territory." He wished Millie was here to hear that he'd been thinking, that he had good ideas. But it was just as well she wasn't, because thinking was as far as he'd gotten. "The old Santa Fe Trail ought to still be clear. It's a longer route, though. I can't drive them myself. And I ain't got money to hire extra hands, even if there was anybody I'd trust."

Last thing most of Zeke's neighbors wanted was to ride onto a government post, looking for trouble. Most folks around E-town came with the thousands clamoring for gold after the war. Lucien Maxwell, who first owned the land, made a few attempts to control the rush of squatters, but never had the heart to make them "square up or git." Maxwell had sold his land, though, a few years back, and the new owners had a mind to enforce their rights. Zeke could sympathize with the squatters, to a point. There wasn't much money to be made in mining or in ranching, and he was no friend of the feuding landlords who lined their satin pockets with his meager profits, but he had too much at stake to risk taking advantage of the situation. Ranching was risky enough.

Jake understood the intricate politics of the region and did him the courtesy of pondering for a bit, not offering a quick solution. "Never herded cattle before, but I'd be willing to come along and help. Could two men do the job?"

"Hardly." Having begun to shuck his burdens, he might as well confess the rest. Zeke wasn't sure he qualified to fill the position of even one man anymore—not a whole one, anyway. "I'm a busted up old cow hand at thirty-five, Jake. Back's all twisted up." He settled his hat back on his head, in part to avoid Jake's eyes.

"How many hands would we need?"

His knowledge was still valuable even if his physical stamina was in question. Trailing cattle was years behind him, but that way of life was as familiar as the feel of a rope in his hand. "When I rode the trails, we used twelve men to drive nigh onto three thousand head, but my herd ain't near that size. We could do with less." He pulled on his lip, counting. He could lead. They'd need a cook and two drovers as outriders with another man to bring up the rear. A wrangler to manage the horses. "I reckon we'd need at least a half dozen men."

"What about the boys?"

A laugh escaped as a snort. "They're just that—boys."

Jake watched him, his eyes keen with intent. "Zeke, how old were you when your Pa died?"

"Thirteen."

"How old is Beau?"

"Fourteen."

"Adam was fourteen last month, and Forrest and Jackson aren't far behind."

"It's different, and you know it," Zeke countered. He'd known Jake as long as he'd owned the ranch—ever since Eliza rode in on the stage from Fort Union with Millie. Jake had stood up for him at their wedding. He knew parts of his life story, but only parts. "When my Pa died, I became man of the house. I had no choice but to grow up. Beau's a good help to me, but Forrest and Jackson are nigh onto useless. Forrest is lost in dreams half the time, nose in his books, and Jackson . . . " He snorted again, this time on purpose. "They'd be more trouble than they're worth, and that's a fact."

Jake tilted his head, rubbing one hand across his whiskers. "I think maybe you don't give them enough credit."

"I know my boys. I ain't saying it's their fault. I never wanted them to struggle like I did, but they have no idea how hard that kind of work is."

"If what you say is true, a trail drive might be just the thing to make men of them." He stared Zeke eye to eye. "Do you have another option?"

Zeke took off his hat again and scratched his head, making the sweaty thatch stand on end and not caring. "Guess not. Still, it rankles me to take help."

"Why? We're friends."

"Feels like charity. I always done for me and mine. Paid my own way."

"I understand. Rufus and Charlotte don't need half as much help as they let on. We're mostly just trying to make ourselves useful because we've got nowhere else to go. You and your sons can return the favor, if you like, by helping me build a new cabin. I could use four good men."

"Whether my boys count as men remains to be seen, but you can count on our help as soon as we get back from Fort Union."

Jake nodded, plucked up his broom, and reached for the door. "Should we put it to the ladies?"

In that instant, Zeke's mind was made up about a great many things. "No."

The word shot out of his mouth cold and sharp as the fall of an axe, and Jake's eyebrows raised for the second time in unspoken question.

Zeke tried for a more moderate tone, but his feelings on the matter were firm. "Millie's got plenty of opinions lately about how I ought to run the ranch, but I know how to manage without any help from her."

Chapter 6

Any hope Millie cherished that this horrible day might be salvaged at the Fourth of July celebration was obviously a delusion.

"You cannot be serious." Millie gaped at her husband, dumbfounded but certainly not dumbstruck. Had Zeke hoped he could do-si-do in and back out smoothly—announcing this audacious idea of his with nary so much as a "care to dance" or "much obliged"? Millie had never suffered a lack of words and vowed Zeke would suffer a bounty of them later, but Rufus and Charlotte's mercantile was not the place to launch her fireworks. Not in public. Zeke was probably counting on that. He might have hoped that if he led, she'd follow, but this shindig was not nearly over. Not by a long shot. For now it would be enough to remind him, in a carefully pleasant tone, "You promised to build a room for Dixie Lee this summer."

"I said I'd get to it when I got time." Zeke's face was stone. "Now is not the time."

She clenched her hands tightly over her swollen stomach. What had gotten into the man? He'd do well to remember that time was of concern to her as well. "When do you propose to leave?"

"First light Monday morning. Jake and I will ride down to Fort

Union to secure a contract and scout a trail."

So this was more than an idea. It was a bona fide plan. The fact that Jake knew more about it than she did rankled her plenty, but it was still just a plan. Two men on good horses could ride to Fort Union and back in three days—maybe another to do business. That would be the end of it unless they got a contract.

Zeke plowed on, oblivious, as if it were a done deal. "It'll take about a week to round up and brand my cattle, but after that there's nothing to stop us."

Millie rubbed her belly and made a frantic count of the weeks until her baby would come. To her, having Zeke home with that date looming was a very big "something". "How long will you be gone?"

"Don't know yet. Depends on which route we pick." His voice was as hard as his eyes, daring her to a challenge.

Well, wasn't that dandy? Her own schedule was not so flexible. The baby was due in early September. But the rent was due by the end of July, so that took precedence—at least in Zeke's mind it seemed to.

With an effort Millie softened her tone, appealing to the tender side of the man she used to trust. "Zeke, most mornings I can barely drag myself from the bed. How will I ever be able to cook and clean and watch your children and take on your share of the ranch work as well?" Though she was painfully aware that their discussion was public, she could not keep her voice from quaking with her growing panic. Could he hear? Did he care?

"You won't have to worry about watching *my* children. I'm taking the boys with me."

Specters of all that could go wrong on a trail drive spiraled from the well of her imagination like bats swarming from a dark cave. The route to Fort Union was full of dangers. Bad roads. Bad luck. Bad men. Zeke, her boys—they could be hurt . . . or killed. Millie's hands cradled her stomach as if by protecting this unborn child she could shield the others as well. "You're taking my boys?"

"So they're *your* boys now? That's just the trouble, Millie. You've never let me make men of them."

Zeke's words stung like a slap. Millie stared at his face but hardly recognized the man behind it. For a second time tears rushed to her eyes, but this time she stood her ground. "No, Zeke." That wasn't the trouble at all. He asked too much—of the boys, of her. The man was a fool for work. She couldn't go at it as long and as hard as he could on her best day, and she hadn't had one of those in months. Her chin began to quiver. She hated her weakness—and came nigh to hating him for airing it publicly—but she couldn't deny the truth of it. "I can't do it."

Zeke pursed his lips.

Maybe he would reconsider—delay the trip at least until the baby came. They could hold out somehow. Hadn't they always?

Instead he shook his head, his disappointment in her obvious. "All right, then. I'll leave you one. Forrest or Jackson. Take your pick."

Her heart tugged in two directions. How could she choose one son to favor? To protect? Forrest—the academic, the dreamer. And Jackson . . . even Millie sometimes had trouble describing her youngest son's bold, headstrong temperament in admirable terms. Forrest would likely prefer to stay home. Jackson, she was sure, would long to go with the men.

Of course Beau was not part of the bargain. No one could have missed that. Zeke considered him indispensable. Good thing her two younger sons weren't present to hear their father voice his preference for their brother. She had to admit it made sense to take the oldest, the strongest. Beau was so like his father. They'd always worked in tandem with few words between them. They were much alike, but her younger sons would not understand that bond. Eager to win their father's praise, they would feel the slight as rejection. Was this not the root of their many squabbles?

In the end, it didn't matter who she picked. Neither boy would be able to run the ranch to Zeke's satisfaction—nor could she, for that matter. The responsibility was a recipe for failure . . . but Jackson. Yes, he might embrace the challenge. Young as he was, he had the will to win over obstacles, the drive to best his brothers. At the very least she could offer him a respite from Zeke's criticism of late. Forrest could look after himself. He knew how to distance himself, to shield his heart. "Leave me Jackson," she said before she could question her decision.

"Done."

Zeke turned on the heel of his boot and strode away.

∞〇〇〇

Millie held a jar of beets for several minutes, staring without seeing. Her eyes blurred, but she willed the tears to stay put. She would not make a scene.

Zeke had already staged quite a spectacular display.

"Can I help you?" Eliza's voice was tender.

Millie knew her friend well enough to know she wasn't offering advice on grocery selections, but pity came at a higher price than she could afford right now. "How much are these?"

Eliza quoted the cost.

Whatever she said, Millie didn't hear. It didn't matter anyway. Whether it was five dollars or five cents, they had no money to replace the produce she'd carefully preserved from last summer's garden. Dry goods would have to get them through, and if the boys grew weary of plain fare, maybe they'd think the next time their tempers flared.

She put the beets back, aligning the jar with the edge of the shelf, turning it so the label faced forward. Then, for good measure, she adjusted the jars on either side. If only she could straighten Zeke out as easily. Keep her children in line. Keep up appearance.

Maybe this turmoil was her fault. Her failure. The only person she had any control over was herself.

Withering under self-recrimination, Millie straightened to confront the probing stare of Safrona Crump, her eyes smirking over the row of jar lids. Safrona Crump, whose gift for gossip was as boundless as the Maxwell Land Grant. Safrona Crump, whose husband was one of several ranchers who took advantage of the general confusion about who owed how much rent to whom to get by with paying nothing to anyone. Safrona Crump, who had apparently been shopping on the other side of the display shelf . . . for how long? How much had she heard? Her sanctimonious gloat indicated she'd heard plenty.

Eliza was still waiting for an answer.

Millie forced a smile. "I believe I'll have a look at the dried beans."

"Very well."

"Flour, too."

"Tell me what you need."

Another veiled invitation? Millie didn't want to talk about her marriage—to air her laundry for public viewing. What she needed was time to think. Time to figure out the change that had come over her husband and what, if anything, she could do about it. "Twenty pounds of flour should be enough for now. And twenty pounds of beans."

Staple dry goods were stored along the wall behind the counter. Eliza propped two sacks of flour against the counter, then lifted the lid off a large barrel and began scooping dull brown beans into a muslin bag.

Snatching up a bolt of fabric seemingly on impulse, Safrona Crump hurried to the counter as well, staying within earshot.

"I can take care of you over here if you're ready, Mrs. Crump," Eliza's aunt Charlotte said, smiling. "My goodness, this will make a lovely dress for someone." Did she mean to provide a welcome distraction?

"For my daughter Adelaide, I think," Fronie chortled. "Four

yards, please, and a yard of that white cotton for bloomers."

Millie bit her lip. It wasn't fair. By cheating on their rent, the Crumps always seemed to have money left over for luxuries. Truth be told, she didn't know if she was more envious of the dress cloth or the snowy white drawers. Adelaide Crump wouldn't have to worry about a stiff breeze lifting her pretty new skirt and displaying an Aztec Flour Mill brand mark on her backside.

Eliza kept scooping beans.

"Can you tell me how much that comes to?" Millie struggled to sound casual. It was going to be a long summer with nothing but beans and biscuits. If there was money left over, maybe she could buy a small sack of split peas just to have something different.

But the price Eliza quoted was already high.

For a fleeting second Millie considered asking her to put back some of the beans. Then they'd have enough for the peas. But she couldn't do it. Appearances, always appearances. She'd seen how little was left when Zeke paid the doctor, had begged him not to call for him the second time, but he'd seemed so worried about her and the baby then. Now he acted like this little one was an unwelcome burden. Like their troubles were her fault. Her eyes smarted, and her vision swam. They could do without the peas. Whatever was troubling Zeke, she'd gain nothing by adding to it.

Finally the store was vacant. No prying eyes. No sharp ears.

"Will you need anything else?" Eliza asked as she knotted the top of the bean sack.

"We'll be fine." Millie's voice contained more confidence than her heart. "Zeke will be in directly to pay for these."

"Do you have time for a cup of tea before he comes to carry these out? Or shall I call Jake to tote them out for you now?"

A moment's indulgence in casual female conversation—just chit-chat, nothing personal—would do as much good as a tonic, but Zeke didn't need to be lifting groceries with his back acting up. And he wouldn't take kindly to having Jake do his work for him. Should she call the boys? She eyed the bags. They didn't look too heavy. No heavier than the Dutch oven she baked in every day or the rugs she hauled out to beat clean or the wet sheets she lifted out of the laundry pot. "No. I think I can get them." She hoisted one sack from the floor before Eliza could object.

Something deep inside her popped.

Pain, sharp and hot, tore through her midsection.

Millie dropped the bag and grabbed her sides as an echoing spasm spread across her bulging belly. She was vaguely aware of the rattle of spilled beans, but her mind was focused on the upheaval within. She'd felt this tightness, this insistent squeezing, before. Six times before, to be exact. Labor. Gentle at first, the contractions would only increase in intensity until . . .

Charlotte and Eliza stared at her with round eyes full of unspoken understanding.

Too early. Far too early.

"Help her to the back," Charlotte ordered, kneeling near the hem of Millie's skirts as if to scrape up the beans. The floor was dry. "Her water hasn't broken. Lay her on my bed and put the kettle on. I'll get my herbs."

All for a sack of beans . . . Millie's conscience flogged her . . . *and Zeke's pride.*

ℴ)(ℛ

With Eliza's strong arm for support, she made it to Rufus and Charlotte's living quarters behind the store. A single room, they crossed in few steps, and Millie sank into the big feather bed.

"Try to relax. It'll help to ease the pain." Eliza positioned the kettle and poked up the fire. "Has this happened before?"

Millie's guilty conscience made her bristle. "Not with this baby." Would she have taken the risk if it had?

Eliza seemed not to notice her defensive tone. "Any other signs?"

39

She thought of her swollen ankles. The persistent morning sickness. This whole pregnancy had been difficult—but no, these weren't signs of early labor.

Eliza peered at her when she hesitated to answer.

She shook her head. "No," she said firmly.

Eliza did not look relieved. "I'd still feel better if we called a doctor."

"No." Another spasm, gripping her tight belly like rough hands, forced the answer from her with more volume than she intended.

Eliza's eyebrows arched.

Millie willed herself to expel a calming breath, then said more evenly, "I can't. Zeke's already called him out to the ranch twice." Would Eliza read between the lines?

"Well, you'll need to rest for a while at least. I can't imagine that a bumpy wagon ride will do this baby any good."

Nor a picnic. Nor a dance. Millie groaned.

Eliza flashed Millie an encouraging smile. "Let me tell Zeke we'll bring you home later."

"No." Millie squeezed the answer between gritted teeth. Zeke must not know.

Eliza cast a questioning glance over her shoulder, slanting her eyes at her, but just then the kettle sang out, and Charlotte came in with her packets of herbs and a bottle of spirits. Whatever questions Eliza had, she set them on the back burner and poured the water for tea as Charlotte stirred the steaming brew and added a splash of whiskey to the cup.

"Drink this," the older woman instructed, and Eliza propped Millie up with pillows so she could.

The infusion had a peculiar aroma, and the taste was strong, but not unpleasant. Millie blew away a tendril of steam and sipped. A soothing warmth filled her and began to work its way out from her core, relaxing every muscle. Sip by sip she drained the cup.

"Better?" Charlotte peered at her closely.

"Much." Her eyelids felt heavy, and her tongue seemed slow. Speaking required an effort, so she didn't.

Charlotte placed a hand on her stomach and watched the carved clock that occupied a shelf beside the door.

It's ticking sounded unnaturally distinct. So did the sound of her own breathing. Millie focused on the sounds of young voices drifting through the open windows on a breeze.

Five minutes passed before Charlotte seemed satisfied. "Just an alarm, perhaps." Her attention shifted to her niece. "Did you ask her to stay?"

"I did, but . . ." Eliza paused to study Millie's face.

"We don't get many opportunities to socialize." Millie made her voice light as she offered an explanation that explained nothing.

"You can't mean . . ." Charlotte began.

"Surely you're not planning to stay for the dance." Eliza's voice had an edge of pleading.

"Oh, my feet are much too swollen to dance, but the children would be disappointed to miss the festivities." Such a shallow answer would fool no one, but the dance had become a desperate charade.

"All right then," Charlotte said, but her eyebrows were still knit with concern. "I'll go on back to the store. You rest a while longer." She rose, letting the doorway curtain fall behind her.

Eliza did not move, nor had she shifted her gaze from studying Millie's face. "Why will you not let Zeke know?"

Millie watched the empty teacup rise and fall from its perch on her stomach, her heart as torn as her belly. "Because I love him. And he loves his land." She might be losing this child, but she was also losing her husband.

Eliza took the cup. Her eyes held no condemnation. Only confusion. "I still don't understand."

"I don't know what's troubling Zeke, but it's clear he blames me. If he thought I was a good wife, wouldn't he trust me? Wouldn't he let me help him? Wouldn't he want to stay and help me?" Her finger traced a pattern over her mounding stomach. "Zeke works hard. He expects me to hold up my end of this yoke, and I can't do that if I'm bedridden."

A tear burned its way down her cheek. Much as she hated this dance of deception, she would follow Zeke's lead. He would never hear the angry words she'd been saving—she'd bite her tongue, if that's what it took—but he wouldn't hear about the trouble with the baby either.

Silence fell. Even the children's voices had moved off toward the street, toward the wagon. From the other side of the doorway curtain, Jake laughed over some unheard comment as boot heels scuffed the pine floors. He and Zeke were loading those wretched beans.

Millie held out her hand—needing both a hand up and a handshake of agreement.

Eliza grasped her hand and stood her to her feet. "I understand what you've told me, but I'm not sure I agree." She set the teacup on the dry sink and returned to help Millie toward the store. "Will you at least let me talk to Jake? Let me tell him what happened today. I feel sure Zeke would never leave you on your own if he thought the baby was in danger."

"I wish you wouldn't." Millie caressed the little lump that now lay still. "For what it's worth, I'm grateful to Jake for helping him."

"I can help you while they're gone. Beth and I can come to the ranch and help with the chores."

Millie nodded. She had to admit their help would be sorely needed. "But only after the men are gone."

If Zeke didn't want her help to save their land, then she didn't need his help to have this baby.

Chapter 7

For a woman who lived for social occasions, Millie was anything but the life of the party today. Zeke snuck a glance at her, sitting reserved and retiring while the children scattered to find their friends. As much as she'd made on over the boys earlier, she didn't even care to walk over and watch them race in the relays. Was she that upset about the ruined pantry goods? He'd told her not to worry about them. He'd always managed to keep his family fed. Been working to do that for as long as he could remember. In fact, he couldn't remember much else. Millie was always badgering him about needing to take time for fun. Well, here they were, and she was having no fun at all. He would never figure this woman out!

As the sun slipped behind the western ridge, the shadows lengthened, stretching across the valley's broad bowl and up toward the eastern rim. Jake and Eliza had promised to join them toward evening when the store closed. Zeke looked out over the crowd to see if they might be coming.

A commotion caught his eye, but it wasn't his friend. It was that blowhard, Cornelius Crump. Ponderous and ham-fisted, the man walked like a bear, shifting his bulk from side to side with each footfall. His wife and daughter walked five steps behind, waving to all and sundry. Together they gave the impression of a three-man parade. He'd seen one once when a circus came to town. And swarming all around, like flies on bear scat, was Crump's usual following of two-bit cowpunchers—squatters and swindlers all.

Zeke felt his lip curl. He couldn't abide the man, but it made no sense to borrow trouble when he had enough already. He looked away, but a shadow fell over him as Cornelius Crump stopped and blocked the sun. What did the man want with him? Zeke might not have gone looking for trouble, but trouble kept finding him anyway.

Crump looked down his nose. "Nice day for a picnic, eh, Pickens? Where's your basket?"

"We came for the festivities."

"Indeed!" Crump dug in his vest pocket and tossed his daughter a nickel without ever looking at her. "There you go, Sweetheart. Go buy yourself a lemonade. Why don't you ask Dixie Lee and her brothers if they wouldn't like some, too? I'll bet their daddy's got a nickel." A slow, oily smile spread over his meaty face as his eyes taunted the challenge.

Zeke refused to take the bait. "My children are fine. We have food in the wagon."

"I'm sure you do." Crump tried another angle, staring brazenly at Millie's bulging belly. "You're looking in the pink there, Mrs. Pickens. How many will this one make?"

Mrs. Crump was looking at Millie in an uppish sort of way. Zeke had to remind himself to pull his horns in as Millie murmured, "Our fifth."

"My, my! That's almost a litter!" Cornelius Crump chortled.

Blood pounded in Zeke's ears. Crump had as much as called him a cur and his wife a b. . . he bit off the thought. His fists curled at his sides, and the veins of his forearms bulged. He was itching to swing, but Zeke couldn't let Crump goad him into a fight. There was too much at stake.

"Tell me you ain't thinking on leaving this little lady alone in her condition this year, Zeke, and braving that washed out canyon road on some fool's errand to make rent in Cimarron."

Crump's cadre of cowboys stared, daring him to answer, but they'd have to look elsewhere if they wanted information. He owed them nothing.

Just as the fringes of Zeke's vision began to burn blood red, Jake arrived. "Zeke's a good deal smarter than that, Cornelius." His friend clapped him on the shoulder and remained to stand beside him.

Zeke hadn't seen him coming, but he was grateful.

Eliza, standing tall next to Millie, chimed in sweetly. "If you'll excuse us, Mr. Crump, I've got a basket of chicken here, and it won't be nearly as good cold." With a nod she sent Adam and Beth off to round up the Pickens brood.

The Crumps and their cohorts ambled off before the children returned, but the backward glances shot over their shoulders let Zeke know that the animosity between him and Cornelius Crump was not over. Not by a long shot. For now, though, he felt oddly at ease. He had the upper hand. Crump had laid his cards out on the table, and it was obvious that he did not know what kind of hand Zeke was holding nor what move he planned to make next. He'd called Crump's bluff. Now he could take his time as things played out if he slipped away quietly and stayed watchful on the trail.

Millie seemed to doubt him, though. She barely picked at her supper, and he'd rarely seen the woman so quiet. A couple of times she and Eliza put their heads together and spoke in low tones. What was that about? Crump must have scared her, but that's what gave bullies like Cornelius their power. They thrived on intimidation and fear. Trick was to deprive them of information and stare them down with confidence. It would help if Millie had a little more confidence in him.

When the music started, but she was reluctant to dance. That he understood. Big as she was, she could hardly see her feet. They joined the grand entry march around the pasture, but Millie's promenade was more of a winded waddle that left her eager to take her seat again.

A momentary pang niggled at him. No wonder she was worried. Farm chores were much more strenuous than dancing. Maybe she was fretting again about how she'd handle them while he was gone. Made no never-mind, though. If he had any hopes of feeding this new little mouth she was carrying, he had to know of a certainty that he'd have land, free and clear, to work and raise his cattle on. If his back held out, he'd leave everything all squared away for her and be down to Fort Union and back in no time.

Two quick trips—just a few days each. Not like the months he'd spent on the trail in his youth. Like as not nothing would go wrong.

Chapter 8

"Jake? Are you asleep?"

Now what kind of question was that? "If I were, could I answer you?"

Eliza snuggled closer.

He stretched out his arm, inviting her to pillow her head against his chest, and she obliged. "What's on your mind?"

"We have a problem."

Jake buried his fingers in his wife's soft hair, a cascade of silky waves freed for his pleasure from the tight braid she wore by day. "You mean helping Zeke and Millie save their ranch, or helping Zeke and Millie save their family?"

She raised up on one elbow. "You knew?" When he nodded, she continued. "Both . . . and more."

Jake studied his wife's face in the moonlight. "Is that what woke you up?"

She shook her head. "Never slept."

Must be bad, then. What could be worse than . . . "Something wrong with the baby?"

"I can't really say." But the truth was in her eyes.

"Zeke will want to be with her . . ." Jake hadn't been there when his first wife died in childbirth. The regret never quite healed. He would spare his friend that plaguing guilt, that pain.

Eliza's head rocked against his shoulder. "She refuses to tell him, and she was quite insistent."

"Well, then, they're a fit match for sure. Can't say I ever knew a man more determined than Zeke Pickens. Downright bullheaded." Jake chuckled, then became sober. "Should I try to convince him to delay our trip?"

Eliza was quiet a moment, considering. "No. I think we're safe for now, but I don't think this baby will go to term. It may be better that you're going soon so you can return more quickly."

Her words urged him to leave, but her fingertips, light on his skin . . . well, he'd just as soon ditch the whole notion of cattle and travel and stay right here. He shifted, rolling to face her. "You know there's something deeper at work here."

"Deeper than stubbornness, miscommunication, and common pride?"

Jake pressed his lips to her forehead. "I think so. A man's got a powerful need to please his wife. If he stops trying . . . well, there's something behind that. I don't know what it is yet, but Zeke's hiding a hurt that's bigger than his need to love and be loved."

"You think he'd talk about it?"

"One way or another. Even if he knows what it is, I doubt he'd name it directly." That wasn't a man's way, but in avoiding the pain, he might talk his way around the edges of it. "You have to study the shape of the holes in a man's conversation—what he doesn't talk about. Or listen to the tales he tells. An incident here. Another there. Seemingly unrelated, but if you connect the dots . . ."

Eliza's eyes glowed with understanding. ". . . the outline comes clear. Yes. Millie's done a bit of that."

"I observed it time and again during the war—men sounding out the hollow places in their souls."

"You reckon, if we're watchful, we can help?"

"Maybe, though often it's not so much a matter of saying the right thing as it is keeping out of God's way while He's whispering to them." He kissed the tip of her nose. "But I 'reckon' we're here for a reason. It's certain I'm no shopkeeper."

"So you'll ride beside our friend and help him save his ranch?" Eliza pressed her hand flat against his chest.

Her touch was electric. It made his skin prickle like the air before a lightning strike. His heart kindled. "Yes, and maybe at the same time he picks up a few clues on how to win back the wife of his youth."

The response from the wife of *his* youth proved her complete agreement, and Jake was content to let the lightning consume him.

Chapter 9
Slim Pickens Ranch
Moreno Valley, New Mexico

Zeke got a firm grip on the rounded knob of the hand plane and, with steady pressure, guided the instrument down a length of pine. The sun had set, but residual light played on the thin curls that rolled like golden butter off his blade. The stack of smooth lumber behind him attested to a good day's labor—that and a growing soreness that shot through his back at the end of each stroke. He set his jaw against the pain and let the rhythmic rasp of the plane and the sweet aroma of resin mesmerize him, evoking memories of a different kind of pain. An old one, buried deep.

He was thirteen years old and planing wood for caskets—one for his father and another for his younger brother, both carried away by the fever his pa contracted in a Yankee prison camp. Pa lingered two weeks after he staggered home from the war. Elijah, who showed signs of the fever ten days after his father's return, succumbed much faster. They died on the same day, leaving his ma bereft and grieving.

Fifteen years his father had plowed the dirt of their east Texas farm, and tomorrow they would plant him in it. Plant him where nothing grows. Little enough ever did.

Zeke had watered that patch of dirt with his sweat as well, taking up the plow and the reins when his father left with a Confederate regiment. He'd hated every minute—sworn he'd never be a farmer—but he'd done his best at the tender age of eleven to provide for his family and keep their stomachs full.

He'd done his best with the caskets too—a last token to honor their loved ones. Ma seemed . . . not pleased, exactly, but comforted. Grateful. He'd stood beside her as neighbors shoveled dirt to fill the holes. Each drum of sod upon the lids made him more aware that nothing could fill the hole in his mother's heart—not even him, though he aimed to try. He bit the inside of his cheek until he tasted blood, willing himself not to cry, offering her what strength he had.

His mother stood erect, holding three-year-old Lizzie by the hand, silent tears washing trails in the dust that blew up from the graves to settle on her thin cheeks.

With the backs of their shovels their friends tamped the dirt in place. Zeke did not miss the finality of the gesture. They tipped their hats and struck out for their own homes, but Ma still stood, staring, but not seeing those fresh-dug mounds.

Lizzy squinted up at her, her eyes filled with unvoiced questions, until Ma nodded to no one in particular and said, "We will make it."

His sister seemed reassured by her words, but Zeke understood the determination behind them. They would survive because they had to. They would keep waking up and doing what had to be done each day because it was the only way to keep what remained of their family together. They would hold on to their land because it would be beyond enduring to lose again what was now planted there.

Zeke straightened and wiped his forehead and his eyes, then shoved his bandana back in his pocket and kneaded the kinks in his back.

"What's this?"

He snapped around at the sound of Millie's voice behind him and immediately wished he'd remembered to move more slowly. Why was it, when something hurt, that everything seemed to conspire to aggravate the injury? With an effort he hid his grimace.

Millie carried a plate.

He vaguely remembered Dixie Lee coming out to call him in to supper. Guess they got tired of waiting.

Fried chicken. A peace offering? He was expecting beans and cornbread, but remembered now that this was Sunday. However bad things might get—even when the smell of meat began to choke her—Millie always cooked his favorite meal on Sunday.

He took the plate and thanked her.

"You've gotten a lot done," she said as he bit into a piece of cold chicken. "How much more will you need for the new room?"

He'd known what she'd think, and the boards *were* for a new room, but her words—implying an expectation he might not be able to fulfill—scraped against his grain. "I told you I ain't got time for that."

For one brief moment her face fell, but then she composed a careful smile. "Oh . . . yes. You surely did. It's just that, when I saw you out here working so hard, I thought maybe . . ."

"These boards are for a chuck box."

Millie cocked her head to one side.

"What?"

"Nothing," she hurried to say. "But aren't you getting the cart—or the chuck wagon—before the horse a bit?" She smiled at her own joke. "I mean, you don't have the contract yet to sell your beef . . ."

Zeke slammed his plate down on the sawbuck and glared at her. "Have a bit of faith, woman. Would it hurt you to believe that I can succeed at something?"

Millie blinked wide eyes, and her chin began to quiver.

He braced himself for the onslaught, but instead she picked up the plate and said, "I'll take this in if you're finished."

"Quite."

Without another word she walked back to the house.

He didn't watch, but heard the door as it closed behind her.

Zeke worked until the last of the long day's light faded, then he lit a lantern hanging just inside the barn door and worked another half hour carrying the planed lumber in to be stacked against the back wall of the barn.

A soft light glowed from the window of the bedroom he shared with Millie, but he was in no hurry to face her. He took time to sharpen and oil the planing blade before blowing out the lantern and heading across the moonlit barnyard toward a darkened house.

As he entered the silent kitchen, regret niggled at his conscience, but he shoved it from his mind. If he had to choose between losing his family or losing his land, there was no choice. He had to keep the land, because the land was the only way to keep the family together.

Chapter 10

Exhausted and aching, still sleep abandoned him. Towards morning, Zeke finally gave up on the attempt.

"Time to get up." He hollered up the hole to the loft like he did every morning.

Like every morning, the response was a chorus of groans.

"Day's wasting." There'd be no second call. They'd heed the first, if they knew what was good for them.

His shoulder rebelled as he shrugged a flannel shirt over the long johns he'd slept in. He ignored his body's complaints like he ignored his sons'. No room for excuses. Jacob Craig would arrive soon to ride with him to Fort Union. There was a lot of work to be done beforehand.

Beau was first down the ladder—yawning, shoes in hand.

Jackson, fully dressed, clambered after him, nearly treading on his brother's fingers in his haste, which set off a shoving match. Everything was a competition with that one.

Forrest, always slow to wake up, slipped down quietly and went straight to the cookstove. He stoked the fire—Zeke never could understand how he did it without making noise—and pumped water, setting the kettle on before unwrapping the tidy bundle of clothes he'd set to warm on a nearby chair. He dressed slowly. Methodically.

Zeke resisted the urge to prod him.

Dixie Lee slid down the ladder without touching the rungs at all—her booted feet skimming the outer edges of the uprights as she used her hands to arrest her fall. She tucked the tails of a too-big shirt into an old pair of Jackson's dungarees just as Millie emerged from the lean-to bedroom. Zeke's wife and daughter squared off, an unspoken challenge hanging between them.

"Please, Ma." Dixie Lee broke first. "No one's gonna see me."

"Mr. Craig is riding out, likely as we speak. I'd prefer you looked like a lady."

Jackson snorted.

Zeke's glare silenced him.

Dixie Lee stuck her tongue out at him anyway. "A lady don't . . ."

"Doesn't," Millie corrected. "'A lady doesn't . . .'"

Dixie Lee sighed. "A lady *doesn't* climb ladders in a dress. If it's short enough I don't step on the hem, then I'm like to show off my . . ."

Millie's raised hand stopped her. "That's enough description." She cast Zeke a look, its meaning perfectly clear. *Your daughter needs a bedroom.*

He could not do everything. Why could she not see that?

He walked out into the welcome stillness, closing the door behind him, and breathed deeply. The sky was just beginning to turn gray. The stars had not yet faded—but they would. Shoving the door open again, he barked a command. "Out."

Beau, Jackson, and Forrest trudged past him and headed for the barn, their boots leaving a trail of darker green in the dew-damp grass. They had livestock to feed and water, stalls to muck, straw to pitch. Dixie Lee tagged along behind, swinging a pail in each hand—one for eggs, the other for milking.

By the time the sky turned pink, Zeke had saddled his horse, tied on his pack and left the bay mare to wait while he filled his stomach with Millie's biscuits and gravy. He ignored the normal clamor around the breakfast table, his mind already miles away—about fifty miles, as the crows fly. Twice the distance of the canyon route over terrain so rough that no seasoned mountain man with half a lick of sense would choose it. What did that say about him? He had to be loco—or desperate.

Hoof beats and a halloo at the gate announced Jake's arrival.

Zeke downed one last swallow of coffee and went out.

The family assembled on the porch as he unwound his mare's reins. He set his boot in the stirrup to mount up, thinking of nothing but the road before him and how best to win the prize at the end of it.

"Zeke . . . " Millie's gentle tone held a note of something more. Accusation? Pleading?

He looked at her, noticing for the first time that she wore one of his old shirts—sleeves rolled up, the bottom two buttons unbuttoned so that the tails flared out over her skirt. Did she expect a kiss? He went back to oblige.

She turned her cheek.

Fine, if that's all she wanted. He'd done his due.

He swung into the saddle and looked down at his brood—Forrest distracted, Dixie Lee barefoot and scowling in a dress, and Jackson munching a biscuit. "Mind your Ma, and do your chores." His gaze and his hopes rested on Beau. "Don't let me down." Then to all, "We should be back in four days—five at the most."

Millie's face darkened.

"What?" he challenged, impatient to be off.

"I was counting on four at most, that's all. I worry for you."

"Ain't no need. Just can't never tell what we might run into." His words didn't seem to calm her any, so he changed the subject. "Whatever you do, don't let word get out where we've gone."

The bay mare was chomping at the bit, anxious to be off. He gathered the reins and tightened them, turning her head toward the ranch gate.

The clop of horseshoes on bare earth was one of the most pleasant sounds he knew. As they rode out, he turned for one last look at his ranch. He'd left everything in good shape.

His family still stood on the porch, waving them through the gate.

"We'll miss you," Millie called after him.

He smirked. They might, but probably not first thing in the mornings. He just hoped they would keep the place running in his absence.

ഇൗൟ

The morning was cool and glorious. Peaceful. The music of rushing water, the creak of saddles, and the song of birds made a welcome contrast to the hullabaloo of home.

The horses nodded amiably as they followed Moreno Creek due south through the broad valley. Bordered by the Cimarron Range to the east and the Taos Mountains on the west, this first part of their journey would be an easy ride, the landmarks as familiar as the points of a compass. Their trail descended some three hundred feet into a basin where Moreno Creek joined Sixmile Creek from the west and Cieneguilla Creek flowing in from the south to form the Cimarron River that drained eastward down the canyon of the same name—a canyon which was now impassable.

"I mean to head south, toward Mora." Zeke had taken the road to Mora before, of course—a rugged route, but beautiful in its wild way. He'd traveled the Santa Fe Trail as well, when it was open, before the new railroad had made the trail from Cimarron to Fort Union more or less obsolete. "Just above Black Lake, we'll scout out the old Manueles Canyon route over the ridge to Ocate. Ought to be easy enough to pick up the main trail at Ocate Crossing." This section of the trail, though less used, had still been cleared and broad enough to get a coach through. At least it had been five years ago. It might be still. He'd never tried it. There'd been no good reason to try such a fool's errand before, and certainly not with a herd of ornery cattle.

Today he would study the route with a cowman's eyes, planning how best to provide for his livestock and protect his investment in the rough terrain. "Back in Texas we'd keep an eye out for watering holes," he said, thinking out loud. Water would not be a worry here, except where there was too much of it. Snow was still visible in the watersheds of the highest peaks, even in summer. The mountains' steep slopes fell in folds like a woman's flaring skirt, hemming them into a narrow trail bordered by somewhat more gradual inclines to the west. "Out here we're looking for safe passage and broad places where the cattle can graze and bed down."

If Zeke sounded like an old schoolmarm, Jake was a willing student. "How far can we drive them in a day?"

Zeke stifled a chuckle. "Well first off, driving cattle is a last resort. Stubborn as they are, you do better to lead them. Best yet, you let them think the whole trip is their idea. Identify the natural leader of the herd, convince him to walk along beside you nice and peaceful like, and the rest will follow right along."

Jake grinned. "Sounds like leading cattle is a lot like raising children."

Zeke knew his friend had spoken in jest, but the words didn't set well. He shook it off. There was something about the open trail—a curious mixture of peace and excitement. The way of it never left a man. Zeke filled his chest with the fresh morning air. He might not know much about much, but this—this he knew.

"On the Chisholm and Sedalia, over broad prairie," Zeke said, "we'd figure on covering ten to twelve miles a day. A cow can walk maybe twenty-five miles in a day, if she's a mind to, and I've chased after a stampede or two at a clip that would amaze you." He laughed now at the memory. "But cattle get edgy if you rush them. Besides, you want them to graze along the way and save their strength so they're nice and fat when you get them to market." He turned in the saddle, surveying the broad alpine meadow behind them, the bottle-necked passage ahead. "I figure we'll average ten miles on days where the way is broad. Maybe as little as six in the tight spots."

It was the tight spots that worried him. Where the trail was narrow and rocky, the cattle would string along for a good distance with only the boys—greenhorn cowhands—to keep them moving. Granted there wasn't much place a cow could stray off to, but one stumble on a loose stone, one scream of a cougar unseen in the woods—the whole herd could panic and run, and there weren't many places where a rider could get around them to stem the tide . . . or get out of their way to avoid being crushed.

Another thing that worried him was the altitude. Once they left the Moreno Valley basin, they'd begun to climb. The headwaters of Cienguilla Creek lay some six hundred feet skyward. Neither man spoke as they picked their way through the treacherous, rocky gap. When they reached the top they stopped to rest their horses.

Jake removed his hat and fanned his face. "This will be one of those six-mile-a-day sections, I take it?"

Zeke nodded soberly. "At best."

After the horses caught their wind, they urged them forward along a section of trail threading through another narrow pass. Stone walls rose close beside them. Just beyond this pinch point, though, they picked up Coyote Creek as it fell away south and east through a comfortable valley, still green from the earlier spring rains.

They pulled up again and took a swig from their canteens as they surveyed the trail behind them. "I'd allow a full day for such a climb, then let the cattle drink their fill from the stream and graze the valley to replenish themselves. That place, there, would make a good camp our second night out." Zeke pointed out a grassy spot a couple miles distant at the base of the valley. At the thought of a campfire, his stomach rumbled like thunder. "You hungry yet?"

Jake glanced at the sky as they started down. The sun was just cresting the towering treetops to the east. It had not quite reached its zenith, but they'd started early. Breakfast was miles behind them. "What's ahead?"

The answer pleased Zeke. Jake would make a trail hand yet. "A third narrow passage, and then Black Lake. That's where we'll head east to join the trail at Ocate."

Jake studied the sun's angle again. "Let's press on. We can eat after we find the cutoff." He opened a pouch that hung from his pommel by leather straps. Drawing out two pieces of jerky, he offered one.

Zeke took the strip of meat and sank his teeth into the smoky spiced venison. Yup. The Yankee mountain man would make a fine partner in this venture. "I meant what I said about helping you rebuild your cabin when we're done."

"Maybe a room for your daughter first, eh?"

Zeke grunted. The comment was an unwelcome reminder of his troubles with Millie—troubles he'd almost managed to forget with the freedom of the trail.

"Might as well," Jake continued. "I'm not sure where I want to build yet."

"Further away from that river, I'd imagine." Zeke had never seen the Red River, much less Bitter Creek. Never visited the cabin Jake had built after they married and left Elizabethtown—always been too tied to his own responsibilities—but 'once burned, twice shy' applied to devastation in any form.

"I might not even stay in the Red River Valley."

"You ain't thinking of settling back down in E-town, are you?" Jake's temperament was not well-suited to town life. He was rugged. Independent. Had disappointment and failure beaten him down until he was ready to be tamed?

His friend laughed. "Naw. I'm not ready to give up yet, but I haven't pulled a trace of gold from that mine shaft in years. Been living off my hunting and trapping, even in the lowlands." He waved his jerky as proof. "But game is scarce where people are plentiful.

Maybe this flood was the Lord's way of giving me a clean slate—a chance to start over that might be more profitable in the long run."

"Where would you go?" Even if they didn't see one another often, Jake was his oldest friend . . . maybe his only friend, since Jake had no part in the land wars that plagued the Maxwell tract. He'd hate to lose a good neighbor.

"Not so far." Jake laughed again. "Up the Moreno Valley—straight up Moreno Creek and through Costilla Pass—there's a valley that'll take your breath away." His eyes never left the trail, but his gaze was distant. Wistful. The land he saw in his mind lay far to the north. "Found it once when I was trapping. It's a climb, I'll warrant you. The pass is higher than any we've crossed today. The height of it will literally steal your breath. Air so thin you can hear a twig snap for miles. But there are places there no man has yet set foot on—not even Indians. Views no other eyes have seen. Streams full of trout and huge herds of elk that call to one another through the pines . . ." He filled his lungs with air and sighed. "If I was to start over anywhere, it would be there."

If he was honest, Zeke didn't see the point, but of course he couldn't say so. "Would Eliza go for that? So far from everything?" Millie wouldn't like it at all. She liked people.

"We've lived mostly by ourselves for all these years. It wouldn't be so different." Jake shrugged. "You live less than ten miles from town, but how often do you socialize?"

Well, that point he did see. In the winter, snow and cold weather made travel difficult. The spring thaw turned the roads into rivers of mud, and calving season kept him busy day and night. By the time the roads were dry enough to travel, the ground was dry enough to plow and plant. He made a few trips into E-town every summer to sell beef and replenish their supplies. Millie always begged to go. She begged him to take her to the big Fourth of July celebrations in town as well, but soon after that he had to think about getting his cattle to market so that he could pay the rent. Then came harvest. There was another brief social season around Thanksgiving. Millie insisted they take the kids to church at least for Thanksgiving whether or not the roads were fit for travel, but by Christmas the snow lay in deep drifts, and the cycle started over again. "We don't see other families above six times in a year, if that. The rest of the time, it's just us."

Jake grinned and nodded. "See? If a man can be happy at home with his family, he doesn't need much else."

Happy. Satisfaction and contentment. Wasn't that what he'd been working for all his life? But the more he pursued it, the more it eluded him. He didn't expect prosperity. He'd settle for sufficiency, but even that lay beyond his grasp.

And that part about not needing much else sure as shooting didn't apply to Millie. She didn't just like people, she seemed to crave them in a way he'd never understood. She rarely seemed satisfied and content just to be at home. He had to admit it was hard not to take that personally. She knew she was marrying a rancher when she said, "Yes."

Zeke checked to see if Jake was waiting for him to respond. He wasn't, and that was good.

He really didn't know what to say.

❦

When Black Lake came into view, glistening in the midday sun, they paused for a meal from their saddlebags.

"That way lies Mora . . ." Zeke fisted a hunk of the bread Millie had packed for him and pointed south beyond the broad water to where the trail was swallowed up by trees. ". . . but fortunately, we ain't going that way."

Black Lake was bordered along most of its eastern shore by a boggy marsh—a sure trap for thirsty cattle. On the south end of Black Lake lay Guadalupita Canyon—half again as long as the one they'd just come through and twice as narrow. Granted there was still

Manueles Canyon to their east to deal with, but once they got through that, the land lay open to the east and south to Fort Union. They should be able to make the trip in five days with the herd, he figured.

Stuffing the chunk of bread into his mouth, Zeke dusted his hands on his pants legs and mounted up again. "Come on," he urged, talking around the last of the crumbs. "I want to get to the crossing by nightfall."

Jake tossed the last half of an uneaten apple into the tree line and swung into the saddle without complaint.

The rift they entered was the longest and most challenging by far, first rising and then plunging almost two thousand feet over the course of six or seven rocky, forested miles. Even their mountain horses grew winded. Zeke rode in grim silence, revising his earlier estimate to add another day. Maybe two. He had to be crazy to think of bringing cattle through here, but what choice did he have?

Might be a moot point, anyway, if he failed to secure a contract at Fort Union tomorrow.

The canyon finally broadened near the community of Ocate, a meager handful of farm huts that barely deserved to be called a village, but any outpost of civilization looked like the Promised Land after their hard ride. The north end of the valley could support an overnight camp with their cattle if they were careful to avoid the grazing pastures of the local farmers.

A man in serape and sombrero stood guarding sheep in one such pasture. Should he take time to attempt to speak? Set things up a bit? The man watched them as they rode past, dark eyes narrowed. *Nah.* In this part of the country, there were still awkward feelings about the territory's transition from Mexican to American rule. Language was more likely to be a fence than a bridge. All too often a gun became the clearest interpreter. Zeke decided not to chance it. Instead he made a mental note of the lay of the land, and they pressed on.

A small church marked the village center, together with a ramshackle trading post and an old adobe structure that had seen better days as a roadhouse when Ocate was a stop on the wagon route to Taos. They rode past these just at dusk. Zeke's backside was feeling saddle-shaped, and his knees ached from bowing around his mare's belly. The aroma of roasted meat, chilies and fry bread made Zeke's mouth water as they passed the old inn, which apparently still managed a brisk business with the locals. A powerful temptation to dismount almost overwhelmed him, but he had no money for such luxuries. Instead he let his eyes and ears sample the offerings—savory food, pungent drink, lively music and dark-haired women.

Light and laughter poured from the windows, but rowdy men poured through the door. Good sense told him to stay clear and keep a tight hold on his life, his gun, his wallet, and his reputation. Still he could not resist a backward glance as they rode off east of town in search of a place to pull up for the night.

"You think it's safe to camp along the road?" Jake voiced Zeke's thoughts.

"Not really." Those men. Something in their eyes, making note of their passing, warned him they were the sort who would rob a man in his sleep. Or worse.

Ocate Crossing lay five miles to the east of the village along Ocate Creek. They found a secluded spot and made camp where an outcrop of rock would hide them from the road. A hastily built campfire kept the specter of thieves and miscreants at bay, and soon a pot of coffee was brewing. They caught trout in the stream and roasted them on sticks, the scents of wood smoke and supper wafting on the cool night air.

Bellies full, they rolled out their blankets. Zeke made a pillow of his saddle and lay back to savor the day. This was the life he'd dreamed of—the one he felt born to live. It had its hardships, to be sure, but the challenges tantalized him with the promise of adventure instead of beating him down to despair.

The stars hung low above the smoke of their fire. The horses on their pickets munched peacefully beside the babbling creek, but the lights and revelry of the village would not leave him. He plucked a blade of grass and chewed one end. "You ever been in a place like that? That roadhouse?"

"More like a saloon, it seemed to me." Jake's choice of words made his conscience squirm a bit. "No. I never did. Like that bog at Black Lake—some things it just seems wiser to steer away from. A man could get stuck—mired down in something he might not get out of."

Well, when he put it like that . . . He'd never think of entering a saloon in Elizabethtown or Cimarron. Never had since the day he married Millie. But on the trail—out here where no one knew him— the lure was strong. Was there always a hook beneath the bait?

"Why'd you ask?" Jake asked.

Why did he? "I don't know. Just curious I guess. After a big sale of stock, the outfit I worked for used to go into town for the evening. Live it up a bit. I was just fifteen when I signed on to go up the trail, though I hadn't been wet behind the ears for at least four years. Still, they left me to wrangle the spare horses. Never got to go along." Had he missed his youth as well as his childhood?

Jake rolled to face the road and pulled the blanket over his shoulder. "Never figured I missed much."

Zeke wasn't so sure.

Chapter 11
Slim Pickens Ranch
Moreno Valley, New Mexico

Zeke had been gone one day—*one day*—and already life was overwhelming. Millie was behind before she got started, filling up the big iron laundry pot on Monday since they'd gone to town on Saturday and stayed for the 4th of July celebration. Not that she'd gotten to enjoy it much. After the misadventure with the beans, she'd mostly sat quietly on the picnic quilt and watched as others socialized.

The memory of her premature contractions was still painfully fresh and frightening. She'd gotten Beau to lift the pot onto its hook for her and asked Jackson to carry wood and lay the fire while she, Forrest, and Dixie Lee toted water from the well in buckets. Then she stood withering, sweating, and swelling over the soapy brew. She'd levered the hot, sopping laundry into the rinsing vat on the end of her stirring stick, then wrung them out by hand before slinging them over the fence rails. By the time they were dry, she'd been too tired and sore to bring them in. The children did that after supper, before their evening chores, then they'd all fallen into bed exhausted.

How would she manage with only Jackson and Dixie Lee if Zeke got this contract?

If she hadn't been so worried about the baby, she'd have been heartbroken about missing most of the celebration. Every year she looked forward to that shindig—lived for it when the days dragged on, long and lonely, and stored up the memories to look back on. This year the only memento she'd brought home was swollen ankles from being on her feet so long, and after stirring laundry with a stick all day yesterday, she couldn't squeeze her feet in her shoes this morning, either.

Today: ironing. *Joy.* The notion of standing to press clothes in the kitchen was unthinkable. Even if she could have stood, the woodstove blazing away beneath the flatirons made the heat in the lean-to oppressive. Instead, she cleared the breakfast dishes and spread an old quilt on the table in the main room so she could sit and iron where it was cooler.

She turned to fetch the laundry basket. Four sets of eyes gaped at her.

"What?" She snapped, impatient.

Forrest appointed himself spokesman. "Where shall we study?"

Fatigue and frustration descended upon her. "I do not care." She enunciated each word with equal emphasis.

The eyes stared, unbelieving.

"Find something that needs doing. Just don't do it here," she said, sinking wearily into a chair and dragging the basket closer.

"Ya-hoo!" Jackson dumped his lesson books on the nearest horizontal surface and was out the back door like a shot.

Beau followed, likely headed for the barn.

Forrest handed his school books off to Dixie Lee and walked quietly into the kitchen. Moments later the clatter of tin plates let her know he was washing the dishes—his own idea—and her heart wrenched a little.

Dixie Lee still stood staring, eye to eye with her. "Are you all right?"

Millie sighed. "Yes, sweetheart. I will be."

"Can I help you?" she asked, woman to woman.

She was a good girl, really. "Trade out this cold iron for a hot one and save me a few steps?" Millie forced a smile to reassure her daughter.

Dixie Lee set the school books on a chair and ran to obey. She returned quickly, taking care to set the fresh iron exactly where the old one had been—a trick Millie had taught her that saved scorched elbows. "Anything else I can do?"

"Did you gather the eggs?"

"Not yet," she confessed. "I only finished the milking." Chores hadn't quite run on schedule this morning with everyone scrambling to make up the extra work.

Dixie Lee grabbed the egg pail from its peg and left out the kitchen door.

A minute later Forrest emerged, gathered his books, nodded wordlessly, and left as well.

Quiet.

Millie breathed in the warm, starchy steam that rose from the ironing table and thought what a wonder it was that a little heat and a little pressure could knock the kinks out of cotton clothing when they had exactly the opposite effect on her day, her plans, and her peace.

The iron grew cold. Millie heaved her bulk from the creaking chair and waddled into the kitchen to swap it for a new one.

A chicken flapped past the open window.

What on earth? Had Dixie Lee forgotten to latch the gate to the chicken yard?

No sooner had she thought it than she heard her daughter's screams. Sliding the flatiron onto the woodstove, Millie ran barefoot out the door and collided with Dixie Lee running in.

"There's a snake! A snake in the hen house, and it's eating the eggs." Millie was already shooing her frazzled daughter toward the chicken coop. "I reached into the nest and put my hand right on it." The child hugged herself with both arms, shivering.

Millie didn't doubt that it had given the girl quite a turn. She'd grown up around snakes, herself, but here in the higher elevations they were rare. A glance told her the boys had their part of the situation already in hand. Beau was coming out of the barn with a hoe, and Jackson was poking around in the nesting box with a long stick. "Here, now," she said, stooping to scoop up one frantic bird, "start grabbing chickens." She tucked the hen under her arm and started after another that ran by.

The hot, dusty chase was over in ten minutes. Millie and Dixie Lee stood waiting outside the coop with two chickens dangling from each hand and flapping in protest at having their legs confined so indelicately. The boys, meanwhile, stood studying what was left of the snake.

"It's a rattler," Beau announced.

"No rattles. More likely a bull snake," Forrest weighed in.

"Bull snakes don't eat eggs, but maybe a king snake . . ." Jackson was still poking at the lifeless critter with his stick.

"Bull snakes eat rats, and rats eat eggs," Forrest reasoned.

"Ugh, now we got rats *and* snakes?" Dixie Lee wailed. "I am never gathering eggs again!"

Millie sighed, exhausted. "Hurry up, boys, and get that thing out of there so we can get these ladies back on their nests."

Beau slipped the blade of the hoe beneath the snake's severed head and flipped the thing deftly over the fence. Jackson looped the snake's body over the stick and held it out to assess the length.

"I'm going to skin it and make me a hatband," he announced.

He couldn't help but pass near them as he carried the snake out through the gate.

Dixie Lee, still in high drama, jumped out of his way and tossed her four chickens in the general direction of the chicken yard before chasing after her brother, suddenly eager for another look at the snake.

Millie sighed and cast her eyes toward heaven's aid as one of Dixie Lee's chickens scooted out again. She entered the chicken yard, bumped the gate shut, and set her hens on their nests—not that they'd be likely to lay after today's scare—then limped after the repeat runaway. Fortunately she and the escaped chicken had both lost their zeal for the chase. The hen allowed herself to be recaptured and came along quietly after just a few minutes.

Millie carried her back to the chicken coop and slipped her into her nesting box. "Now stay put, you," she scolded.

The chicken acquiesced.

She should have such luck with the children.

Millie latched the gate and trudged back up the hill to the house, wiping at the dust that clung to her sweaty forearms. Maybe now she could get back to the ironing.

"Ma! Wagon's coming!"

Then again, maybe not . . . still, visitors were a rarity and welcome even on the worst-timed occasions. She glanced at her reflection in the kitchen window, plucked a russet feather from her windblown hair, then ran her fingers through the unruly curls and tried to tuck the worst of them into place. "Can you see who it is?"

"A lady . . . and a girl, looks like."

"Eliza and Beth?" It would be like her friend to ride out to check on her. Millie tied on a fresh apron and headed into the cabin's main room to have a look for herself.

Dixie Lee squinted out the front window. "No, ma'am. It looks more like Miz Crump and Adelaide."

Millie's heart sank. Her bulging belly lifted the hem of her rumpled skirt, exposing two dusty, swollen feet sticking out beneath. The front room was a mess with books and ironing piled high, but any company was company. Besides, after the fracas on Saturday, she needed to do what she could to smooth things over. She stepped out onto the porch to greet them.

The wagon rumbled to a stop, and Safrona Crump looked down at her. "Millicent, you poor dear!"

Her name wasn't Millicent . . . nor Mildred, nor Amelia, nor any of the other fancy names Safrona Crump called her, depending on the whim of the day. It was just plain Millie, but there was no point in correcting her again.

"Welcome, Safrona. Come rock on the porch for a spell. The breeze helps take the heat." If she could contrive to keep her out of the house, Fronie Crump would have no tales to tell about her housekeeping skills.

Mother and daughter alighted from their wagon.

Dixie Lee bounced on her toes. "You look nice, Adelaide," she said before she remembered to curtsey to Mrs. Crump. "I like your dress."

"What, this old thing?" the girl said, lip curled. "You can have it, if you like it. Mama's making me a new one." She tossed her brown curls. "Where's your brother?"

"Which one?"

"It doesn't much matter."

Millie found the coy response rather shocking from one so young. A distraction was in order. "Dixie Lee, would you pump us some water, please? Adelaide can go with you. Maybe she'd like to see the new chicks."

The girls ran off around the house, Adelaide clearly craning her neck for some sign of the boys.

Millie sank into a rocker, indicating that Fronie should take the one next to it.

"My dear, are you entirely miserable? I mean, when I saw you at the celebration Saturday, I could not believe how very large you've gotten."

Millie tucked her puffy bare feet beneath her skirts. "I'm fine, really."

Fronie leaned forward to pat her hand. "Well, you look ready to burst. I said to Cornelius, I said, 'She must be due any day.' Are you? Due any day now?"

Millie forced a tight smile. "Not quite. Should be sometime in early September."

"Oh, my! I don't remember you being this large with your others . . . but then that's been a while. I might have forgotten. Your girl's the same age as mine. Twelve, yes?" Safrona Crump's tone was conversational, but insincerity seemed to lurk just beneath her words. *Like a snake in the nesting box.* She'd never troubled herself to visit before. Why now?

"Ten." Short answers seemed best. Safest.

"Ah! You see? I did forget. You had them all so quickly. Why, Beauregard must be fourteen already. You had him the very year you and Zeke were married—the year Zeke and Cornelius and the others filed for their land."

"Yes." The conversation was definitely edging toward dangerous territory. Millie tried to keep her voice light and pleasant, but Safrona had obviously come to pries out the information her husband had failed to secure from Zeke.

"Where is your husband, by the way? I'd think with you being 'great with child' as you are, he'd be staying close by to attend to you."

Zeke wasn't exactly the 'attending' kind, but Millie wasn't about to reveal that to the likes of Safrona Crump. She wasn't going to reveal anything about him riding down to Fort Union to get a contract for his cattle, either. Anything she said to Mrs. Crump was certain to make its way home to Mr. Crump, who was none too happy with Zeke for paying out his lease and making the squatters look bad. Millie made her tone casual. "Oh, Jake Craig rode out this morning to help him with the cattle. They'll be back directly."

Safrona Crump rocked forward in her chair and peered around the edge of the porch to take in the view of the cattle grazing quietly on the hillside and the boys loafing in the barnyard. "If he needed help with the cattle, I'd have thought he'd have taken your boys with him."

Millie forced another smile to hide her exasperation. Without divulging more information than prudence allowed, there seemed no way to answer the woman's prying questions, and she prayed there'd be no more.

Dixie Lee reappeared as an apparent answer to her prayers, walking carefully heel and toe so as not to slosh the cool well water from the two tin cups she carried.

Adelaide Crump walked primly behind her.

"I brung y'all the water, Ma," Dixie Lee announced.

"'Brought'," Millie corrected. "'I have brought the water.'"

Holding out the tin cups, Dixie Lee tried again. "I have brought the water."

"Never mind, dear," Safrona Crump said, rising. "We really must be going." And then she smiled a false and calculating smile that made Millie's blood run cold.

Chapter 12

Up at first light after a night on the trail, Zeke stretched and rubbed his shoulder. The ground seemed harder than he remembered it being twenty years ago. It took an effort to hide his stiffness. His weakness.

Mounted once more, they had no difficulty finding the wagon ruts of the old Santa Fe mountain route. This would be their main trail. Turning south, they found it still passable—broad and clear.

They rode into Fort Union before noon. Even though the old fort was well past its heyday, the sheer size and finery of it had Zeke craning his neck like a greenhorn. The dirt road surrounding the parade ground was swarming with enlisted men, busy about their duties.

Zeke drew up next to the first one they encountered and touched his hand to the brim of his hat in casual greeting. "Would you mind directing us to the quartermaster depot?"

The young sergeant pointed the way and walked briskly on without a word.

Zeke looked at Jake, who shrugged. He spurred his horse in the direction the man had indicated and eventually saw a gate with wagons coming in and going out. "This must be the place."

They fell in line behind an oxcart loaded with sacks of flour from the Aztec Mill. Though he'd pondered what he ought to say for most of the last week, Zeke drew a deep breath and focused his thoughts once more upon his plan. He would sound calm. Confident.

Equipped to supply the needs of this outpost and many others, the quartermaster's complex was extensive. Surely with so many people to feed, there'd be a good market for his beef. They searched for the commissary officer and found him in one of the storehouses, checking supplies against a long list of requisitions.

"Yes?" The officer acknowledged their presence without looking up from his forms.

Zeke introduced himself and put his offer to the man quickly, before he had a chance to talk himself out of what might be a fool's venture.

The response was quick and curt. "Don't need any more cattle this year."

For a moment, Zeke couldn't respond. Couldn't acknowledge the meaning of the words that seemed to ring in his ears. Couldn't believe that his only hope of saving his ranch—all he'd worked toward for fifteen years—could be over in fifteen seconds. "Sir?"

The commissary officer, a captain by the look of his bars, turned briefly to address him. "See here, I'm sorry to turn away a man in need, but we've got all the cattle we can use, what with the drought. Whole country, seems like. Cattlemen like yourself desperate to sell off their herds before they starve."

Maybe it was desperation, like the man said. Maybe it was pride, but the captain's insinuation lodged like a stone in the hoof. He might in fact be desperate, but he would never admit to being needy. Zeke straightened his spine. "Sir, you mistake me."

"How's that?" The officer had already returned to his lists.

The casual dismissal fueled Zeke's determination. "I'm not here to sell off a herd of rangy, starving cows. No, sir." His voice shook with passion he hoped would not be mistaken for pleading. "I'll grant you the rain's been scarce in the lowlands this spring, but there was plenty of snow in the higher elevations last winter. It's cooler in the northern valleys. My longhorns are grass fed, fat and sleek." His chest puffed out a bit with the telling.

The Army officer's pencil hovered motionless above his paperwork.

Like a cutting horse sighting a tiny break in a herd that had been headed the wrong direction, Zeke recognized his opportunity and hurried to turn the course in the conversation. "Them other cattle may fill your subsistence quotas, but for the officer's mess?" He let the suggestion and the possibilities hang in the air between them.

He'd gained the man's attention. Slowly the commissary officer turned to face him. "How many beeves?"

If he was going to try to lasso the moon, he might as well go for the stars in the bargain. "A hundred head—half steers of good weight and the rest she-cattle." The number very nearly accounted for his entire herd, but what matter?

The captain raised an eyebrow. It was unusual to offer so many breeding cows, but what good would it do to save the cattle and lose the land? He'd built his herd from a handful before. If he could only manage to get clear title to the ranch, he could build it again.

The officer was likely as good a judge of men as he was of beef. He studied Zeke's face for what seemed an eternity.

Zeke didn't flinch.

"All right, then." He named a price—barely half the going rate last year.

Half insulted, Zeke did not answer. Had he sounded desperate after all?

Instead, seeming to misread Zeke's silence as a challenge, the commissary officer bumped his offer up a bit—only a little, but it was better than nothing.

Zeke ciphered in his head. His cattle were fat, and he had faith in his ability to get them to market in good shape at a good weight.

With what he'd managed to save and hang onto, the new offer would be enough to pay off the land. There wouldn't be much left, but he wasn't likely to get a better price. He'd pressed his luck already. "Deal." He stuck out his hand.

The Army official took it. "When can you deliver?"

"Three weeks." The man was practically drooling in anticipation of a steak that wouldn't taste like an old boot. It seemed wise to close the deal before anything changed his mind. Two days home. A week to round up the cattle, sort the herd, and stock provisions. That left him a full week to trail the herd down—plenty of time to graze them along the way, and he'd still have time to pay his rent in Cimarron before the end of July.

"Done." The commissary officer made a note in the back of his ledger. "I'll have my clerk draw up the contract. You can pick it up in the morning."

The deal was as good as money in the bank. Maybe, just maybe, his luck had finally turned.

Chapter 13
Slim Pickens Ranch
Moreno Valley, New Mexico

Night was falling, and the children were in the barn tending to chores when Zeke returned, dropping his government contract on the table the way a cat drops a dead mouse on the doorstep.

He stood there grinning and proud of himself.

Millie didn't have to read the paper to know what it meant. Only one question remained. "How soon?"

"Gotta have 'em there in just under three weeks. We'll leave next Monday." As he watched her face, his grin wobbled. "You don't look pleased."

"No, I am. Honestly." She dared not discourage him, but even this short absence had been more difficult than she'd anticipated, and that was saying a lot. She got up earlier each morning in hopes the nausea would pass and leave her time to direct the children in their chores before the day became warm. They all worked hard, but her energy seemed to evaporate with the dew. Each night she was more exhausted. Each day, more fatigued.

At least there'd been few contractions. She sent up a silent prayer of thanks and counted the weeks in her head like she'd done a hundred times. Maybe things would work out. If she stayed quiet, maybe the baby would stay still. Zeke would deliver the beef and pay the rent, and there'd still be four weeks left before she delivered in September. "It's what you wanted, right?"

He nodded, one eye squinted as he studied her face. "It is, but you don't look happy."

". . . it's not that." He'd ridden in tired but smiling—happier than she'd seen him in months. It seemed as if one man left and a different man returned. A new one—or, rather, the old one.

The Zeke she fell in love with.

The Zeke who would take on any challenge.

She didn't want this Zeke to leave again, but his smile was not for her. She knew that. The land was what he loved—like a mistress. Oh, he'd do his duty by her and the children, but it was his blasted work that made him happy in a way she never could. If she cherished any hope of holding him she must not stand in his way, even as he left her. "I just miss you, that's all."

Her eyes filled with tears. Pregnancy always made her emotional.

Zeke stepped near and took her in his arms.

The baby forced a physical distance between them—a tangible reminder of all the other ways they'd grown apart.

Poor little thing. If he made it alive into this world, would his father see him as just one more responsibility? And if he did not . . . the dread of that loss, that failure, was too much to consider. And if Zeke did not return? She couldn't think of that, either.

"I'm scared for you, Zeke. Fronie Crump came calling while you were gone, poking around to see what she could find out."

Zeke set her at arms' length, his face wearing the same expression he often used with Jackson. "What did you tell her?"

"Nothing! I didn't tell her anything." Didn't he trust her at all? She had some semblance of sense.

His expression softened into tiredness, and he embraced her again. "Well, things are what they are." He stroked her back absently, and she began to take heart. "Whatever you told her, I'm sure you didn't mean to. I'll just have to be careful."

Millie stiffened. If *she* told? If Crump knew anything, it was Zeke who'd spilled the beans boasting about his great plan in Rufus and Charlotte's store. She *knew* Safrona's sharp ears had to have picked up on that.

Millie let the tears fall, a damp spot spreading beneath the place where her cheek rested on Zeke's shirt. His words hurt, but it wasn't worth arguing over anymore.

Whether he stayed or went, she feared she was losing him.

※

Back at home in his own bed, a firm contract safe in hand, Zeke should have slept like a man spared the gallows.

Instead he stared at the ceiling. Sleep would not come.

This grand idea of his . . . could he pull it off?

He needed to hire on at least one new rider—someone to replace Jackson—but there was no money to do it. He'd known that before, but the low bid on his contract confirmed it.

He ought to be grateful for the sale, but *knowing* he ought to be grateful chaffed his pride. It wasn't right to take the product of a man's hard labor—all he had in the world—and make him grovel in thanks for a meager profit that seemed a pittance compared to the work expended.

Across too many years, his father's voice echoed in his head. *No one ever said life was fair.*

. . . Right—and look where that had gotten *him*.

Zeke flopped onto his side and punched up the pillow. There was still work aplenty and only one week to do it all.

. . . and Millie did not share his excitement. She'd cried herself to sleep. That, more than anything, made him feel like his plan was falling apart before he ever got the cattle out the gate.

No matter how hard he tried, he could never seem to make things come together and stay where he put them—a bad trait in a cattleman.

Bed ropes squeaked up in the loft, and a trickle of dirt drifted through the gaps between the boards above him.

Zeke brushed at his face. The house seemed sound enough when he built it, but the years had dried the wood. Shrunk and warped it. No wonder dirt and noise drifted through the cracks.

His whole life seemed like those boards. Nothing was working out like he'd planned. The daring dreams of his youth had shrunk somehow, twisting and turning when they should've gone straight. He turned again, pressing his back against the straw tick mattress, trying to ease out the kinks—yet another example of something twisted when it ought to be straight. It seemed even his strength threatened to dry up, and no amount of effort could hold things in place.

In the still of the night hoof beats hammered, echoing his thoughts—distant at first, but growing nearer.

Riders on the road.

On his land.

Zeke threw back the quilt and yanked his dungarees from the bedpost.

Horses pulled up in the yard, stamping and blowing.

He shoved his legs into his pants and reached for his rifle.

A glance reassured him that Millie still slept.

Spurs jangled as men dismounted. Crump's men?

Zeke's bare feet made no noise as he slipped from the bedroom in the lean-to through the kitchen and across the floor of the main room.

Boots thumped on the porch.

Positioned behind the door, Zeke could almost hear the intruders breathing on the other side. He cocked his rifle, knowing that whoever stood outside would hear him with equal clarity and deduce his warning.

"Zeke Pickens?"

He did not recognize the voice that whispered roughly.

"We ain't come looking for trouble."

Anyone who pounded on a man's door in the dark of night had surely either encountered trouble or come to cause some. He eased back the hammer. An echoing click served as his second warning.

"We're here on lawful business."

Zeke flattened himself against the thick log wall. "I do my business by the light of day."

"We've been retained by the Maxwell Land Grant and Railway Company to remove unauthorized occupants."

And to frighten folks from their beds? "My rent's paid up. Get off my land."

"No need to get feisty, Pickens. This is a simple courtesy call. You pay on time, and no one will come around to collect."

Any rents these vigilantes collected were unlikely to reach the home office in Cimarron. They had no case with him, and they knew it. "You wake up my family, and you'll be paying perdition. Now get off my land."

The ruffians mounted and rode away with a chorus of yips and hoo-ahs to prove they took orders from no one.

Zeke stole through the quiet house and slipped back into bed.

Millie stirred.

"You're awake?"

"Who could sleep through all that?" she answered. "What's amiss?"

No need to frighten her or give her one more reason to argue that he should stay. "Nothing. A misunderstanding. I took care of it." These men had come and said their piece. Unlikely they'd come again or cause more trouble . . . unless he didn't pay up, and that wasn't going to happen. If anything, their coming made clear the vital need for his mission.

If Millie doubted his explanation, she didn't say so. Just rolled over and laid still.

He tried to go back to sleep, himself, but the incident had stoked a fire within him. An ember of fear smoldered to fuel his anger. How dare they come onto his land and threaten all he'd worked for when he'd done no wrong to them? He lay unmoving, listening to the familiar pops and creaks of the house he'd built with his own hands, but now each noise seemed to be the sound of another nail pulling loose, another threat over which he had no control.

Yup. Things were falling apart. But he would save the ranch or die trying. This land was his only way to feed his family. Put a roof over their heads. Keep them warm in winter. Give them roots and leave his sons a legacy.

They might not see it that way, but that's the way it was.

That's the way it had always been.

∞)(∞

The creak of bedsprings woke Millie at dawn.

Zeke was up with the sunrise—headed for the barn. He left without saying a word about last night.

Millie dragged herself into the kitchen to fry eggs and start coffee, half dreading the week ahead—the pretenses she'd have to keep up when she barely had the energy to prop herself upright—but all day Friday and Saturday, at least, the house was blessedly quiet as Zeke kept the boys busy dragging fallen logs from the tree lot and stacking them to repair the holding pens.

He spent Sunday in the barn as well, working on his chuck box. He seemed proud of it—something about designing it to fit a horse instead of a wagon—but Millie couldn't bring herself to make a trip out to see it. She was too tired. Besides, those planks would have made beautiful flooring for Dixie Lee's new room. . .

Bright and early Monday morning, Jake and Adam arrived to help round the cattle up off the mountain. It took two days to find them all, drive them to the holding pens, and check brands as each one entered. Wouldn't do to sell a neighbor's cattle in with their own.

On Wednesday Beau, Forrest, Jackson—even Dixie Lee— attempted to teach Adam the fine points of calf roping as they prepared to brand this year's calves. Millie watched from the kitchen window as she rolled out biscuits, laughing at Jake and Adam's failed attempts, then stopping her mouth with the back of a floury hand to halt a sudden rush of tears. *Blast these emotions!* But Lord, she prayed there'd be no trouble on the trail. There was no way to teach the needed skills in a day or a week or even all the days on the trail put together. As earnestly as Jake and Adam tried, these abilities had to be honed over time, and delusions of proficiency could be dangerous in a crisis.

Now Zeke—there was a man proficient at his trade. He certainly worked at it hard enough . . . Millie huffed, but a smile teased her lips without permission. She used to love to watch the branding, mostly because she loved the way Zeke filled out a pair of chaps. In fact . . .

She popped the tray of biscuits into the oven. They wouldn't be ready for a while. She could walk out and call the crew to lunch then stay to watch Zeke work for a few minutes.

But as soon as she stepped out the kitchen door, the smell of burning hair and charring flesh assaulted her. She pinched her nose and yanked on the rawhide bell string. Five good clangs of the dinner bell, and she dashed back inside the house where she stayed the rest of the day.

On Thursday, she could not have left the house even if she'd wanted to. With so many extra mouths to feed, she had desperate need of Dixie Lee's help, but today the girl was more a hindrance, pestering the life out of her.

Aching to join the men and not getting the answer she wanted from her mother, Dixie Lee launched her pleas at Zeke when they broke mid-morning, and he granted instant permission. He didn't think to ask whether Millie had already told their daughter no. More likely he was flattered that the girl shared his love for cows.

Dixie Lee shot her mother a victorious glance.

Millie protested. "I do not want her culling cattle." Things could get rough as the men drove the longhorns through a chute, separating the ones they'd sell from the ones they'd drive back into the mountain pastures tomorrow so that they would not follow the herd. The cow pens were no place for a girl.

"All right, then," he said, tugging her blonde braids, "you can be our tally man. All you gotta do is sit up on the fence and count heads."

Dixie Lee tossed her braids and put on a pretty pout for her father. "That's work for greenhorns. Hardly more exciting than washing dishes."

"If it's excitement you want . . ." Forrest gave his sister a playful nudge ". . . you can always count the hooves and divide by four."

The whole lot of them trooped back out to the cattle pens, then broke at noon and again at sundown to devour large quantities of food and leave behind a pile of dirty dishes.

Millie spent the day on her feet, alone, in the kitchen. She pulled her shoe laces tight to control the swelling, but she had to take them off at night.

Zeke didn't seem to notice or care how the extra work taxed her. He came in late, fell into bed exhausted, and was up again before dawn.

By Friday her back throbbed, and her feet looked like boiled potatoes—cracked and red. It was Forrest who noticed and offered to help with breakfast. Millie set the coffeepot to boil then insisted on Dixie Lee's help so she could retreat to her rocking chair for a few moments' rest. The creak of the rockers on the wooden floor marked time as it slipped past. There was work to do, but it would have to wait. Millie focused on the rhythm of the chair, of her breath, of the spasms that had returned in the night.

A morning breeze from the open windows brought with it the crunch of wagon wheels.

Dixie Lee shot past her and ran to the front window to peer down the lane from the main road. "Beth!" She jerked the front door open and let it slam behind her with a bang.

Millie struggled to her feet and did a fair job of composing herself before Eliza arrived.

"How are you?" Eliza hugged Millie and then held her at arms' length for a good look. Her eyes narrowed.

Before she could speak Millie stopped her with a quick shake of her head. Zeke, Jake, and the boys were still talking out on the porch. "They'll want coffee."

Eliza followed her to the kitchen. "How bad?"

Millie cracked an egg into the coffeepot to settle the grounds, grabbed a dishtowel and snatched a pan of biscuits from the oven. "No worse than before." And then in response to Eliza's scolding glare, "I've been resting." She dropped the hot pan onto the drain board, already exhausted.

"I can see that," Eliza quipped.

Millie whirled to face her. "That's not fair. Forrest made these. I only gave instructions from my chair."

"So the children know you're having trouble?"

She caressed her hard, bulging stomach and shook her head. "They noticed a few things, that's all" . . . and their father did not. But if she spoke openly about the baby, about the danger, the children would naturally assume their father knew about the risks, as well. And then they'd talk with him about it, and then . . . "It wouldn't be fair to ask them to keep secrets."

"But you still ask me to."

It wasn't that simple. "The rent is due. If we pay this last installment, the land becomes ours. If we don't, we have nothing." Eliza should understand well enough about having nothing. "I won't put Zeke in that quandary unless I have to."

86

"What quandary? If he had to choose between his work and his wife, is there any question where Zeke would stand?"

That was exactly the problem. There was no question.

None at all.

Chapter 14

He had to do it, but that didn't make it easy.

Zeke put the confrontation off until Sunday, broaching the subject while he and Jackson pitched hay alone, but maybe that was a mistake.

"Please take me, Pa. Please." Jackson stared up with desperate eyes, talking fast. Pleading his case. "Wasn't I a help to you, bringing down the cows from the high meadow? Did you see me when that ol' muley broke for the brush? It was me brung him in, Pa. I can carry my own truck on the trail."

No doubt he'd try . . . but no telling what else he might try.

"I'm sure you could, boy, but I need you here." Zeke ruffled his son's straw-colored thatch. Most days it seemed like the only thing they had in common.

Jackson batted his hand away. "I'm not a kid." His quivering chin belied the point.

Aw, now, don't cry. And don't beg, neither. It wouldn't do a lick of good. Zeke smothered a sigh. "Son, I need you here to take care of your mother. I'm counting on you. You're the man around this place until I get back, eh?"

His son's eyes welled with tears, but the muscles in his jaw clenched as he straightened his shoulders. "Yes, sir." He blinked and swallowed hard. "If you're done with me, can I leave?"

Zeke nodded.

The boy turned on his heel and strode from the barn, holding his emotions close until he was out of sight, then Zeke heard his boots pound the dirt as he lit out for the house.

It wasn't fair, the boy blaming him for that decision. It was Millie who made a fuss about needing him at home. And hadn't he confirmed his faith in the boy? Told him what his own Pa had told him when he was about the same age.

He'd been a few weeks shy of twelve when his daddy left with the Marshall Guard, riding out of Texas to join the Confederate cause. *"Take care of your mother." "You're the man until I get back." "I'm counting on you."* And he'd done his best, hadn't he? He had, and if Jackson wanted to prove himself a man, he could step up and do the same.

Zeke packed the chuck box by lamplight, reveling in the silence.

The box was a clever contraption. He'd designed it himself. He'd shaped it, measured it, cut each piece to fit just as he pleased. Now he stocked it with dry beans and cornmeal, flour and lard. Arbuckle's Coffee. Black Cat Baking Powder. Even the cooking utensils fit neatly in the places he assigned them.

Building a chuck box was not at all like building a family.

At home, nothing seemed to fit.

The quarter moon was setting as he made his way back to the house.

He took his boots off at the door, not wanting to wake Millie. Padding through the kitchen, the sound of muffled crying sifted down through the cracks from the loft above him.

Zeke grabbed a leftover biscuit from the warming shelf and stood, listening.

"What's the matter, Dixie Lee?" Even when he whispered, Jackson's voice carried like the bugle of a bull elk. "Can I come in?"

"No." The sniffles recommenced.

"C'mon. Don't be miserable all by yourself."

"You'll laugh at me."

"I swear I won't."

Zeke heard the sharp heel strikes of childish footsteps and then a creak of rope as she drew the quilt divider back.

"It ain't fair. I can ride and rope as good as you . . ." his daughter hiccupped ". . . but Pa won't let me drive cattle 'cause I'm a girl . . . like girls ain't no count."

"I'm getting left behind too." Jackson's low tone was full of injury. "You think you're no count . . . He's leaving me with the women, and I ain't even a girl. He don't want me, neither."

That hurt. True, he didn't trust his rowdy, rebellious son on the trail, but did the boy really believe the rejection was personal?

"You assume a correlation that isn't necessarily valid." Forrest might be next to useless when it came to ranch work, but Zeke trusted him to see the logic of the situation.

"I don't know what those highfalutin five-dollar words mean," Jackson retorted.

Forrest translated. "Pa's taking me, but that doesn't mean he wants me along any more than he wants the two of you."

"Aw, Forrest, you know Pa loves you." It was Dixie Lee's turn to offer comfort.

"Sure I do, but that doesn't mean he has much use for me."

". . . or trusts me to have sense enough to get out of my own way," Jackson added.

The last bite of biscuit stuck in Zeke's throat. Their words stung.

"Keep it down, you three." Beau would talk some sense into them. "You'll have him hollerin' up here at all of us." The bed frame creaked as he rolled over. "Look, aren't any of us likely to enjoy this much, but we're in it until the job's done." His son laughed—a humorless snort he recognized as an echo of his own. "Ain't likely Pa's gonna let up on any of us any time before that, and maybe not after."

Not exactly the defense he'd hoped for, but apparently the best he was likely to get.

So be it.

Life was hard and full of disappointments. Maybe it was time they learned.

෨෬

Jake and Adam rode in at first light Monday trailing one spare horse.

Zeke met them on the porch with Beau and Forrest. The spare nag didn't flinch when he stroked her cheek then slipped his thumb to lift her lip. She was looking a little long in the tooth. Probably spent her better days hauling Rufus' delivery wagon and better suited for retirement than the trail, but she'd do. Beggars couldn't afford to be choosy. He gave her neck a resigned pat.

By the time Zeke pulled on his work gloves, Millie and Dixie Lee had joined them.

"Where's Jackson?" His son hadn't come down to breakfast. Zeke instinctively glanced toward the barn. Would the boy dare to saddle up and defy him in front of their friends? But there was no sign of that.

Millie shrugged. She looked tired and unwell.

Zeke looked at her closely for the first time all week and wished women were as easy to read as horses. Hard to tell about women, sometimes—at least with this one. She generally talked like her tongue had a loose hinge. When she was mad, she talked more. But when she was livid, determined, or sad she clammed up entirely. Millie'd been mighty quiet of late, and he was placing no bets as to the cause.

She offered her cheek.

He pecked it, and she flashed him a weak smile. At least she didn't seem peevish about the cattle drive. Perhaps she was just worried about Jackson.

Zeke had no time to bother with his son's theatrics. He gave Dixie Lee's pigtails a tug and saddled up.

Beau ran to lift the rails that barred the entrance to the cattle pen, and Zeke rode in.

He knew just the steer he was looking for—a big roan with a splash of white speckles across his rump. He was clearly a leader, with a strong will and the horns to back it—long and curved and as thick at the base as a man's arm—but all Zeke had to do was issue an invitation, and he'd come along easy and be proud to do it.

Spotting the roan at a distance, Zeke circled the herd and cut him out. They sized each other up for a while, and if it had been man against beef, the steer might have won. But Zeke's horse had a lot of good cow sense. Together, they had the steer outnumbered. With whistles and a few flicks of his lasso Zeke worked him through the gate.

They stood at a distance, him and that steer, while the other four cut in around the edges of the pen—Beau and Adam circling around the right side while Jake and Forrest took the left. The cattle began to bunch toward the center, then, as the riders pressed in from the rear, the herd commenced to move through the gate, following that big roan steer.

They rode away with Zeke in the lead.

He turned to tip his hat to Millie.

She waved.

Jackson was beside her, standing straight as a ramrod with his rifle by his side. No telling where the boy had been, but standing there now he reminded Zeke of the way he'd stood by his own mother.

Zeke caught his son's eye and nodded, offering a man's encouragement—a sign of faith and trust.

His son's chin jerked up in slight acknowledgement of the gesture, but his stony expression did not change.

Fine, then. If Jackson was bent on proving he was a man at thirteen, here was his chance.

Once the cattle were out of the pen, Beau rode up to take the swing position on the brand side while Adam took the other flank. Jake and Forrest brought up the rear. With whistles and gentle waves of their coiled lariats they got the cattle drifting south.

From his position at point, Zeke looked back over the loose string.

A hundred head of cattle, plus a few, and five men—mostly green—to drive them through the mountain passes.

No wrangler to manage the relief horses. Perhaps it was fortunate, then, that they had few spares. Jake led their sparse *remuda*.

No cook nor chuck wagon, either, but that, too, was for the best. A wagon would slow them down where the route got narrow and rocky—little more than the stream bed in places. Instead Forrest led an Indian pony sturdy enough to pack their chuck box over the high passes. The contraption Zeke designed was a leather box that fit over a sawbuck frame. Small and lightweight, it spared the wood planks he'd planed, and it was all they'd need. This wasn't like going up the Shawnee Trail or the Chisholm where an outfit might have to feed themselves for a couple of months or more. They'd be gone just two weeks, for all Millie's fussing—less if they got up to Cimarron after the sale and found the canyon road passable on horseback. Still, the trip would be tiring with man and beast alike taking on double duties.

Had he done right to leave Jackson home?

The question riled him. That he questioned his decision at all was irksome. Why couldn't he be as confident at home as he was on the ranch and on the trail—assessing situations, making decisions, and riding them out? He'd never once doubted his decision to sell off his herd nor the price he'd agreed to take for them. In a time of necessity, he'd done what was needful.

Zeke had to admit, though, that he knew more about cattle than he knew about being a father. Past the tender age of eleven, he had no pattern to follow. No model. His father had been gone . . . or dead. Every day he was trying to create something he'd never seen up close, and he felt about as helpless as a glass-eyed nag walking a ledge in a howling storm.

Driving cattle . . . that was different. He rode beside some of the best bosses on the trail. They'd been strict teachers. On the trail, foolishness could get a man killed and was, therefore, not tolerated. But they'd taught him how to be a man. And maybe, on the trail, his sons would learn a thing or two . . . the ones that were with him.

By mid-morning, the trail had worked its way with him, burning away anxious thoughts of his troubles at home like the rising sun burned away the morning dew.

Zeke settled into an easy rhythm. These first days, especially, it was important to give the cattle time to adjust—let them get comfortable with the idea of traveling. Besides, the Army was paying him by the pound, not the head, so he needed these critters to look fat and sleek as promised when they arrived. They'd take it slow.

Jogging along at an easy pace Zeke had time to relish his role as trail boss. The dreams he'd entertained back in the day, the youthful fantasies he'd set aside—this one seemed to have come to him at last.

With all hands fresh and the cattle moving smoothly, a stop for lunch seemed like an invitation for trouble. He didn't know if the others shared his contentment, but if they had any gripes, they kept them to themselves. They all had venison jerky and hardtack biscuits in their saddle pouches, courtesy of Jake. If they were hungry, they knew how to fend for themselves. The cattle, though, were another matter. They'd need water.

He slowed the pace toward mid-afternoon to give the herd time to drink from the stream. Zeke took the opportunity to whistle and motion for Forrest to ride up beside him.

"Head on down toward the pass, son, and stake us out a spot near the river—some place with high ground and good grazing where we can settle in for the night. Then get a fire started and get supper on."

Leading the pack pony, Forrest spurred his mount to a gentle trot, but even at that pace they soon outdistanced the herd, grazing along slow-like.

As the sun slipped behind the western peaks, Forrest's campfire was like a beacon at the bottom of a great grassy bowl, guiding them in to a place the locals called Agua Fria—"cold water."

They made that first camp well before nightfall. By the time the herd ambled into the valley pasture and began to graze, Forrest had bacon frying and coffee brewing. The boy'd even managed biscuits, wrapping the dough around sticks to bake.

Zeke plucked one up and tasted it. Not bad. "How'd you learn to make these?"

"I watched Ma."

He was impressed, but he didn't say so. Too early for praise. It might go to the boy's head. But he could brag a bit on the biscuits. "Come and tuck one of these under your ribs," he called, and the others came readily enough.

They ate like men who'd worked hard and skipped lunch, and Forrest kept the grub coming. It was some time before they went for their bedrolls and laid back around the fire for a last cup of coffee. With a bandana wrapped around the handle of the coffeepot, Forrest topped off each cup.

Zeke blew off a thread of steam and savored the thick black brew. "Mmmm . . . thick as casket varnish." He winked. "You learned all this from watching your Ma?"

"Yes, sir." Forrest grinned. "Are you finished?"

"I am, indeed . . ." Zeke returned his grin ". . . but you're not. Dishes." He winked and gave his son a coffee cup salute.

The boy shrugged and set to collecting the tin plates. "I don't mind."

"Really? How do you explain this newfound enthusiasm you have for the trail?" his brother teased.

"I've been reading. Did you know a good cook is highly valued and may receive twice the pay of the other cowboys in his outfit?"

Beau's wide-eyed gaze swung from his brother to his father. "Is that true?"

Zeke took a slow draw from his cup, then grinned. "Yup."

"You're really gonna pay him double?" Adam jumped in.

"I am," Zeke said, earnest as a preacher.

Beau scowled.

Adam jumped up to clap his friend on the back, but stopped when Forrest halted mid-stride to slant his eyes at his father. "What's wrong?"

"He's gonna pay me double, all right," Forrest sighed, "but he's paying you nothing."

Jake sputtered with laughter as Beau cocked his head. Adam prompted him. "Twice nothing is . . ."

Beau's face brightened. "Still nothing!" Then he howled with laughter as well. "Little brother, I think I like this trail drive better than I imagined."

Forrest just shook his head as he set out the dishpan and filled the coffeepot with fresh water.

"So, Pa, is this like the trail drives you remember?" Beau settled back, expecting a story.

Zeke pondered a bit. "Well, it's very different to be head honcho. A far cry from my first ride, I'll tell you that."

"You were fifteen?" Jake prompted.

"Barely." He hadn't expected his friend to remember—couldn't remember telling this story in years. "A lot has changed, but one thing hasn't. I signed on because we needed the money." Then, as now, his best efforts were barely enough to feed his family and keep a roof over their heads. "My Ma, she . . . well, let's just say she had strong objections and saw to it that I heard all of them." She'd cried for days, but he'd already signed his name to the contract, and he wasn't about to go back on his word. His mother's response hadn't been so different from Millie's, come to think of it. Both afraid. Both worried how they'd make it alone without him. But both times, he'd had no choice.

"I thought you had to be sixteen to ride the trails?" Forrest *had* been reading.

"I lied." Zeke shrugged. "Had no other option. Like I said, we needed the money." He finished his coffee and tossed the tin cup to Forrest, who caught it deftly. "I think the cow boss knew, but . . . well, I begged. Wrangler. Cook's helper. I was willing to do anything."

"Did anyone else find out? That you were too young, I mean," Beau asked.

"Oh, I suspect they knew . . ."

The *segundo's* voice was clear in his memory. "What's your name, boy?"

He'd told them. Ezekiel Pickens.

And oh, how they'd laughed.

Zeke's face had burned. "What's the matter with my name?" Wasn't right to laugh at a man's name, nor anything else he couldn't help.

"E-zekiel Pickens," the cook had drawled, shifting a length of straw that dangled from his lips. "E ... Z Pickens."

". . . and I was 'Easy Pickens' to every man in the outfit from that day forth."

But not now. Now he was in charge, and he liked the feel of it.

୫୬୦୯

With everything packed, they settled in for the night.

Zeke took first watch and woke Forrest for the second. Together they took the night ride around the herd, then checked on the horses.

Zeke pulled off his boots and slipped his aching legs into his bedroll. "You won't fall asleep on watch, will you?"

"No, sir. I won't." Forrest pulled a harmonica from his pocket. "Same music that helps me stay awake should help them sleep, right?"

Zeke nodded. "Where'd you get that?"

"I bartered Mr. Rufus for it last summer in exchange for helping out at the store." He blew a few trills, then a familiar tune, soft and soothing, floated onto the night air.

"Never heard you play before." Zeke couldn't figure any way the boy might have picked *that* up from a book.

Forrest shrugged. "Couldn't play much worth listening to, at first. I practiced in private, mostly, but then I read that cows like music— that it keeps them calm—so I thought I'd try. It's all right, isn't it?"

"Yes. That's a very fine idea you had."

Even in the dim glow of the fire, Zeke could see the gleam of his son's smile.

Boy might not be exactly wilderness material, but at least he wasn't useless.

Chapter 15
Slim Pickens Ranch
Moreno Valley, New Mexico

Aunt Charlotte's wagon rattled through the gate shortly after noon. She'd come to deliver Eliza and Beth now that the men were away.

This time Millie insisted that Dixie Lee wait for their guests to arrive rather than tearing off down the lane, but she flew into action, herself, the instant they were through the door.

"Jackson, bring the ladies' bags in, please," she directed over her shoulder as she scurried to the lean-to and reached down a new jar of cherry conserve that had somehow escaped devastation. There were plenty of biscuits left from breakfast, and from a sealed tin she brought forth her carefully rationed stash of loose leaf tea. It's exotic aroma filled the kitchen. "You'll stay for a cup, won't you?"

Her invitation accepted, she followed Jackson as he carried Eliza's satchel into the bedroom off the kitchen. Her bulging belly made kneeling difficult, but she succeeded in dragging a small square hatbox from beneath the bed. She held it triumphantly at arms' length for a moment, then blew off a layer of dust and struggled to her feet.

Huffing a bit, she carried the box to the kitchen, set it on the drain board, and untied the crumpled satin ribbon. She set the box lid aside and felt through several cushioning layers of paper, then smiled as a china cup emerged.

"How lovely!" Charlotte examined the dainty piece.

Sunlight poured through the kitchen window, making the thin bone china glow, illuminating its painted floral pattern. Five more cups soon joined the first and six saucers wreathed with matching garlands.

Eliza and Dixie Lee carried the cups and spoons into the main room where Millie laid a crocheted cloth and arranged them on the table.

"Better let me take mine in a tin cup," Jackson said, hanging his hat on the ladder back chair. "Ain't you afraid I might break that?"

"No. I am not." Millie caressed his head on pretense of smoothing his hair. "Sit."

She set out the biscuits, jam, and sugar and lit the kerosene lamp—even though it was broad daylight—just because it made the table sparkle.

She took off her apron.

Then she poured the tea.

"I declare, Millie, I forget sometimes how much we need to take a rest now and again and enjoy a special occasion in good company." Charlotte's eyelids drifted shut as she sipped. "Mmmm . . . it does a body good."

Eliza lifted her cup in toast to her aunt's wisdom. "Body *and* soul."

Millie joined in agreement, and the girls, who had been watching to see how this was done, now giggled and joined them, holding their pinkies aloft.

Jackson snorted and reached for a biscuit.

"You disagree?" Charlotte asked as Millie shot him a glare of warning. *Behave.*

Jackson reached for the jam. "Well, I do and I don't," he said, spooning a gooey glob onto his plate. "This sort of socializing, ma'am ... it's all well and good for girls and womenfolk, but men ain't got the time for it. A man's gotta work mighty hard."

"Mighty big talk . . . and yet here you sit." Dixie Lee turned up her nose and rolled her eyes at him.

Millie shot her daughter a warning glare as well, but not, apparently, in time to stop Jackson from giving her a good swift kick beneath the table. She had it coming.

With a lift of her brows as if to say *Twist the bull's tail, and that's what you get*, Millie turned a softer gaze back to her son. "Is that what your Pa told you, Jackson? That you were to be a man while he's away?" Seemed like an awful lot of responsibility to lay on a boy's shoulders.

"No, ma'am. He just said he needed me here."

Warmth flooded her heart. She'd like to think Zeke meant it—that he needed this errant son and had placed his trust in him. Somehow she doubted that, but the boy seemed to have given his father's words full faith and credit. "He does. And I do."

"Yes, ma'am. I mean to make him proud of me."

"I'm sure you'll do just fine."

The boy leaned his chair back on two legs and popped a last bite of biscuit in his mouth, grinning at her around the crumbs. "Already did." His chest puffed out as he said it.

"Did what?" Dixie Lee challenged.

"Well this morning . . ."

"You mean when you nearly missed telling Pa good-bye?"

The chair plopped down, and he stared at his sister with a puzzled expression then turned to Millie with horrified eyes. "Is that what you thought? That I was off pouting?"

She hated to answer, so she just said, "I wasn't feeling particularly perky this morning, Jackson. I don't know what I thought."

He seemed on the verge of tears. "Is that what he thought? Pa?"

"Well, son, I don't know. He was busy too . . ."

"No!" Jackson's voice bore an edge of panic. "I heard something. Last night. The chickens . . . they were all fidgety-like." His words tumbled over one another. "I knew Pa was tired, but I was scared maybe some ol' bear was trying to get into the cow pens. So I got my gun, and I snuck out to look."

The ladder to the loft was right outside their bedroom door. It creaked—always had. Zeke meant for years to fix it someday when he got time, but as the boys grew older, he'd decided maybe it was better to leave it like it was. How did the boy . . .

"I went out the window."

Had he read her mind?

"Been doing it for years." Jackson blushed.

Millie stared at him. "Are you telling me you snuck out your window alone to shoot a bear in the dark of night? What if it had been a cougar?" Mountain lions were more stealthy than bears, and quicker, too.

He hung his head. "Yes'm." But looking up quickly he said, "You don't have to worry, though, cause it weren't no bear. Just a dumb ol' coyote. I didn't even have to shoot. Followed him a good ways, though, to make sure he wasn't planning to circle back around for another go at the livestock."

Millie had no words . . . and no air in her to say them if she had.

Eliza peered at her over the rim of her teacup. "I dare say you're not looking 'particularly perky' even now, Millie."

Under scrutiny, Millie's hands went to her stomach.

"How do you feel? The truth, please."

She lowered her gaze. "There've been twinges."

Beth and Dixie Lee brightened and clapped their hands, but Charlotte motioned for them to be quiet. Wide eyed, the girls looked at each other, then to Jackson, and then all three looked to Eliza.

"No need to frighten them," Millie interjected quickly.

"I don't intend to," Eliza said, her voice calm, "but not knowing something you need to know can also cause fear." She watched until

Millie nodded reluctant consent, then addressed the children once more. "This baby has been trying to be born too early."

Dixie Lee's brows furrowed. "What do you mean?"

"Only that the baby is too little to be strong if it's born now. That's why I've come to help your Ma while your Pa's away—so I can do the cooking and cleaning and your Ma can rest and take care of your baby brother."

". . . or sister." Dixie Lee looked sober.

"Or sister." Eliza nodded.

"You children will need to help, as well . . ." Charlotte addressed her niece, but her message clearly included all three ". . . by being as quiet and useful as you can." She paused to let that sink in, then set down her teacup. "And now, I'd best be getting back to help Rufus close up shop."

Jackson was the first to jump up. He half escorted, half dragged his mother to her rocker while the girls cleared the table. Charlotte and Eliza washed up, and then the wagon rolled away.

"Where will I sleep?" Beth asked with satchel in hand.

Dixie Lee grabbed for it. "In the loft with me." She tugged her friend toward the ladder.

"Oh . . ." Millie's hand flew to her mouth as everyone looked to Jackson. "I . . ."

"It's all right," he said. "I'd just as soon sleep out in the barn so I can listen for trouble."

Far from looking cast out, it seemed to Millie he was right proud of the honor.

Chapter 16

Zeke rocked along in the saddle, feeling the powerful plodding muscles of the horse beneath him, smelling the pine and the dust, the leather and the livestock. The mid-July sun beat down on his back as they picked their way along the long climb up Cieneguilla Creek. This second day out, the plodding pace was enough to lull a greenhorn into a stupor, but this was not his first trip up the trail. He stayed watchful. A cattle drive consisted of long stretches of boredom interspersed with unexpected bursts of sheer panic.

Cattle trail's a lot like life . . .

Trouble was, you seldom saw real trouble coming. The dark clouds that began to build over the western range in late afternoon gave plenty of warning, but rain was a mere inconvenience.

His horse twitched her ears, and he patted her sweating withers. "You'll get to cool off in a bit."

Her skin flinched in response.

His skin was a bit crawly, too, come to that. All day he'd been unable to shake the feeling of being watched. Squinting, he searched the shadows at the wood's edge and listened for any snap of wood or scrape of stone that could not be accounted for.

Nothing.

Not that he could see, anyway.

Still the feeling wouldn't leave him.

He shook it off and turned his attention back to the gathering storm clouds.

Zeke drew his lips tight across his teeth and whistled, the sound bouncing between the canyon walls. "Fixin' to get drenched," he shouted, and heads turned to where he pointed. "Forrest, ride ahead and rustle up something quick for grub. Not too far, and nothing fancy."

The boy rode up, taking care not to alarm the plodding cattle as he passed, then loped around a bend and out of sight. So far he'd shown good sense. Hopefully, he'd remember to find a campsite with high ground tonight.

Zeke kept a close watch on the sky. The thunderheads piled up, thick and black.

He led the cattle from the little canyon an hour later. A small valley, surrounded by trees, opened before them with Black Lake a silver ribbon at the southern end. A good stream ran the length of the valley, separating a gentle slope from a broader meadow. As long as they could keep the cattle bunched up at this end and out of the bog that bordered the lake, all would be well. There wasn't much grass for grazing, but it would be enough for the night.

Though they'd followed the bed of Coyote Creek for the better part of the day, the steady pace of the drive prevented the cattle from drinking deeply. Now, smelling both water and rain, they hurried to quench their thirst at the stream. When they were satisfied, they ate a few mouthfuls of the sweet meadow grass, but seemed in a hurry to lay down and chew their cuds.

Zeke was pleased to see that Forrest had secured his horse and the Indian pony on pickets well up the hillside beneath the shelter of the trees. Down by the creek a cooking fire glowed and snapped. Tendrils of blue smoke beckoned the hungry cowhands to coffee, beans, and cornbread. He dismounted, but as soon as his boots touched earth a clap of thunder dashed any hope of a hot meal and a warm bed.

The storm broke. Huge drops of icy rain pelted his face and pummeled his back and shoulders, stinging wherever they struck.

"Up here!" He shouted over another roll of thunder, pointing to high ground. "Get them saddles off and covered, then rig cover for the bedrolls." Wet blankets could be borne, but a wet saddle would be a misery to man and beast.

Hat brims pulled low to shed the rain, Zeke and Jake lashed a rope between two pines and tossed a slicker over the top. "Drag that deadwood over to hold the loose end," Zeke shouted over the downpour, and the boys squelched off to obey. With any luck it would keep the shelter from flapping. Two picket lines held the rain fly out in front, but nothing could stop the rain that blew in at the sides.

"Now haul the tack up here," Zeke shouted.

The boys ducked their heads against the torrents and went to it with a will, shuttling the last of their gear under cover. Then, drenched to the skin, they huddled shivering under the shelter.

"You're as wet as you're gonna get, and you won't get no wetter," Zeke chided them. "I'd suggest you rig up another lean-to."

Adam cocked his head. "You're joking, aren't you, Mr. Pickens?" His voice was barely audible over the drumming of the rain on their tarp.

"I am not," Zeke assured him. Saddles and tack littered the square patch of semi-dry ground where they stood dripping. "There's barely room to stand in here, much less lie down. We're going to get mighty cramped if we mean to get any sleep before this blows over."

His own sons gaped at him, but no one moved.

"Get to it." He roared like the thunder.

His order was met with moans and grumbling. Zeke felt the heat rising to his face. How dare they defy and embarrass him publically? "When I was your age . . ."

"When you were our age, you were our age," Beau shot back. His eyes widened a bit with the shock of his own words, but with arms at his sides his fists clenched, and the muscles in his jaw tightened as he stood there dripping and glaring a challenge.

His oldest son had never mouthed off like that before. The response stunned Zeke so that it was a moment before he could answer. "Move!" he barked, then turned his back and sloshed off to retrieve their meal.

Jake sloshed after him down to the creek bank.

The fire was doused, the ashes sodden and steaming, but the coffeepot and Dutch oven came with lids for a reason. Zeke grabbed both. Almost an inch of rainwater covered the cornbread in the skillet. Jake drained it off, and they struggled back up the hill. By the time they returned, the boys had rigged up another shelter, but echoes of the earlier tension remained—like the rumble of thunder after a lightning strike. Sullen, they crowded together beneath the tarp and dipped out lukewarm servings of the half-cooked meal.

"The beans are crunchy." Beau curled his lip and glared an accusation at his brother.

"Never mind," said Adam. "The cornbread's soggy enough to balance them out."

"Very funny." Forrest tossed at least half his serving into the undergrowth, then held his plate out to take advantage of a stream of water draining from the rain fly. "At least the dishes will be easy to clean."

৪১৪৩

Zeke took the first look-out.

The cattle were edgy, and he reckoned he knew how they felt.

Despite the earlier grumbling, no sound came from the next lean-to. The boys slept soundly despite wet ground, wet clothes, and wet bedrolls. Hard work would do that for a fellow young enough not to fully understand the danger around him. What did these three know? They were wet behind the ears as well.

Even if they'd snored like thunder, he wouldn't have heard them over the pounding rain.

And that's what made him edgy.

He couldn't shake the feeling of being watched, and since he couldn't talk himself out of it, he decided to listen to the voice of warning . . . and to any other sound that seemed amiss, but with this downpour he couldn't hear a dog-gone thing, though he strained his ears until he thought they would bleed. A whole troop of ne'er-do-wells could be slinking through the tree line right behind him, and he wouldn't even know they were there until it was all over but the shoutin' and the shootin'.

A cold hand gripped his shoulder, and Zeke nearly jumped out of his skin. He turned, ready to swing, and grabbed for his gun before recognition sank in.

Jake threw both hands up and ducked. "Sorry." His voice was low, barely audible.

"Don't be," Zeke said, rubbing the catch in his shoulder. The damp made it ache like the dickens. "My fault. Just jumpy, I guess. Can't you sleep?"

"Been thinking . . ."

Did Jake feel it too? That crawly, skin-prickling foreboding—like a trickle of icy rain down a man's spine . . . "'Bout what?"

"What you said about leading cattle instead of driving them."

Huh. That wasn't what he'd expected. Jake had picked up on the reference before. It rubbed Zeke the wrong way then as it did now, but he stayed quiet, allowing Jake to continue.

"Take this for what it's worth, friend, but I'm thinking cows and boys may not be such different animals."

Zeke rubbed again at the nagging muscle in his back. "What are you saying?" Whatever it was, he wished he'd just get to the point.

"Sometimes it may be wise to let a young man think the journey to manhood is 'all his own idea' and just invite him to come up beside you on the adventure."

Zeke felt his hackles rise. "You saying I got no need to take charge and crack the whip now and again?"

His friend shrugged. "I'm saying most young bulls feel they've got something to prove, and it seems to scare them some. Intimidate them, and they may show you their horns." Jake grinned, shrugged, and gave Zeke's slicker a backhanded slap, raising a spray of droplets. "I'm not challenging your way of doing things. You're the boss in this outfit . . . but think on it?"

Zeke grunted and turned his eyes back to the look-out. He *was* the boss in this outfit, and he rather resented any suggestion that he wasn't up to the task—with the cattle or with his sons.

Jake rose from his haunches. "Let me know when you've had enough." The sound of his footsteps was soon obscured by the storm.

Zeke hunched his back to the pounding rain, not knowing whether Jake made reference to the night watch or something else.

Chapter 17
Slim Pickens Ranch
Moreno Valley, New Mexico

Millie loved the sound of rain on the roof. Warm and dry in the cabin Zeke built she felt safe, but her thoughts were not tucked away within the snug walls. Her heart was troubled with thoughts of the men, out on the trail in this downpour.

She timed the rhythm of her knitting to the creak of her chair's rockers and the little thump they made as they crossed the joints of the pine floorboards. The babe in her belly seemed to time its kicking with both, as if it sensed her fretting.

Jackson headed out to the barn hours ago, intent on feeding the animals and finding his bed in the loft before the storm broke. For all his father's criticism, the boy could take care of himself . . . and often of others as well.

Eliza had climbed the ladder to the girls' garret bedroom to see them tucked in. Millie heard her shoes scrape the rungs on the way back down and her footsteps as she crossed the kitchen before her face became visible in the glow of the oil lamp.

Her friend took a seat where Zeke usually sat and took up her own workbasket. They worked in companionable silence until the small scraping and giggling noises stilled above. Then Eliza rested her hands in her lap. "Can you tell me now why you would not tell Zeke about the problems you're having with this baby?"

Millie sighed. The trouble between Zeke and her was a private matter, and she would not speak of it, but a less direct answer to Eliza's question was old news. "You've never met my parents, have you?"

The question was rhetorical. Eliza and Millie had met years ago on the stage from Cimarron when both came west alone—she from Louisiana, and Eliza from Texas.

"I only know that your mother sent an entire trousseau in three trunks." And then, as if she thought she needed to put in a good word for Zeke she added, "Your husband-to-be hauled them without a word of complaint, as I recall."

Millie laughed without humor. "*Ma mère* has a rare gift for keeping up appearances." The baby gave her a good swift kick, and so did her conscience. Had she not done the same thing? Keeping up the appearance of an untroubled marriage? But her goals were not the same as her mother's motives. In fact, they were quite the opposite.

"You told me once that the Yankees destroyed your father's plantation during the Red River Campaign. Perhaps that might explain your mother's need to defend the family pride?"

"I never said he owned a plantation." A common inference, but inaccurate. Millie paused for a moment to let the correction sink in. "It was just a nice little farm in Louisiana, but Mama aspired to be a lady of leisure. The war made a convenient explanation for my father's perceived failures . . . with a little bending of the truth. You see, my Mama blamed my Papa for losing more than they ever had. The only pride she defended was her own." She looked up to meet Eliza's astonished gaze. "Instead of thanking God for the good man He gave her, my mother goaded him constantly and spent money they didn't have to impress people who weren't interested and only succeeded in making herself look ridiculous." She might be disobeying the commandment to "Honor thy father and thy mother," but that was the bald-faced truth of things, and she knew from experience that the truth was important . . . and often unpopular. The anger that welled up in Millie even after all these years surprised her. "Papa worked and worked to make her happy, but she never was." It had made an old man of him. "He was faithful, but there was no love in our house."

Eliza nodded, saying nothing, and went back to her stitching, her expression unreadable.

Millie had heard her friend tell often enough how her own mother had died during the war, succumbing to a fever she caught from a sick child she'd attended. What must she think, hearing Millie speak so dispassionately of a mother who still lived? "To lose a loved one is heartbreaking, but to watch love itself die, the victim of constant faultfinding . . ." Millie looked down, rubbing her mounding belly to caress the restless infant in her womb. "I vowed my marriage would be different."

When Eliza looked up again, her eyes reflected the lamplight, shining softly with understanding and compassion. "I've known women who manipulated their husbands by airing every worry and burden, using their discontent to keep their men serving them."

Exactly. "Crying and carrying on until they get their way . . . and destroying their marriages in the process." Millie's hand came down with a smack on the rocker's carved armrest. Embarrassed by her passionate outburst, she rubbed the spot where her palm still tingled then ducked her head as she tucked the offending hand beneath her skirt. "That's why I couldn't let Zeke know. I couldn't use this baby to make sure I got my own way."

Eliza looked thoughtful. "But don't most men have a powerful desire to provide for their families and protect them when the needs are real? When we women insist that we don't need their help, I wonder if our men might not hear, 'I don't need *you.*'" She fixed Millie with her gaze. "You are not your mother."

Eyes welling, Millie shook her head. "I won't take the risk of becoming like her."

"You weren't imagining the risks with this baby. Surely in a strong marriage husband and wife can work as a team, each knowing what's at stake?" As Millie shook her head again, a tear ran down her cheek. "I saw what it did to my father to lose our farm. It was never a grand plantation, but it was his. When he went back to sharecropping on other men's land . . . well, I can't see that happen to Zeke. He'd never forgive me. He doesn't seem to think I care about the ranch, but I do. I know he has to sell his stock, or we'll lose everything we've both worked for. It's hard enough to think of building the herd over."

If only he would trust her to help him now.

Suddenly the room seemed entirely too quiet. To lighten the mood, she said, ". . . and if he stayed, he wouldn't be worth living with anyway." That much was true. There'd just be more days like last week and the week before. More arguments. More division. "I say, 'Let him go,' and the longer he stays gone, the better!"

Chapter 18

When a cold boot nudged Zeke's bedroll, he woke up quick and angry. Angry at the way the damp cold made the ache in his shoulder so much worse. Angry that he'd let himself sleep so deep and so late. Angry at the boot and at its owner who stood grinning at him in the gray of predawn, a tin cup of coffee in each fist.

"You've been jumpy for days," Jake commented as he offered him one.

Smoke hung, wet and heavy, on the humid morning air.

"Mmmmph." Zeke took the mug. Wrapping stiff fingers around its soothing warmth, he took his first sip and swallowed, feeling the steaming brew warm its way to his guts. Didn't feel like talking though. In view of last night's assault on his character, maybe it was best to hold his tongue. Where'd Jake get off telling him how to raise his own sons? He knew the words were well intended, and he and his boys *did* seem to have more than their share of fracases of late, but . . . well, it didn't sit well. Ruffled his feathers, and he was feeling madder'n an ol' wet hen anyway, just in general.

He still couldn't shake the feeling they were being watched. A cold shiver took him, like someone had walked over his grave. He hoped it wasn't an omen. A man would have to have some kind of burr under his saddle to cache up in the woods and lie in wait all night through a mountain storm, but he could think of a dozen or so right offhand who were riled enough to chance it. "Can't shake the feeling someone's trailing us."

Jake eyed him over the rim of his cup as he blew off a thread of steam. "How long's that been going on?"

"Ever since we left, actually."

"Any reason you think so?"

"You mean like something solid?" Maybe he was just getting worked up over his own apprehensions. "Nah."

"Any other reason?" Jake prodded.

"Maybe," Zeke acknowledged, trying to sound casual. "Had a midnight call a few nights ago from some gunslingers claiming to represent the Maxwell Land Grant company. A warning to pay up or else. And Millie said Safrona Crump rode out to poke around for more information. Either side or both would oppose what we're doing, so take your pick."

Jake made a noise in his throat to indicate that he understood.

"I'd appreciate it if you wouldn't mention it to the boys, though. Like as not I'm just taking counsel from my own fears. They don't need that distraction—need to keep their minds on doing their jobs." He took another slug of the strong coffee. "Just help me keep an eye out."

Jake nodded.

∞∞

They dispensed with breakfast as quickly as possible and saddled up.

The herd was up and grazing by then. They circled around behind to bunch them up some, then Zeke took up the lead, and they began to move out. His sons, riding beside him, looked to him for directions.

"Down there a ways the road makes a fork, just shy of Black Lake beyond them trees."

Forrest squinted to look where his father pointed, then nodded.

"Head down yonder and take the left fork—the Manueles Canyon cutoff. That road'll take us to Ocate where we hook up with the Mountain Route." With all the unforeseen issues that had gone awry and those that might yet, Zeke was glad he'd had a chance to scout the trail. As long as they stayed on the old Santa Fe trail, they should make good time. "Put three good miles behind you and start looking for a likely spot to pull up for lunch."

Forrest nodded again, clucked his cheek to spur his mount, and headed off at a trot with the little Indian pony in tow.

Zeke had been pondering his next orders to Beau, and he paused again now to make sure it was worth the tongue lashing Millie would give him if she knew before he reached for his gun belt, unbuckling it with his free hand.

Beau's eyes grew wide as his father handed over his Colt.

"You know what to do with this." It was a statement rather than a question. He'd taught each of his sons the proper use and safety of firearms and made sure each of them could hit the broad side of a barn . . . without actually firing at *his* barn . . . before allowing them to hunt.

"Yessir."

"And more importantly you know what *not* to do."

Beau quirked an eyebrow at him. "Sir?"

How could he explain the foreboding that had set him on edge since they left? A good cowhand knew not to spook the cattle. A good trail boss should take the same care not to spook the hands. "I mean, should we run across danger and need to protect the herd, you know you've only got six shots." Zeke hoped he'd never need them, but he paused for effect to let the sobering caution sink in just in case. "Make 'em count."

"Yes, sir!" Beau's chest expanded some as he buckled the firearm around his own slim hips.

That done, Zeke turned to check and see how Jake and Adam fared at the rear of the herd that trailed off behind him.

He caught the flash of motion from the fringe of his field of vision.

Before he could cry out, half a dozen men poured from the cover of the forest, guns blazing.

The white-rimmed eyes of men and beasts turned toward the noise.

In a split second while time seemed suspended, Zeke saw alarm light a fire in his son's eyes. Saw him draw his revolver and offer it back to him. "Keep it!" he shouted as he reached to pull his rifle from its saddle scabbard.

The words of caution that had left his lips just moments before mocked him now. Beau had only six shots. He had but two. And it didn't matter. In either case, it wasn't likely to be nearly enough.

The cattle bawled in fright and began to stampede, nearly climbing over one another in their panic to escape.

This was his worst fear.

"Pa!" Beau shouted to be heard above the rumble. "What do I do?"

"Stay in front," he shouted back, "and stay out of their way!"

And then the charging cattle were upon them—all horns and hooves.

A fire of adrenaline surged through his veins. He goaded his mare's sides and swung wide to the right, doubling back a bit to stem the course of the herd. The marsh along the eastern perimeter of Black Lake—after last night's rain the ground would be treacherous. Perhaps he could turn the cattle away from the swamp and back in the direction of the Manueles cutoff.

The cutoff! Forrest!

Zeke scanned the eastern slope. Caught sight of his son, pulling frantically at the little pack pony's lead. Watched in horror as a masked rider barreled toward him. Saw Beau put spurs to his gelding's flanks in a race to reach his brother. Gauged the distance as the cattle bore down upon them all, and his heart leapt into his throat.

At the last moment, Beau raised his pistol and fired into the air.

The report echoed off the mountainsides.

The stranger's horse reared, throwing its rider before tearing off after Zeke's *remuda*.

The masked rider landed hard and stayed down.

The cattle turned. Now they came barreling toward Zeke again, heading straight for the bog, but his sons were safe.

Beau swung wide of the herd then surged forward, inching ahead of them.

To Zeke's horror, Forrest dismounted. *Never, never . . .* but he ceased his mental scolding as he watched his son deftly relieve the motionless reprobate of his guns and remount just as quickly.

With that crisis in hand, he tore his eyes from his younger son and turned his mount south in the direction his cattle were heading. South, not east. South. Toward Mora.

Riding right flank, Jake managed to split the herd and was attempting to route a portion of the cattle down the drier and safer west bank of Black Lake. His efforts worked, for the most part, but at least five head forged into the lake anyway and soon became mired in the soft mud.

Zeke saw one founder.

The ones that headed down the west bank kept right on a'running, charging up the low slope and into the trees. He could hear them crashing through the undergrowth, but at least it would slow them up some.

There were still more coming. Jake had circled to the rear where Adam was fighting to restrain and calm the reserve horses—guns drawn to guard them from would-be thieves. Lord help any man who tried. Jake was a dead shot.

Zeke positioned himself east of Black Lake and west of the herd—a barrier between his cattle and the marsh. It was a treacherous spot, to be sure, but it was the vantage where he could do the most good and also take the most direct route back to the lead. If he could get ahead of some of them before they passed the lake, he had one last chance of turning them back east, cross-country, to rejoin the trail.

It was not to be.

South of the lake, the cattle forged into a narrowing valley, forcing him to detour into the tree line.

He lay his head alongside his mare's neck to protect himself from low-hanging branches. One snagged his hat and ripped it from him. The stampede string cut painfully into his neck before it gave way, but he stayed in the saddle.

The sloping sides of the canyon were slick, and the creek rushed with unusual force. The cattle slid and splashed, falling and rising. It would be a wonder if any number of them weren't trampled. They ran in a blind panic long after they began to froth, and their tongues hung out.

He'd lost sight of Beau.

And then, about a quarter mile up ahead, he heard a shot and then another. The crack of pistol fire echoed up the narrow valley.

The cattle turned back on themselves, giving the back riders time to bunch them back up a bit. They churned about in the creek a while, but gradually calmed, the fight gone out of them.

The four of them—Zeke, Beau, Jake and Adam—circled them until they went to drinking. By the time the cattle had slaked the powerful thirst they'd worked up, Forrest and the pack pony had caught up with them.

"What was that about?" Adam asked, his eyes still wide.

"Do you recollect what I said about long stretches of boredom with unexpected bursts of sheer panic?" Zeke turned to humor to dispel the fear and to hide the shaking that had taken over his limbs now that the crisis was averted. "That would be one of those bursts."

A round of nervous laughter rippled through his little outfit.

Zeke reached for his canteen, and the others did the same.

"So what do we do now?" Jake asked when he'd wet his whistle.

"Well, we could head back up the trail, couldn't we?" Beau suggested. "Get back on the road we intended."

"We're going to have to head back north one way or another to round up the strays and see about the ones that got theirselves stuck in the mud," Zeke allowed, "but I don't know that I'm inclined to take that route. Might be better to get this lot settled down and fetch the others to join them." He looked up and down the trail, trying to gauge his location. "If I'm not totally bamboozled, there's a small meadow just south of here, 'bout halfway to Guadalupita." This was unscouted terrain, though both he and Jake had ridden this road on horseback many times before. He turned to him now. "What do you think?"

Jake studied a bit. "You might be right, and if that's the way of it, it'd be six of one and half a dozen of the other."

Zeke nodded agreement. "That's my thinking on it, too. On the one hand, this route is steeper, narrower. We'll have to move a little slower. But after their run, the cattle will need to drink and graze to put some weight back on them." He paused, sobered. "Especially if we come up shy a few." He didn't know yet how many had died in the swamp, how many might have gone feral, or whether some might have been stolen . . . which was another thing. "On the other hand, we don't know who those men were, but we do know they're back yonder. I'd as soon sneak in, grab what's mine, and head in an opposite direction."

Jake pulled at his lower lip. "You think rustlers, maybe?"

"I hope."

Adam's mouth gaped. "You hope it was rustlers, Mr. Pickens?"

"Yes, because if it wasn't, then it was either the land grant posse or Crump trying to keep me from paying off my lease." Whoever assailed them had not shot directly at them, and they hadn't given chase to risk being shot in return, so the chances were they didn't want any evidence to lead to their discovery. Zeke supposed he should thank God for small miracles, but if their assailants' goal was to stop the drive, they might still be lurking. Following. "Anyone see which way they went?"

Beau hung his head. "Sorry, Pa. I was concentrating on turning the herd."

"Don't be sorry." Zeke clapped his son's shoulder. "That's exactly where I expected you to focus your attention—on the herd and on helping your brother."

The boy looked tentatively pleased.

It would be wrong to encourage him, so Zeke said, rather tersely, "You did your job."

Beau sobered. "Yes, Pa. I tried."

To Jake he said, "We'll be able to scout for their tracks when we go back to look for our cattle. They were behind the stampede, so their tracks should be clear. Untrampled."

If the same could be said for all men and beasts, that would be cause for praise.

೮ೂ೧೩

They made for the meadow, which lay just over the rise and around a bend in the road where they expected to find it, and there they pitched camp. After a late lunch, Adam and Forrest—with his newly acquired pistols—were left to guard the remains of the herd while Zeke, Jake and Beau struck out to rescue the strays. "Play your harmonica for them, son," Zeke advised in parting.

He couldn't help but notice the look that slunk over Jake's face.

"What?" he asked as soon as they were out of earshot.

"Nothing," came the answer. "Just noticing the boys looked mighty pleased with themselves. All of them. They're growing in skill and confidence."

"Mmmmph." He had to allow that he'd noticed the same. He'd also noticed that he didn't worry much about the possibility that they might have to leave the boys to guard the herd overnight since they'd almost surely lose their light before they found the last of their cattle. After seeing how they'd handled themselves today, he reckoned they were up to the task, though he still keenly felt the need for more and experienced men.

They had a number of head to round up. He'd counted over lunch and compared the tally with Forrest's. Seventy head. Nearly a third of his herd was missing. Without them, he would not make enough to cover his rent. Even with them it'd be a squeeze, since they likely ran off several pounds in their little jaunt.

Zeke tallied up the days as well. He'd need all the time he could get to amble the cattle along the way to Fort Union so they could fatten back up a bit.

At least they'd gained a horse—the companion to those revolvers Forrest now wore. He hadn't wanted to say anything to upset the boys, but now he spoke in low tones to Jake. "You recognize that mount?"

"The piebald? Yup."

"You reckon it's still got an owner walking this earth?"

"Dunno. Once we find your cattle, if the valley's all clear, we ought to check." Before Zeke ever signed up for his first trail drive, Jake was scouting trails for the army—the "wrong side," but still, he had plenty of experience at tracking.

"For a body, you mean? If he was just hurt, they'll have carried him out, same as if he was dead. Either way, there'll be no trace of him."

"One thing's for sure . . ."

"How's that?"

"You can't ride back to E-town with that man's horse and saddle."

A paint horse with those distinctive patches? Zeke agreed. "No, nor his guns." His adversaries would spin the tale to their advantage—claim that it was stolen. Zeke was disinclined to trust the goodwill of most of his neighbors. He didn't trust the "land war" courts, either, and horse thieving was still a hanging offense. "I'll break the news to Forrest."

Might be a stroke of good fortune, though, come to that. If those sons-of-the-devil had deprived him of several thousand pounds of beef, at least he had a horse, a saddle, and a fine brace of Colts to even up the score a bit.

☙❧

Their path took them back uphill over rough terrain, but they took their time. Their slow progress gave them time to scan the forest and look for lost cattle—thirty-four, to be exact. Zeke needed every one of them.

Some came willingly enough, ambling out of the undergrowth when they heard the calm clop of familiar hoof beats. Others remained gun shy, lurking in the shadows. Beau went after these, deftly swinging his lasso. Often that was enough to let the cattle know he meant business, and they trotted back to join the herd without further coercion. A few, though, he had to rope around their broad horns—no small feat in the limited clearance of forested valley and ridge.

Zeke couldn't help feeling proud . . . and old. With his twisted back and stiff shoulder, were his roping days over?

At a chokepoint in the trail they came upon the trampled remains of a yearling steer. Zeke had seen before what hundreds of pounding hooves could do to flesh, but the sight was no less ghastly. In some ways it brought back the horror, and he shuddered.

"You think they just outran him, Pa?" Beau asked.

"No. Look here at his neck." A gaping wound had torn the flesh just below the jaw line. "He got gored. Long horns and narrow

123

spaces are a bad combination."

Beau gulped and nodded.

Zeke did, too, but likely for a different reason. Beau had ridden down this same valley, past this very chokepoint, in his attempt to get ahead of the herd and turn them. One slip . . . he gulped again. He'd seen men trampled before. They wound up the same as this poor critter. One—a man he'd worked with every day for a month—had been recognizable only by the fragments of color that had been his shirt and his boots just minutes before. So easily this could have been his son.

By the time they reached Black Lake, they'd recovered twenty strays. In the meadow beside the lake they found five more—two whose flanks were caked with mud—and two still bogged down in the mire. Zeke had seen five go into the swamp and watched one go down before his eyes. That one must not have made it. If he could get this steer and one ol' shelly out, that would bring the count to twenty-seven. With one gored and one drowned, that left only five unaccounted for.

Again he had to call on Beau to rope the she-cow around the horns. She'd long since ceased to struggle and thrash, so the boy got her on his first attempt.

That was the easy part.

The hard part was hauling her out. One rope was not enough.

Jake did himself credit by landing a lasso around her neck on his third try.

Zeke waited until last, hoping a third rope would not be necessary, but in the end there was nothing for it. He had to try, and he hoped he could succeed. The thought of disgracing himself in front of his son was might-near unbearable.

He measured out a loop but had barely started his wind-up when a sharp pain took him—radiating through his shoulder and down his arm. He doubled over in the saddle, clutching his elbow.

"Pa!" Beau shouted. He rode alongside his father and waited

anxiously.

It was hard to tell what hurt worse—his arm or his pride.

Zeke handed over his lariat. It almost killed him to do it. He felt like a part of his life—of himself—had died.

"I'll get her, Pa." Beau swung the lasso then handed the lariat back to his father.

The boy said nothing and acted as if he'd done nothing out of the ordinary.

Still, Zeke could not look his son in the eyes. He owed him thanks, but could not say it. Instead he looped the rope ends around his saddle horn, and the other two men followed suit. Spacing themselves, they began to back slowly away from the marsh.

"The trick's in the tension." Zeke coached as they pulled. "Too loose, and this ol' cow ain't gonna budge from where she stands. Too tight, and we could break her neck."

They pulled for upward of two hours as the cow bawled and thrashed. More than once she fell, but each time she struggled to her feet again and made a few inches of progress.

Zeke really couldn't fault her for resisting. Did she know where she was headed and suspect the fate awaiting her at the end of the journey? It seemed a shame to have lived so long in the pleasant mountain pastures only to endure an arduous trek and wind up on someone's plate. It wasn't that he was sentimental, but he'd known these cattle a long time—delivered some himself. Selling them all like this sometimes felt like a sort of betrayal.

He shoved the thought out of his mind, dug in his heels, and pulled hard against the rope.

By the time the aging cow emerged from the muck to set hoof on solid ground, men and beasts were exhausted.

One down. One to go.

They loosed their lariats, and Beau shooed the beast toward the meadow where the others grazed. Then he mounted up again. He laid a loop around the steer's neck then lassoed him again with his own rope before returning Zeke's—again without a word.

It was a gracious act—a kindness. His son had truly become his right hand man. Why did that hurt?

The steer was closer to firm ground than the shelly had been. This time Zeke and Beau pulled alone while Jake coaxed from the nearest shore.

They had him out and grazing with the others in far less time than before, but there was no way they would be able to find the remaining cattle, scout for tracks, and trail the cattle down to join the others before nightfall.

Jake squinted at the western sun, sinking quickly behind the mountains. "What do you think, boss?"

Zeke shook his head. "Ain't nothing for it but to stay put and head back tomorrow. Adam and Forrest are on their own." At least he knew Forrest could cook. "Sorry, fellas," he said. "Looks like it's going to be a long, hungry night."

Jake surveyed the valley where the cattle now grazed as if nothing had happened. "Not for them," he grinned, "and not for us, either. I've still got jerky and hardtack."

"I suggest we hit the sack early, then, so we can ride at first light."

They led their horses to drink at the stream and refilled their canteens, then unsaddled two of the mounts and set them out on pickets before rolling out their blankets.

Volunteering for first watch, Zeke left his mare saddled in case of need during the night. Jake and Beau stretched out fully clothed with their boots on for the same reason.

Zeke dared not get comfortable. He was too tired, and sleep was sure to slip up on him. Instead he settled in on a damp boulder near his mount, pulled at a stick of jerky with his teeth, and watched the stars come out.

All was quiet—not even the popping of a fire this night.

He leaned his back against a tree and watched his cattle by the light of a waxing moon. In many ways, he was right back where he'd started this morning, less five head of beef. *Was it really only this morning?*

It had been a long day. A very long day.

Chapter 19

Beau offered to take the second watch, slipping up quietly with his horse already saddled. He even offered to unsaddle Zeke's horse for him.

Zeke laid back against the saddle, stretched out his legs, and crossed his arms over his chest. It felt dangerous and unsettling to relinquish control, but his body demanded rest. Willing or not, he surrendered to sleep and knew nothing until morning.

He woke refreshed just before sunrise.

Jake broke out the hardtack.

They made a quick breakfast and began scouting for tracks at the north end of the valley. It was easy enough to spot Forrest's trail veering off to the east. The little Indian pony's hoof prints were much smaller than the other horses'. Riding point, any prints left by Zeke's mare would have been wiped out by the cloven-hoofed tracks of the herd. That left the tracks of Beau's and Jake's mounts riding flank, and Adam's leading the *remuda* all together.

At the far north end of the valley, they found the place where a group of six horsemen had lurked in the shelter of the trees before descending on their prey. These rode higher on the slopes, well out of reach of the herd.

"What do you make of that?" Jake asked.

"They came from the direction of E-Town." From where he squatted beside the evidence, Zeke looked up. "I'm thinking if they were rustlers, they'd have ridden in closer and shot truer." He rocked back on his heels. "Our first instincts seem to prove out. Whoever this was didn't want us dead, and they didn't want our cattle. They just didn't want *us* to have our cattle."

"Riding that piebald was a mistake," Jake said. "Masks or no masks, only one man in the territory has a horse like that, and he rides with Crump."

"*Had* a horse like that," Beau amended. "He's ours now, isn't he, Pa?"

Zeke pushed to his feet. "For the moment. Can't keep him, though. The horse is known. It'd be our word against Crump's how we came to acquire him, and I'd rather not risk my neck with the local judges."

"The more important question," Jake observed, "is whether they're still dogging us."

Mounted once more, they followed the tracks of the six riders as they split to spook the herd. They found the spot where the piebald's rider had fallen. There was no blood, which was good. It was confirmation that Beau had not shot him—though he'd have been well within his rights to do so. Still, it wasn't necessarily proof of whether the man lived or died. He could have broken his neck. Either way, it was plain to see the tracks of his mount where it spooked and fled to join the *remuda*, and the tracks of another horse coming and going. Someone had removed the injured rider and headed back north.

Indeed, there seemed to be three sets of hoof prints heading north. Two more sets headed east toward Manueles Canyon.

Zeke dismounted again and fingered the tracks. "That's not good. Once the riders reach Ocate Crossing, they can turn north and lie in wait for us at Cimarron or south to try to intercept us before we reach Fort Union." He punched to his feet. "We'll need to stay sharp," he said, "but we're safe enough for now."

They scouted the area for anything that might indicate who they should watch for—a bit of shirt material torn on a bush or maybe a few hairs from mane or tail—but found no sign.

"Let's split up to look for the five strays we're still missing," Zeke said. "Jake, it'd probably be best if you stayed with the ones we found. Beau, you take the west side of the lake, and I'll head further east toward the cut-off." He deliberately assigned himself the more dangerous route where he'd be least likely to find the strays. These days he was better at slinging a gun than swinging a rope. Holding his hand out at arm's length, he used his fingers to measure the sun's height above the rim of the mountain range to the east. "We'll meet back here in an hour," he said, stacking a second hand above the first.

The others nodded, and they parted ways.

When they regrouped at the end of the hour, Beau drove two young steers to join the others in Jake's care.

"Just three missing now, Pa. Do you want to re-ride?"

Zeke gauged the sun's height. "Morning's well on. We've lost a day already, and the route through Mora is longer . . ." He counted up the days in his head, weighing the need for timely delivery against the need to present a full roster of cattle at good weight. There seemed no way to accomplish both, but if he sold off his entire heard and still lost the ranch by falling short . . . what would be the point? "Yes. Re-ride, but we'll switch sides so we can slap fresh eyes on the search." He felt reasonably sure that their assailants had ridden on and were well on their way by now. His son would be safe.

Beau rode east, and Zeke rode west, cutting a broad circle through the forest beyond the meadow. There'd been no cloven hoof tracks heading back north with Crump's henchmen, so he knew the cattle had not been rustled. They were out here somewhere. He listened carefully for any sound of snapping twigs or lowing that might indicate distress, but at the end of another two hours he rode back empty.

Beau returned alone, as well. "Shall we search again?"

Zeke had to admire his son's dogged persistence. He searched the sky again. The sun was, by now, nearly above them. "I think not." His voice rumbled with grudging resignation.

This trip had already taken much longer than expected. They were behind schedule, and many miles still lay ahead of them on a longer, unscouted trail. He knew the general lay of the land, but he also knew that the route through Mora was drier than the Mountain Route. He'd have to detour out of his way each night to find grazing places where his herd could fatten back up without agitating any uncharitable lowland farmers. The locals weren't likely to be eager to share their water with a hundred head of thirsty cattle.

Ninety-nine. He made the correction in his head.

This little jaunt had cost him dearly, but he'd been lucky for all that. Real lucky.

☙Cஐ

They took their time trailing the twenty-nine head they'd recovered down the rocky river road to the meadow above Guadalupita. The way was exceedingly narrow with steep cliffs beside and below them at various points. At any other time, in a different situation, Zeke would have admired the rugged beauty of it—the layers of exposed stone jutting at angles from some prehistoric upheaval, the fringe of pine and aspen, and the underlying layer of saplings, moss, and fern. He had no time or attention to spare today on birdsong or the scent of rain-drenched earth. All he smelled was danger.

As they approached the chokepoint where the yearling steer had been gored and trampled, Beau moved up alongside his father.

"Will the cattle balk or spook if they see the carcass of a fallen comrade?"

Zeke tried not to show his amusement. "It depends. The others may walk by and take a look or a sniff. In a pasture, they won't settle in and graze or rest near the body . . . unless it's a cow and calf. If a calf dies, the mama cow usually stands nearby and calls to it, soft and low. Grieving. If the cow is dead, her calf will stay nearby or lie down next to her. But otherwise they just move over to the other side of the pasture and go right on eating. For herd animals, cows stay pretty much taken up with their own affairs." *Such as they are.* Then thinking of the narrow trail he added, "Don't matter, anyway, since there's no place else to go."

But when they reached the spot, the carcass was gone.

"Wolves?" Beau asked.

Zeke nodded. " Or carrion crows. Or even mountain lions." *Take your pick.* There was no shortage of danger and opposition on a trail drive. He prayed they'd make it the rest of the way to Fort Union with what remained of his herd intact.

An early dusk had fallen between the ridges by the time they reached the meadow to rejoin the herd. The twenty-nine strays, famished from their walk with no forage and little water, hurried to join the others as they grazed beside the little river that slowed to a trickle in this broader valley.

Adam, mounted, rode in slow circles around the herd, and Forrest had a good fire going.

Nights were chilly even in mid-summer. The scouting party was glad to warm their hands at the fire. The aroma of a hot meal cooking smelled like heaven to men who'd subsisted on jerky and hardtack and missed lunch altogether.

They prepared early for sleep with Beau offering to take first watch. He was a fine boy. *Turning into a fine man.*

Jake ambled over to where Zeke had unrolled his bedroll, gnawing on a leftover biscuit with a cup of coffee in hand. "The boys did well. Acquitted themselves like men . . ."

"They did," Zeke admitted. "I have to own that I'm pleased."

Jake said nothing. Just waited.

Zeke went back to arranging his blanket. "I can't tell them that, though."

Jake took a bite and washed it down with a swill from his cup. "Why not?" His voice held neither accusation nor challenge. Just a simple question between friends.

It riled Zeke anyway. "Because it might go to their heads. Build false confidence. A little fear will keep them cautious, and I think we've seen the need for caution several times these last two days, haven't we?" Try as he might, he could not keep the note of challenge out of his own voice. "We've been shot at and ambushed, and there's still two of them out there somewhere. We ain't safe until we sell these cattle and get the payroll to the land office in Cimarron."

If Jake took umbrage, he didn't show it. "I see your point—about the fear, I mean."

Zeke humphed in derision as he laid back on his blanket and pulled his hat down over his eyes. As far as he was concerned, this conversation was over.

There was a splash as Jake tossed the remains of his coffee into the brush. "Just don't wait too long. Life is dangerous . . . and too soon over."

The words echoed in Zeke's mind, and there was no way to shut them out.

☙❧

They finally reached Mora on Saturday night. The town was alive with revelry.

Mora was a sizeable village—not as large as Elizabethtown, and strung out along the two main roads rather than laid out in neat blocks—but it was civilization nonetheless. The locals were mostly

133

Hispanic, but a larger-than-usual selection of saloons and cantinas served as evidence that Anglo visitors had always been welcomed at this crossroads outpost. Several were owned by men who had once been cowboys but had fallen for the wiles of some dark-eyed *señorita* and decided to stay.

Zeke could sympathize. The thought of stopping in at one of the local taverns—just to sample the experience—was tempting, but he didn't want his boys around such things. He didn't want them to see *him* around such things, either. *If word ever got back to Millie . . .*

Instead he urged his cattle across the Mora River and west of town. The detour added a mile to their trip, and they'd have to backtrack that mile come morning, but it was important to avoid trouble as well as temptation. He would respect the local water and grazing rights and try not to tempt fate with would-be rustlers. Besides, where there were saloons there was fighting, and where there was fighting there were often guns. One stampede was quite enough.

"How much further to Fort Union?" Beau asked over supper.

"Maybe twenty miles yonder as the crow flies," Zeke pointed with the knife he used to pick the remains of fish from his teeth.

"Three days, then?" Adam asked hopefully.

"Four . . ." Zeke had already weighed his options. ". . . 'cause cows can't fly." He winked at the boys, though he didn't really feel much humor. "The next village is La Cueva—nice little town 'bout like this one. Nice mill there by the stream." He sketched the road in the dirt with the tip of his knife. "We'd make our delivery date easily if we could go straight to Fort Union from there."

"But we can't, can we, Pa?" Forrest interrupted. "There's a canyon. Deep one. I saw it on a map."

"Yup." Zeke scratched the obstacle to their route. "We'll turn off and head toward Buena Vista . . . then Golondrinas . . . past Loma Parda . . . and then northeast to Fort Union." He marked each landmark with an X in the dust. "Four days," he said, resigned.

Every night they delayed gave the rustlers another opportunity to ambush the herd . . . or worse.

"We can push through," Beau said. Urgency gave his voice an edge. "We don't mind the work."

"I know you don't." Zeke stole a quick glance at Jake. "You boys have worked well. Ain't you that needs to take it slow. I dare not push these cattle, that's all. If we push them, the best we can do is to drag in late Tuesday, sweaty and haggard—man and beast alike. Like as not the quartermaster compound will be closed by then, anyway, and it'd all be for naught." He'd played out every scenario in his mind, and this was his best option. "We'll make camp once we get past Loma Parda and trail them in first thing Wednesday morning— fat, sleek, and rested. It's our best chance of getting top dollar, and that still leaves us two days to get the payment to the land office in Cimarron."

He only hoped it would be enough.

Chapter 20
Slim Pickens Ranch
Moreno Valley, New Mexico

Millie plunged her hands into the dishpan and sighed. The warmth of the sudsy water relaxed her arms all the way up to her shoulders. She stretched her neck, letting her head roll in slow circles, and sighed again as the day's tension oozed out of her. Outside the kitchen window, the setting sun painted the sky with glowing color. She loved the peace of early evening. If she had to wash dishes to earn the chance to stand still and enjoy it, then so be it.

Nine days. She'd kept a tally in her head of the days since Zeke left for Fort Union the same way she counted the weeks of her pregnancy. Nearly eight months for the babe. Both father and child would be here soon, but Zeke should be safely home in good time for the delivery.

Days on the ranch had settled into a familiar, if challenging, rhythm. Millie offered a prayer of praise for her two youngest and for the friends who had come to help. She could not have managed without them.

Eliza and Jackson headed out to the barn after supper to tend the livestock.

Beth and Dixie Lee had gone early to the loft without a bit of prompting. The quiet up there was unnatural, but she was too grateful for it to allow suspicion to ruin the moment.

As if they could hear her thinking, a peel of giggles rained down.

Millie picked up a plate, fished out her dishrag, and smiled.

More giggles drifted down the ladder, then "Let me see that. You've had your turn."

"I'm not done yet."

"Gimme!"

It was Dixie Lee's voice she heard, growing loud and demanding. "Are you remembering to be a good hostess?" Millie called over her shoulder.

The only answer was the sound of scuffling.

"You have one to look at."

"Yes, but yours is better."

Shoes scraped against the boards overhead, the bedding rustled, and paper crumpled.

"Girls, do I need to come up there?" Millie sincerely hoped not. Her bulging belly would make climbing the ladder to the loft very difficult.

"No, ma'am," her daughter answered sweetly, but then whispered coarsely, "I want it."

Did they think she was deaf?

Next came the unmistakable sound of pages ripping.

That snuffed it. She was going to have to go up there.

Millie hoisted herself up the ladder, scraping her stomach on each rung, until her head poked through the scuttle hole. "What's going on up here?"

Both girls jerked upright to sit primly on the edge of Jackson's disheveled bed. Beth kept her hands hidden behind her, but Dixie Lee scrambled to shove a fistful of pages beneath the rumpled pillow.

Millie heaved an exasperated sigh and lifted her eyes to heaven . . . *from whence my help must come.* Apparently they thought she was blind as well. "What have you got?"

The quarrelers merely blinked at her and moved closer together, closing ranks—their disagreement suddenly mended.

She was getting nowhere. Millie looked back down the scuttle hole into the kitchen. There was no sight nor sound of Eliza and Jackson. She'd have to go up herself.

Palms flat on the rough plank floor, elbows bent almost even with her ears, she dragged herself through the opening and sat on the ledge to catch her breath.

The girls just watched her, eyes rounded.

Whatever they've got, it must be bad. She rolled to her knees then straightened them, bumping her backside against the sloping joists of the roof.

The girls tittered, but one glare from her stilled them.

She grabbed the roof joist and hauled herself to a standing position. "Now, then, young ladies, I will know the cause of the argument that's forced me to climb up here." She used her sternest tone, and truly, by this time, she was inconvenienced enough to mean it.

Beth broke first, drawing her hand from behind her, clutching a roll of well-worn pages.

Millie recognized what she held from the cheap binding. "A paperback novel?"

She held out her hand, and Beth laid the offending item in it. The pages unfurled to reveal a tawdry illustration depicting a maid of improbable proportions, swathed in some gauzy getup. Millie was repulsed even before she read the title—*Dewitt's Ten Cent Romances.* She wanted to fling it, but Dixie Lee, red-faced, was already shoving her own contraband toward her.

Millie stared at the pages, yellowed with age and bedraggled from repeated readings. "*The Privateer? The Bride of Pomfret Hall?*" Her hands fell limp to her sides. "Where on earth did you get such things?"

And then the excuses began to pour out, hot and fast.

"We only found them . . ."

". . . under Jackson's bed."

If that was meant to pass for confessions and repentance, their excuses were as thinly veiled as the women on the books' covers.

Millie stood deliberating for what felt like an eternity. It was hard to think about what to say to the children, how to deal with this situation, when this whole ordeal brought back all the frustrations she felt toward Zeke. Wasn't this clear proof why Dixie Lee needed a room of her own? If she and Beth hadn't been sleeping in the loft where the boys stayed . . . if she wasn't with them all the time, observing their mischief and picking up their rough habits . . . if her daughter could have had a little space of her own where Millie might have watched more closely . . .

A door slammed below.

"Jackson!"

Her son's head popped from the scuttle hole, posthaste. He wore a quizzical expression, but a hint of knowing, which Millie recognized as the dread of discovery, lurked in his eyes.

Millie displayed the incriminating publications. "Perhaps you'd care to explain how these came to be here."

Dixie Lee's obvious relief bordered upon gloating, though Beth squirmed in apparent sympathy for Jackson.

The boy blushed furiously. "Ma, I didn't . . ." He scrambled up into the loft and took the paperbacks from her as if to gallantly relieve her of a burden. "Adelaide Crump brought them." He lifted the corner of his mattress and retrieved three more, which he added to the stack.

"She's sweet on Beau," Dixie Lee put in, "but he don't like her. He wouldn't take 'em."

Millie threw her daughter a warning glance.

By this time, Eliza's head had also popped through the ladder hole.

With all the witnesses assembled against him, Jackson's

mortification was now complete. "I only read them for the stories, Ma. Honest." His eyes pleaded with her to believe him.

"And you didn't even look at the pictures?" his sister taunted, seemingly unable to resist the opportunity to shuffle blame from herself.

A glare from both her mother and her brother silenced the girl.

Millie drew a deep breath and rested a hand across her stomach—her constant reminder of the melodrama playing out in her own home. "I don't know but what the stories bother me more than the pictures."

All three children stared at her until Beth quietly asked, "Why, Ma'am?"

How could she explain? "Because these stories are all fiction. Real life and real love are much harder."

"And a much greater adventure, as well." Eliza smiled up at her.

Millie nodded. She'd allow that was true—or that it could be. "What we're trying to say is that grown-up life isn't always romance and roses."

The baby kicked furiously.

Millie rubbed her belly as she focused on Jackson's face. "You store up images of what the perfect woman should look like, but a real woman is more than just an ideal on paper." She shifted her gaze to the two girls who shuffled their feet, hands clasped contritely. "And you like to read stories about perfect men who always know just the right things to say and who always behave heroically. Well, real men aren't like that, either."

"Most do the best they can to be kind and brave," Eliza added, "but in real life there's no author to put all the right words in people's mouths and make sure that things end happily ever after."

"That's right," Millie said, though right now she was hoping desperately that her and Zeke's story would end well. "I don't want you children to cut your teeth on stories like these and grow up pining after perfection." Her mother had done that, and she'd nearly destroyed a marriage that could have been very satisfying by trying to force a good man to live up to an ideal forged of fantasies.

Eliza was still perched halfway up the ladder—her chin resting on her crossed hands. "What we want you to understand is that happiness isn't so much about getting everything you can think of to want as it is about learning to appreciate what you've already got."

Her words caught Millie's mind up in a whirl of fragmented thoughts that skipped like dust devils from scene to scene. Zeke, forced to head a house when he was barely older than Jackson. Always responsible to be brave for others, he'd lost his childhood trying to live up to the ideals of a father who was larger than life and then was gone. He was beat up and worn down, yet he kept working. He'd always worked. And without meaning to, she'd implied that he should do more. Be more.

Dixie Lee's room could wait.

"I didn't marry your father because he was perfect. I loved him even though I knew perfectly well that he wasn't—that he had faults, same as me." And suddenly her heart seemed to swell until it felt too large to fit beneath her ribs. "But he's kind and brave, and he's true to me. That's real love, and it's not what you see written in stories like this."

The children stared at their shoes for a bit, and when they looked up their eyes were shining.

Eliza disappeared, climbing back down the ladder—signaling a successful end to the conversation.

Jackson handed the little stack of dime novels back to Millie. "Here, Ma. I don't want these. You can burn 'em or give them back to Adelaide or Mrs. Crump."

Now there was a thought. Where had that child gotten such a lot of tripe? As little as Millie thought of Safrona Crump, she doubted the woman knew what her daughter was reading or that she would approve. Some of the mercantiles in Elizabethtown carried such things. They appealed to the cowboys and mining men, but where would Adelaide have gotten the money? And how could she have bought them, unseen? Besides, some of these copies were battered with age and use. Could the child have pilfered them from her father or from his men? If so, returning them might open a hornet's nest. Best to leave things as they were for now.

Millie accepted the novels. She could decide what to do with them later. "Thank you, Jackson." She turned toward the ladder.

"And Ma . . ."

She paused.

". . . I'm sorry I disappointed you."

Her heart swelled still larger, and her eyes welled with tears. If only his father could see how much their trouble-prone son was like him. "You haven't disappointed me, Jackson. I can always count on you to do the right thing in the end."

With that she felt with her foot for the rung of the ladder, heard the scrape of her sole as she missed the step she could not see, and then she had barely time to acknowledge her quick descent before she was lost in a sea of pain.

"Ma!"

A chorus of screams rang out above her, and then the world went black.

སོགཞ

Millie's eyes fluttered open, and a ring of frightened faces slowly came into focus. She hurt in so many places it was hard to take them all into account. To better take stock, she tried to raise her head.

"No, no." Eliza reached out a hand to stay her. "Lie still. Where do you hurt?"

"My head. My ankle." Millie became aware of its throbbing . . . and of another rhythmic pain. She could not hold back her panic. "The baby!" Her contractions had started up again, and she felt the warmth of wetness spreading beneath her.

Her gaze locked with Eliza's, asking unspoken questions, and receiving all too plainly the answer she feared.

Her friend spoke calmly. "Jackson, sweetheart, we are going to be needing Aunt Charlotte. Do you think you can saddle the horse and find your way to town in the dark?"

Her son's eyes were sober with concern. "Yes, ma'am. I'll take the barn lantern. Should I come back to help you, or stay the night and bring Miz Charlotte at first light?"

Eliza shook her head. "We'll need her tonight. You can help Uncle Rufus hitch up the wagon, and Aunt Charlotte can drive it."

He nodded, took up his hat and gun, and was gone. The pounding of his horse's hooves echoed through the thin night air.

Chapter 21

Looping strong arms beneath Millie's head and armpits, Eliza helped her to a stand.

"Oh!" She cried out as her weight came down on a badly sprained ankle . . . and as the baby's weight settled low in her belly, bringing on a fresh contraction.

"Get a fresh rag and pump up some cool water," Eliza directed her daughter, and the girl hurried to obey.

Leaning heavily on her friend's arm, Millie limped into the bedroom.

Eliza closed the door behind them.

Millie propped herself, shaking, against the bedstead while her friend spread a fresh quilt—old, but clean—over the bed and rummaged for a clean nightgown. Eliza worked quickly, but the effort of standing even for a few minutes caused Millie to break out in a cold sweat. Unable even to stand up straight, she pressed her lips together against the pain as Eliza untied her skirt and petticoat and unbuttoned the shirt she'd pilfered from Zeke. She had to let go of the bedpost for just a moment so that Eliza could pop the nightdress over her head, but even those few seconds of effort caused the darkness to close in from the edges of her vision.

Once dressed, the springs creaked as Millie eased her weight onto the mattress and sagged forward to prop her head on her hands.

Eliza let her collect her breath for a few seconds while she opened the door again.

Dixie Lee slipped in quietly to fluff and stack the pillows for her mother's sore head, and Millie lay back upon them.

Eliza gathered her feet and lifted them onto the bed then straightened her nightgown. Her shoes were still on. It seemed odd that Eliza didn't remove them, but Millie was too tired to bother asking why.

Beth returned with a damp cloth as instructed, and Dixie Lee followed, carefully balancing a full pitcher of water for the washstand.

Eliza laid the cool cloth across Millie's brow.

It felt good. Millie allowed her eyes to flutter closed, but when she closed out other distractions, the throbbing of her head and ankle and the distinct, rhythmic sensation that gripped her bulging midsection overwhelmed her. She snapped her eyes open again.

Eliza moved to the other side of the bed. She sat, resting one hand softly on Millie's stomach and feeling for her pulse with the other. "You have quite a knot on your head, I'm afraid. Try not to fall asleep."

As if she could. Millie lay still, searching her mind for calming, pleasant thoughts. She pictured her first view of the ranch the day that Zeke had fetched her and Eliza from the stage in Cimarron . . . but that was the day they'd found Eliza's Uncle Rufus robbed and beaten along the road. He'd had quite a lump on his head, too, that day, and they'd been unable to awaken him. And now Zeke was gone on account of this blasted ranch that seemed to have started with trouble and ended the same way, with little but trouble in between. Just thinking about it made her head and pulse pound. No, her introduction to the ranch wasn't such a calming memory after all.

She cast about in her mind, searching for another memory, and recalled a mountain lake she and Zeke had hiked to in the first days of their marriage—back when it was just the two of them. They'd been so young back then and so much in love . . .

That thought was interrupted by a kick and another contraction. Her eyes darted to meet Eliza's.

She nodded. She'd felt it, too.

Millie was glad her friend was counting. She was too tired, and her head felt dense and fuzzy. Gathering her thoughts once more she envisioned the mountain meadow where she and Zeke had picked flowers for their wedding. That was an entirely pleasant day. So long ago . . . but it would do. She focused her mind on recollecting every detail—the sound the creek made as it flowed over the rocks, and the wind in the meadow grasses, and the blue sky arching overhead—then drew in a deep breath, and released it slowly.

Beth and Dixie Lee had scooted out of the way and now hovered in the doorway, hands clasped and eyes large.

Dixie Lee whimpered. "I'm so sorry, Mama. This is all my fault." She hiccupped. "If I hadn't sneaked out them ol' books . . . if you hadn't had to come up to the loft . . ." The girl's confession came out in a rush, words tumbling over one another. Her face contorted with genuine remorse, and her tears flowed freely.

Millie tried to lift her head to look at her daughter. "Don't do that, child—berating yourself like that." It took great effort to keep her voice calm and reassuring while her stomach felt as if it were being squeezed in a vice.

Eliza pressed her head back onto the pillow, which was good because even small movements caused Millie's head to throb with a dizzying vengeance.

She took a calming breath as the contraction ended. "You cannot undo what's done. Hard things happen, and they don't have to be anybody's fault. Trouble just comes, sometimes, and there's not always anything you can do to get out of its way."

Hadn't they had a rash of that kind of trouble? She'd tried to

shield the children from as many of their difficulties as she could—
Zeke would say too much—but they'd be grown soon enough with
troubles of their own. It was enough that they should observe the
truths of life now and the way adults handled problems without
having to bear all the world's ills on such young shoulders.

And what kind of example were their children observing? She and
Zeke had a tendency to face their challenges alone rather than
working together. She saw that clearly now, and the consequences of
their errors. He was off saving their ranch by himself . . . and she was
here having this baby by herself. How foolish she'd been. *Forgive me,
Lord. Deliver this child safely, please. Let this baby thrive, and please, Lord, let
me live to raise it.*

"Now, then—dry your tears and trust in God . . . and go light the
lamps and set them in the front windows so help can find us."

୫୨୦୨

An anxious hour passed before they heard pounding hoof beats
and the rattle of wagon wheels crossing the bridge before the gate.
Help would arrive soon.

Jackson escorted Aunt Charlotte through the cabin to the
bedroom in the lean-to . . . and was ushered right back out by Dixie
Lee and Beth.

Millie tried to remember what condition she'd left her house in.
This afternoon seemed like days ago. It didn't matter, anyway.

Eliza rose from the bed to make a place for her aunt and closed
the door behind the children before refreshing the damp rag on
Millie's forehead with cool water from the pitcher in the washbasin.

Drawing a pocket watch from her apron, Charlotte placed one
hand on Millie's belly and focused intently on the sweeping second
hand.

The house became unnaturally quiet. The clockworks, ticking off
the seconds through one birth pang and then another, were like a

mechanical heartbeat racing to match her own.

Finally Charlotte stood and placed her hands on her hips. "Contractions every five minutes. How far along are you?"

"Almost thirty-five weeks, by my count. At least five weeks early. Maybe six." Millie moved her hand to cover the spot—suddenly cool—where Charlotte's hand had been. "My time coming this early and having delivered so many before, I'm surprised my labor hasn't progressed any further." *Surprised, but relieved.* She laughed to cover her nervousness. "At first I wasn't sure you'd get here in time. I mean, the baby must be small . . ." *Hopefully not too small.*

Charlotte smoothed her hair with a motherly touch. "Perhaps not so small. How were the weights of your other babies?"

"Each a bit larger than the last, except for Dixie Lee."

Charlotte nodded and offered a consoling smile. "That's often the case. This little fellow may have a bit of weight on him, and he'll need every ounce of it." She thought for a while. "Had the baby dropped?"

"Not until I fell."

"And that's when your water broke?"

Millie nodded miserably.

"Have you felt the babe kick since?"

"Yes!" That had to be a good sign.

"Where?"

"Low. Here." Millie pointed out the spot.

"May I?" Charlotte asked and waited for Millie's nod before placing both hands on the little mound that now lay still.

She felt about for a while—pushing here, poking there. Then she took Millie's hand in hers and placed it just beneath her ribs. "Do you feel that? That hard spot?"

Millie nodded and smiled.

"That's your baby's head." She moved Millie's hand lower and centered. "And that? That's your baby's backside."

Giggles from the other side of the door let Millie know that the girls were listening, and the sound of pacing boots made it clear how

Jackson was passing the time.

"The feet are over here—where you felt the kick," Charlotte said. Standing up, she placed her hands on her hips and scowled. "Your baby is breech."

Was that so bad? "Jackson was breech. Came into the world feet first, and he's been landing on his feet ever since." Her youngest son took more risks and tempted fate more often than either of his parents found comfortable, but so far he'd always come out on the winning side of things.

Charlotte smiled, then sobered. "This little one isn't trying to come feet first." She tapped the spot earlier where Millie had felt the baby's backside.

Millie caressed her stomach, feeling the way her baby was positioned. *Not good.* She'd known women who died in childbirth when a babe like this had trouble being born. She had so many questions—questions she was afraid to ask.

"You can deliver him like this, but it will be difficult . . . and painful." As if reading her mind, Charlotte began to supply answers. "There's also a risk that the cord will be crushed before the baby is safely out."

Jake's first wife and child . . . She glanced at Eliza, wondering if they shared the same foreboding. Apprehension threatened to choke her. Why had she thought she wouldn't care if Zeke weren't here? She longed for him now—for the reassurance of his strong presence.

"There is another option."

Millie raised her eyebrows, encouraging Charlotte to continue. At this point, she was very much in the market for options.

"We can turn the baby."

Yes, she'd heard of that being done. Sometimes successful, sometimes not, the process was uncomfortable, but it seemed her best choice under the circumstances.

She nodded assent. "I'm willing to try."

"Good, but first let's finish getting you ready." Then to Eliza she said, "I'm surprised you didn't get her shoes off first thing." She began to unlace one boot while her niece took the other.

"She sprained her ankle when she fell," Eliza explained as they tugged at the shoestrings. "Has a goose egg on the back of her head, too. With everything else we had to deal with, I figured the shoes could wait. Might even hold down the swelling."

Millie winced and cried out as the shoe came off. Pain shot through her, bringing on a wave of nausea. She glimpsed her ankle—already purple with bruising—as the two women lifted her feet and placed them under the blanket.

"Now, then . . ." Charlotte began to roll up her sleeves. Making eye contact with Eliza, she jerked her head toward the door. "Best send those children to their beds. This may be a long night."

Eliza's footsteps sounded unnaturally loud on the wooden floor boards as she crossed the room. When she opened the door, three sets of anxious eyes peered in.

"Y'all might as well go on to bed," she said, as if the children had not already heard that much with their ears pressed to the door. "We'll call you when there's need."

"But . . ." Dixie Lee began to protest.

"No buts." Eliza shut down her arguing. "We'll let you know when anything important happens. It's not like you can't hear as well through the ceiling as you can through the door."

"But I can't," Jackson protested. "I won't be able to hear nothing out in the barn." He straightened to his full height and squared his shoulders. "Pa told me to take care of Mama while he was gone."

"What could *you* do?" Dixie Lee snapped. "If I gotta go to bed, you do, too, so you'd best git like Miz Eliza said."

Jackson ignored his sister. "Please let me help," he begged.

Millie heard genuine alarm in her son's voice—different than her daughter's sass and anxiety. *Provide and protect.* A man's natural instincts ran strong through her son, despite his youth. *Best give him something useful to do, or he'll hound the life out of us.*

"Jackson?" She made her voice calm so he wouldn't worry more. "We may need some hot water. You could pump some and build up a fire in the stove to warm it." In all her life, she'd never heard of a birthing where anybody actually needed boiling water, but she'd heard of many men sent to boil some. Now she knew why.

"Yes, ma'am." He sounded grateful.

"And after that you can unhitch Uncle Rufus' horse from the wagon and take her to the barn with yours. They'll be wanting feed and water by now. Can you do that?"

Jackson gave a hearty "Yes, ma'am!" and was out the door.

Dixie Lee poked her lip out and put both hands on her hips. "I want to do something, too."

Millie started to heave a sigh, but a strong birth pang morphed it into a groan. She gritted her teeth and grabbed the bedposts with a white-knuckled grip.

Both girls' eyes flew open with alarm.

Eliza intervened. "Why don't you see if you can find some soft blankets for your new little brother or sister?" And then when the girls stood blinking, she added, "I'm sure you have some. They'll be small." She indicated the size with her hands. "Maybe your Ma lent them to you for your dolls?"

Understanding dawned. Dixie Lee nodded and scurried off with Beth close behind. They soon returned with a small stack of receiving blankets.

Eliza took the little stack from them. "Thank you, girls. Now, go to bed . . . or at least to the loft . . . and try to sleep."

"I need something else to do," Dixie Lee argued. "Jackson got two things to do."

"Then pray," Eliza told her. "Truly, that's the best thing any of us can do."

§⟩⟨₰

Through the thin lawn of Millie's nightdress, Charlotte felt again the mound where the baby lay. Rubbing her hands to warm them, she placed one palm on either side of Millie's stomach. She closed her eyes, concentrating on the shapes beneath her hands.

"Head . . . rump . . . feet . . . back . . ."

Her light touch tickled Millie's belly.

"Clockwise, I think, and his back should come to the front." She pushed her sleeves up over her elbows and locked eyes with her patient. "Are you ready?"

Millie bit her lip and nodded.

They waited through the next contraction, then Charlotte said, "This may get rough . . ."

She placed one hand firmly on the hard lump that indicated the baby's head. With the other, she dug her fingers in beneath its rump.

Millie scrunched up her eyes and bit her lip harder. She mustn't cry out and alarm the girls. Instead she shifted her attention to the sounds outside her room. The soft, bare-footed patter above let her know the girls had at least begun to prepare for bed. The clank of the door to the woodstove marked Jackson's progress with his assigned tasks.

Charlotte's hands pressed in—hard—and twisted.

Millie gasped, then held her breath as the pressure continued.

Outside the bedroom, Jackson's boots crossed the main room of the cabin. The front door hinges creaked softly, then there was a gentle click as the door closed. He'd be heading to the barn now. *Good.*

Charlotte pushed again, shoving the baby into position.

Millie held her breath until she thought she might explode. Her belly felt as if it would burst, her muscles tightening in rebellion.

"Relax," Charlotte ordered.

As if she could. Millie searched her mind again for that flowered meadow.

Suddenly the babe in her womb turned with a belly-heaving roll and, as if on cue, another contraction seized her—a hard one.

Millie cried out in spite of herself.

Almost instantly there came a frantic rapping on the bedroom window, and Jackson's anxious face appeared sandwiched beneath two long, gentle muzzles. His face pressed between the two horses, and all of them staring with such earnest concern—the scene was so comical Millie would have laughed if she hadn't been struggling not to scream.

Eliza opened the sash.

"Ma . . ."

"Shhh! She's fine." Her friend spoke in a low whisper. "Go on, now, and tend to the horses, and let us tend to your ma."

"But I want to help," he pleaded. "I need to help."

Eliza heaved an exasperated sigh. "Jackson, there's nothing you can do. Now please go tend to those horses like we asked." Her voice carried a sharp edge, and she closed the window with a firm thump intended to end any further discussion.

She's tired, no doubt, and worried. Still Millie wished Eliza hadn't snapped at the boy, wished she hadn't cried out and alarmed her son, wished she could have reassured him. He only meant to help.

Just then another contraction began to grip her belly—invisible fingers squeezing insistently. The pangs were coming closer together now. For good or for ill, this baby would not delay its entrance into the world much longer. As the pain sharpened she cried out again despite her resolve.

Outside the cabin hoof beats rang on the hard-packed earth, coming from the direction of the barn and pounding toward the front gate where they changed pitch as the rider crossed the bridge over Moreno Creek at full speed.

Jackson.

Through the window a full moon glowed high in the sky. It was long past midnight.

Millie moaned and unscrunched one eye to meet Eliza's troubled gaze. Where did he think he was going at this hour?

Aunt Charlotte never turned her attention from Millie, but Eliza stepped away long enough to call through the floorboards above them. "Girls, are you still dressed?"

"Yes, ma'am," came the guilty confession. "We were sort of hoping . . ."

There was no time to waste on childish excuses. "Get your shoes on, then, and see if Jackson's got the horses in their stalls, please."

. . . but Millie knew at least one would be missing.

Whatever their questions, to their credit the girls didn't waste time asking them. For once they obeyed immediately. Clomping boots caused a small shower of dust to filter through the boards of the ceiling above the bed. Then there was a clamber and scrape on the loft ladder, and the back door squeaked open on its hinges and slammed shut again. Footsteps raced toward the barn, and in a few moments came pounding back—a rhythmic bass accompanied by a treble of children's shouts.

Millie wished they wouldn't yell so. Her head had begun to pound again. As they neared the house, their alarm was clear, but she couldn't quite distinguish their words.

The backdoor squeaked and slammed again. "Ma! Ma!" Dixie Lee had worked herself up to a frenzy.

Eliza rushed to open the door, and the girls tumbled into the bedroom.

"He's gone!" Dixie Lee exclaimed, "and he took the horse with him." Red-faced, Dixie Lee swiped away tears.

Was she angry? Scared? Both? Millie could well imagine the rush of emotions that must be coursing through her daughter. She was experiencing the same, and resenting deeply the timing of her son's theatrical exit.

At least he took the horse, and his gun was likely still in the saddle holster. Wherever he'd gone, Jackson had a better chance on horseback than he did on foot. But where could he have gone?

Beth reached into her pocket and pulled out a folded paper. "He left this," she said as she handed the scrap to her mother, who handed it to Millie.

The letters swam before her face, but she could make no sense of them just now. Millie waved off the effort and handed the message back to Eliza, who opened the note and read it in the lamplight.

Gone to fetch Pa home. Don't worry. Love, Jackson.

Millie's hand fell limp to the mattress. Surely he would not attempt to catch up with his father on the unfamiliar road south to Fort Union, but would he risk taking the canyon route with all its treacherous tumbled stones?

She swallowed hard as tears welled in her eyes and spilled over to run down her cheeks. Tears of frustration. Tears of anger. "He's a child!" A boy of twelve. Alone. In the dark. *What was he thinking? Likely he wasn't . . . as usual.*

Then in a blaze of insight she understood. Jackson *was* thinking, but he was thinking differently—not as a child, but as a man. Protecting. Providing. That's the way he showed his love . . . and he'd learned it from his father.

The tears still flowed, coupled with prayers for safety, but her anger was gone. These were tears of love.

What an amazing transformation she'd experienced this night . . . or had it begun before? Soon . . . with God's grace . . . she would meet a new child, tiny and helpless as Jackson had once been. She shook her head in wonder as the truth sank in. The journey from infancy to manhood was a leap across a broad chasm, but sometime in the last month her twelve-year-old son had decided to take a run at it.

The risks were huge, but there was nothing she could do now but pray a blessing over him, over the baby, and over herself.

Lord, protect my son. Protect us all!

Then she did her best to turn her mind from the child trying to grow up back to the child trying to be born.

Jackson had always landed on his feet before.

Chapter 22
Fort Union, New Mexico

Zeke rode tall in the saddle as his bay mare passed through the gates of the supply compound at Fort Union trailing ninety-nine head of longhorn cattle and feeling like he owned the world. He might be heading a two-bit outfit with a rag-tag *remuda*, but today it just didn't matter none. He was the cowman. The cattle boss.

At his whistle, Jake and the boys bunched up the cattle, and Zeke rode a slow circle around them, surveying and feeling himself surveyed. He'd made it. In spite of rain, rough terrain, green hands and the outright attack of his adversaries, he'd made it. He'd earned the right to enjoy the admiring glances of other men. Hungry men. Men who understood the difficulty of his work and what it meant to their lives.

But the two people whose admiration he most craved would never see this. His father was dead, and Millie was comfortable at home. Today he would sell off might near everything he owned. Lord willing, it would be enough. A two-day ride would put him in Cimarron where he'd pay off his land to make sure his family would continue to live safe and secure—if Crump's men didn't bushwhack and waylay them before they could get there. Then he'd return home, broke as ever, and start all over again, building a new herd from scratch. That's how Millie would see him—penniless and struggling. How could it be otherwise?

For what it was worth, he wished he could make her proud.

One young private indicated an empty stock pen.

They drove the cattle in, and the soldier dropped the rail behind them.

Jake and the boys waited as Zeke dismounted.

He found the commissary officer in the storehouses of the quartermaster depot, like before.

"Mr. Pickens," the man stuck out his hand. "I expected you the first of this week. We were beginning to think you'd gone AWOL on us."

A shadow tarnished the shine of Zeke's esteem, and a kink knotted his stomach a bit. He took the man's hand. "No, sir. Just ran into a patch of trouble along the way, is all. We did agree on three weeks, did we not?"

The captain flipped through a stack of paperwork until he came to his copy of their contract. "Three weeks passed yesterday."

The commissary officer didn't look angry, but that didn't stop Zeke's hands from sweating. "Yes, sir, three weeks from the afternoon we struck our deal, but I didn't sign the paperwork until three weeks ago this morning. Do we still have a contract?"

"Oh, indeed." The officer chuckled and gave his stomach a meaningful pat. "Not to sound unsympathetic, but my concerns were of a purely personal nature."

Zeke laughed, too, but it came out high and unnatural sounding.

Together they walked to the stock pens. Zeke tried to look composed and confident as the officer counted the beeves and compared his tally with the young sergeant who was stationed there. They selected three cattle at random—a steer, a cow, and a yearling—and measured the heart girth of each and took their length from the brisket to the pin bone, just below the tail.

The commissary officer ciphered for a while in his notebook. Then he looked up. "Ninety-nine. Is that right?"

"Yes, sir. I lost a couple head during that patch of trouble I told you about." He'd lost more than a couple, and even if they were destined for the slaughterhouse, it made him sick to lose them for nothing.

"A pity," he said, tapping his pencil against his ledger. "Still, these look as fine as you promised they would. Based on my estimate of their weight, I can pay you . . ."

The total he rattled off was fair, and Zeke knew it. More than fair, in fact, considering the lost weight of the cow he left in the bog, the one gored, and the three they never found. "Fair enough."

They shook on it, and Zeke signed the requisition, though his heart dropped into his boots.

It wasn't enough. Even together with all he'd saved and brought with him, he still fell shy of the final mortgage amount.

They shook again, and the commissary officer clapped him on the shoulder in parting.

Zeke kept his face and his back straight as he walked back to the *remuda*.

Jake held his horse's reins and studied Zeke's face as he mounted up. "Well?"

Zeke settled his hat low on his brow and cinched up the chin strap. "Like we said, couldn't have taken that fine horse back to E-town with us, anyway."

⁎⁎⁎

They made for Watrous, a railroad town boasting a tavern where meals, hot and hearty, could be had for a reasonable price. A quarter more bought them baths in a whiskey barrel out back, but they had to share the water. They did that first, so they could eat like civilized men.

The barkeeper's wife, a well-rounded woman with wind-reddened cheeks, brought bowls of steaming stew along with two loaves of fresh bread, butter and jam.

Chairs scraped the wood floor as they pulled up close to the table, stuffed their napkins in their neckbands and tucked in. Then there was no sound at all, except for chewing.

She was back in a minute with a pot of hot coffee. "You boys let me know if you're needing anything else," she said.

Zeke couldn't thank her properly with a mouth full of stew, so he just grinned and grunted.

When she left, he swallowed. "You boys did good." He swallowed again. Praise came hard, but this was well-earned and long due. His sons' stunned stillness made him a might angry, hinting plainly that he was miserly with appreciation. "I mean it. I think we all know we couldn't have pulled this off without Jake and Adam to help us, and I thank you for that, friend."

Jake nodded acceptance, but something else. Encouragement. There was more to say.

Zeke turned his gaze to his sons. "Beau, I been right proud of how you stood by me to learn the trade, but the gumption and level-headedness you showed during the stampede . . . well, no telling how far they'd 'a run if you hadn't turned them like you did." He had a lump in his throat, and he couldn't hardly stand the way his boys stared at him. Were kind words from him that rare?

Zeke took another bite to break the tension and give himself an excuse to look down. When he looked back up, they were still staring.

On with it, then. "And the way you saved your brother. I was afraid he was gonna get trampled for sure." Visions of the gored yearling leapt to his memory, and he shook his head to clear his brain. His eyes stung and swam, but he had to get through this. "That was quick thinking, son, and I'm grateful."

Beau looked pleased and proud, but ducked his head modestly.

Forrest fisted his brother's arm. "I'm grateful, too, and glad to still be here. Between the two of us, Beau always did have the common sense."

Zeke turned to his second son, seeing the boy—and the beginnings of a good man—through new eyes. "That ain't entirely true, son."

Forrest quirked an eyebrow, stunned, but had the good grace to wait and hear what would come next.

"I saw you dismount and disarm the man that rushed you."

"Well, that wasn't very sensible, sir, now that I look back on it. I wanted to make sure he wasn't dead, but what if he'd just been playing possum? I'd have been looking down the business end of his side iron."

Zeke chuckled. Maybe not the brightest move after all, but at least the intention showed a good heart. "It was a mighty brave thing to do, nonetheless." That was a good start, but more was needed. "I'm proud of you, son. And I may need to ask you a favor."

"Yes, sir. Anything."

Could his trust be won again so simply? The boy really was a better man than he knew. "We lost five head in that dust up, and I come up short. I aim to sell the horse and saddle we acquired from that no 'count—I figure he owes me for five cows and more—but I may need to ask you if I can sell his pistols too, if it comes to that. I mean, they're yours by rights . . ."

The boy was already unbuckling his gun belt. The revolvers made a distinctive clank on the table, causing many heads to turn as he slid them across without question.

Zeke had never felt so humbled nor so honored in all his days. "Thank you" came easier than he would have imagined. "Now eat up!" He shoveled another spoon load of stew into his maw. "Mmmm . . . much as I love my cows, boys, this sure ain't no longhorn stew."

"How can you know that, Mister Pickens?"

Adam looked such an easy mark it almost hurt to take him.

"Because there's no horseshoe in it."

The boy looked more confused than ever.

"Why son, that's how you cook longhorn beef. Throw it in a pot of water and throw a horseshoe in after it, then boil it until the horseshoe gets tender."

They all laughed.

How long had it been since he'd laughed? Since he'd heard his children laugh? It was a heartwarming sound—one Zeke decided he'd like to hear more often.

When it came time to pay up, Zeke was careful to count his money out under the table. It made no sense to flash a large fold of bills and invite trouble.

They stood to leave. Zeke asked the barkeep where he might sell a horse, tack and guns, and the man gave directions to a livery down the road a ways and to the local mercantile.

"Want us to wait while you do your business?" Jake asked.

Zeke thought for a moment. "No. The boys have earned an afternoon of fishing, I think. If you're willing, why don't you take them and head back toward Fort Union?" He was stalling, but the words came easy. "We'll be safe enough there for the night. Find us a likely place to camp along Wolf Creek, and get a campfire started. I'll find you later." He kept his tone casual.

Jake smiled and nodded. The boys mounted up in good spirits, and together they headed north leading the spare horses.

Zeke kept the piebald, tack, and pistols. He'd linger in town long enough to sell what was needful.

Tomorrow they'd ride further north—forty miles or so—up the Santa Fe Trail to Cimarron. The trail they'd meant to take from Ocate. The trail where—somewhere—two of Crump's riders laid in wait.

But tonight there was something else he needed to do—something he wasn't willing to talk about.

Chapter 23

Zeke dispensed with his business by mid-afternoon. He'd made a good deal. Sold the whole lot to some fella headed for Santa Fe—a greenhorn—who left mightily pleased with himself and saved Zeke the trouble of explaining back home how he came by a piebald horse with very distinctive markings. Favored him, too, with enough money to make up what he'd lost and more.

Enough to buy Forrest a gun to replace the set he'd sacrificed for the cause.

Enough to set back against need in the coming year, if they were careful.

Enough, perhaps, for a bit of fun.

And what harm would it do? Who would know? The boys were safe enough with Jake back on the river. Filling their bellies with fried trout and cornpone, no doubt.

This one experience was still lacking from his growing up years. Tonight he would find out what he'd missed all those times *he* was the youngster left to guard the horses while the men went to town after a big sale.

Where would he go to celebrate his success?

There was the tavern where they'd had lunch in Watrous, but that would not do. He was known there. Besides, the air about the place seemed too . . . he started to say "too respectable" but quickly amended the thought to "family-like." That term suited his conscience better. Of course he wasn't looking to do anything disreputable or foolish. He just wanted to bathe in the waters of success for a change instead of sharing a domesticated rain barrel of frugality.

There were other taverns in Watrous, but perhaps it would be better to dust out of this town entirely. Not only had he come here after selling his herd, but he'd lingered to sell a horse and equipment as well. Asked questions. Been seen. He'd kept a careful watch for any face that seemed familiar—that might have one of Crump's cronies behind it—and had seen no one to alarm him, but the locals might have noticed that he had money on him. If asked by someone who'd escaped his notice, they might point him out. No. It would be foolish to stay too long around here.

Loma Parda, then. They'd watered their cattle at the Mora crossing just after noon yesterday before driving them through the village to the place where they made camp three or four miles beyond—about halfway to Fort Union—so as to arrive early this morning. Despite the early hour, there'd been plenty of customers patronizing the half a dozen saloons and dance halls numbered among the stone and adobe buildings that lined the road. As a town, Loma Parda had barely existed before the fort was built, then it suddenly sprang to life as a favored destination for rest and relaxation. He'd snuck a glance at the infamous Baca Dance Hall— "Sodom on the Mora"—where the pine *vigas* shook with the noise of the crowd on payday weekends. He'd even seen the little "pens" out back—one-room oases of perverted pleasure in many a soldier's desert of solitude. The knowledge of what went on inside stirred a titillating sensation—half thrilling, half shameful—but he would not go there. *Not looking to do anything disreputable or foolish.* The other places, though . . . they should be safe enough. He could lose himself among the traveling merchants and off-duty soldiers. It seemed unlikely he'd encounter anyone in Loma Parda who might recognize him—no one he was ever likely to see again.

He'd be back at their campsite before the night was full dark, ready to head out at first light come morning. They had two days' ride ahead of them to reach Cimarron before the land office closed.

The ride to Loma Parda was easy, the road well-traveled. He passed the first saloon in favor of the second. The establishment was little more than an adobe hut, but the afternoon sun glowed warmly on the windows, and the sound of laughter bid him welcome.

The man behind the bar jerked a nod in Zeke's direction before casting a meaningful glance across the room where several seats were available.

Zeke chose a seat at an empty corner table from which he could watch all the goings on.

A sanguine *señorita* all dressed in satin and smelling as sweet as rosewater came to take his order. The barkeeper's daughter? Dark eyed and red lipped, she was the most beautiful woman Zeke had ever laid eyes on, but she kept her distance—respectable-like.

There was nothing about a bunged up ol' cowpoke like him that would attract a lady like her.

He ordered a drink and watched the sway of her skirts as she went off to fetch it.

She came back with the drink and to collect what he owed her.

Zeke had taken the precaution of burying the stash of folded government bills that comprised the mortgage deep in a pocket where his vest would hide their thickness. He'd stowed the remaining portion—mostly coins—in a small leather pouch he stuffed on top, but there weren't no need to count his money under the table this time. This little woman couldn't do him any harm, and no one else was paying him the slightest attention. Reaching inside his vest where the folded bills made his pocket bulge, he pulled out the leather pouch and counted out what was needed, then tossed a few extra coins onto the table with a flourish, just because he could.

Her eyes grew round and took on a fetching sparkle. "Gracias, *señor.*" She picked the coins up one by one with finely manicured fingertips and tucked them into the top of her blouse where the lace and frills hung low over her . . .

He knew he shouldn't be looking, so Zeke looked away.

But then her hand lit soft and warm upon his shoulder, and all the soreness seemed to drain out of him. All the years and all the worry.

All the sense, too, mayhap.

He saluted her with his glass and tossed back his drink. The liquor burned a brand down his throat like a liquid running iron.

She smiled.

It was hard to say whether the liquor or her smile warmed him more. He ordered another shot—a double.

She laughed and sauntered off to get it, slanting dark eyes at him across the room as she waited at the bar.

Except to fill the order, the barkeeper largely ignored her. The girl was somebody's daughter, but apparently not his.

Her gaze never left Zeke as she returned with the drink.

Again he paid her from the little leather pouch.

Again she tucked the coins away. Slowly. Enticingly.

Again she lingered, watching him drink.

This time he sipped more slowly.

She moved to stand behind his chair, her graceful movements slow and smooth as quicksilver.

Zeke could feel her cool breath ruffling his hair. He nearly jumped as her fingers trailed up his neck and fondled with his ear a bit, sending waves of ice and lightning down his spine.

Maybe he'd given himself too little credit. Maybe he wasn't camping as close to boot hill as he felt most mornings.

Maybe she didn't understand that he was married. *Very married.* He should tell her. *Then again, maybe later.* The way she'd begun to play with a lock of his hair made his face heat up.

She must have seen him blush. She giggled. The light sound of her laughter reminded him of the little bells he'd seen on a fine Mexican harness one time.

Why *had* he married so young? Was this a taste of what he'd missed? Seemed like he'd been working as long as he could remember, with hungry cattle and a herd of hungry young-uns looking to him for food. It felt mighty fine to be on his own, to do as he liked—at least for an evening—and to have no one wanting anything from him but a few moments of pleasure.

. . . but it wasn't right, and he knew it. *T'ain't fair. I ain't even done nothing yet* . . . but his conscience was gigging him.

The girl had draped herself around his shoulders now and was toying with his buttons .

She had to stop. He had to stop her. He took her hand—it was as soft as a new calf's ear—and gave it a little pat. "No, now. You can't be doing that." There weren't no need to hurt her feelings.

"No?" she repeated, poking her ruby red lips into a pout.

He hated to disappoint her so, but . . . *Millie*. "No," he said more firmly.

She tossed back her dark curls and laughed at him. "*Sí!*" she exulted, and throwing both arms around his neck she swung herself down into his lap.

Zeke jumped out of his seat. "Now see here . . ." This was getting way out of hand. His collar felt too tight, and his neck was kinda sweaty.

All eyes were upon them.

She just laughed again as she let her fingers skip up his shirt from button to button before walking them across his chest. "Oooo . . ." she cooed, "so big."

Did she mean his muscles, which he'd never considered were anything above average, or the wad of bills he was keeping in his vest pocket?

"You buy me . . . ?"

Well, if she needed something. Stood to reason. The girl must be on her own. No respectable young lady would work in a place like this unless she was in desperate need. "What? Buy you what?"

She smiled, and Zeke thought he'd never seen an expression more sultry and more coldly calculating at the same time. "You. Buy. Me!"

She slipped her hand inside his vest—inside his vest pocket—and he grabbed it. "No, now. I said no!"

And that sweet *señorita* turned on the tears like a waterfall at spring thaw.

At the sound of her wailing there was an almighty scrape as three burly *vaqueros* leapt from their chairs to defend the soiled dove's honor. An unmistakable click rang through the sudden silence in the room—the sound of the hammers drawing back on at least three revolvers.

With a jeering chorus of laughter behind him, Zeke lit a shuck out of there . . . bursting through the open doorway and out into the street

. . . where he ran straight into Jake

. . . and Jackson.

Chapter 24

Zeke's boots left twin trails in the dusty road as he skidded to a stop, not believing his eyes. Surely he hadn't had that much to drink. He blinked first at his son, then stared into the face of his friend.

Jake's face didn't look very friendly.

Overcome by impulse, Zeke pulled down the brim of his hat to shadow his face. *What use was that?* He was caught sure as a coyote in a steel-jawed trap. They'd seen him—his friend *and* his son. Seen where he'd been, and likely guessed what he'd been doing in there. He swallowed, tasting the liquor on his breath. He felt a fool—and a cowardly fool, at that. Ducking his head, he yanked the hat off and slapped it against his thigh in frustration.

Shame seeped through him, igniting an anger that bloomed into a wildfire, surging faster.

He turned on Jake. "What are you doing here?" he demanded.

"I could ask the same," Jake began, his voice calm but cold as a mountain stream.

Zeke barely heard him. He'd already turned on Jackson. "And what are *you* doing here? I thought I left you to take care of your mother!"

Jackson brisked up, his face brewing with storm clouds to match the glowering tempest in his father's features. "I am taking care of my mother!" he shouted, ears red and spit flying.

Now just how do you figure that? Zeke scoffed, but had little time to wonder as Jackson's barrage of words continued.

"You're the one who ain't where he's supposed to be, Pa! You were supposed to be in Cimarron saving our land or at Fort Union selling our cattle, but instead we had to search halfway to Glory to find you frittering away your time and money playing where you got no reason to be in the first place." He discharged his words like lightning, then stood heaving with rage.

Each accusation struck Zeke's heart with deadly accuracy. It was exactly what he would have said if their situations had been reversed, but he could not abide such impudence—such disrespect. He allowed his anger to sear his conscience. Raising a threatening finger, he pointed it in Jackson's face just inches from the boy's nose and prepared to fire back.

Jake intervened with a backhand to his chest.

Zeke turned as his friend gestured to the door of the saloon where the three *caballeros*, guns drawn, had emerged along with the barkeeper, who cocked a Winchester. Snuffing his rage and resentment, he melted into solidarity with Jake and Jackson to stare the men down.

The barkeeper eyed Jake and pointed toward Zeke with the business end of his rifle. "You having problems with this *hombre?*"

Tension crackled through the space between them as the *vaqueros* stood ready to enforce their own brand of peace in the streets.

Jake delayed. *He must be even madder'n he let on.* He turned to Zeke and looked him up and down with maddeningly slow deliberation before saying, "No. We'll take him home now." Then, as if he were the only adult present, Jake turned to Jackson and said, "Round up the horses, son."

೫೦೦೫

The six mile ride to Wolf Creek was a quiet one.

Jake and Jackson rode in front, which made sense because they were the ones who knew where to find the camp.

And how did Jackson find it? Zeke was plenty vexed to admit, even to himself, that if he'd stayed in the saloon another hour there was no guarantee he'd have been able to find his way to camp in the dark. His thinking was a little swimmy as it was.

Neither his friend nor his son looked back at him. Jake rode casually, as if nothing had happened—or as if whatever *had* happened could wait for a later discussion. Jackson sat rigid in the saddle, his spine stiff as a poker.

He'd find no mercy with that one . . . not that he'd ever offered his youngest son much by way of example.

Darkness was gathering as they passed Fort Union. Was it really only this morning that he'd ridden in sitting so high in his saddle, feeling such pride? The money was still in his pocket, and thank the Lord for that! However far he'd fallen in the eyes of others . . . or in his own . . . he still had what he'd come for. What he'd sacrificed to gain. He hadn't lost the money or the ranch. Only his integrity.

The stars popped out one by one as they headed north, following the old wagon ruts of the Santa Fe Trail. A night wind whispered in the tall grass, and the fragrance of the air changed subtly. The smell of dust settled, and Zeke picked up the scent of pine on the breeze, blowing down from the mountains . . . from home—where Millie was, alone.

Zeke silently cursed his son's defiance, but he had to give him credit for grit. It was two days' hard ride through Cimarron Canyon to Fort Union—a fool's errand for a grown man, an unbelievable feat for a mere boy. His first instinct had been to mark it up to simple willfulness, but now a sense of foreboding pricked at the skin on his neck.

I am taking care of my mother!

His son's words rang in Zeke's head. He hadn't given the boy a chance to explain back there on the street in Loma Parda. What if something had gone wrong at home? Another visit from the Maxwell Land agents or an open confrontation from Crump?

He needed to know.

Was it his imagination, or did Jackson's anger seem to be burning itself out? The boy seemed less stiff . . . less sullen. He'd take a chance. "How was your mother when you left her?"

His son did not turn in the saddle. "Crying and scared," he said, resentment still smoldering in his voice.

Zeke's blood chilled. "Why was she scared? Was she hurt?"

"She was having the baby. Something about it being turned wrong . . ." Jackson's tone shifted from resentment to worry. "It's too early, isn't it, Pa? Way too early . . ."

Dread filled him. A moon just past its fullness had by this time risen, and suddenly Millie seemed almost as far away as that moon above him. She could be dying, having his baby. It had never occurred to him that she might not be there when he got back. Sure they'd lost two babies, but he'd never considered that he could lose his wife. Other mothers died in childbirth sometimes—he knew about Jake's first wife—but Millie took birthing babies in stride. She'd never made on much over it . . . until this time.

The onslaught of fear prompted an urge to defend himself. How could he have known? He'd called the doctor, hadn't he? Twice! If Millie had forgotten to take the tonic, or run out, or if she'd had further trouble . . . she'd have told him, wouldn't she?

His conscience goaded him when he remembered the fuss he'd made over the last bill . . . how hurt she'd been when he joked about her popping out yet another young 'un. He'd been worried about the ranch, about keeping their land, but he'd never meant to imply that she . . .

What had she done? What had *he* done?

Guilt and frustration competed for space in the parts of his mind that were functional. What came out was another heated accusation.

"And you left her? Alone?" He wanted to snatch the words back as soon as they left his lips, but of course it was too late for that . . . too late for a lot of things.

Jackson's reply was terse. "I did not leave my mother alone. Miz Eliza, Beth, Dixie Lee and I been doing most of the work since you left . . ."

"Wait," Zeke stopped him and turned to Jake. "Did you know about this?"

He saw the silhouette of Jake's hat bob in affirmation. "Part of it. Why don't you let the boy finish?"

"Go on, then," Zeke said, grudgingly.

Jackson took up where he'd left off. "Ma sent me to fetch Miz Charlotte from town when her pains started up again."

Zeke struggled to take in this new information and seized on the last bit. "Again?"

"Yes, sir." It sounded as if Jackson strained the words through gritted teeth. "She's been hurting on and off since the Fourth of July, and . . ."

Zeke interrupted his story again. "How did you know?" . . . and how had he not?

"She sits a lot, and her feet get swollen. She goes barefoot 'cause her shoes don't fit good." Jackson ticked of his boyish observations easily with just a hint of resentment that his father had to ask— hadn't noticed. "She presses her lips together sometimes until they go all thin and white, and she screws up her forehead like this." Despite the darkness he half turned his head, and Zeke guessed the boy was arranging his own features in demonstration before summing up. "She just looks worried."

That much he'd noticed, but he'd attributed his wife's anxiety to his own failings and her lack of faith in him. Zeke suffered another pang of self-reproach. If Millie had been one of his cows and gone into distress while calving, he'd have taken notice and known the cause, but he'd failed to spot the signs in his own wife.

His anger was fading, but his son's pig-headedness still rankled him plenty. "So you figured you'd help by disobeying me and likely scaring the women half to death, running away like you did?"

"No, sir!" Jackson's voice, full of offense, rang out in the still night.

Jake reigned in his horse and laid a hand on Jackson's arm. "Keep it civil, boy," he warned, then to Zeke he said, "Let him finish."

"Pa, I did all I could to take care of Ma, just like you told me, but then the womenfolk said there wasn't nothing more I could do. I knew you'd want to be there, so I figured maybe that'd be something I could do to help. I left a note, and I came to fetch you home to Ma."

The dark stillness swallowed them. For a moment there was no sound, then Zeke asked, "When did all this happen?"

"Monday night. Around midnight."

It was Wednesday.

"And had your Ma had the baby when you left?"

"No, sir." Fear gave Jackson's voice an edge, and he swallowed hard. "Once I saw the way of things, I didn't waste no time."

Zeke shook his head slowly. "Do you mean to tell me you made your way down Cimarron Canyon alone in the dark?"

"Yes, sir," he answered. "Well, no, sir—not exactly. I brought the mare." He rushed on. "I knew you'd headed south, so I rode east, thinking to catch you in Cimarron."

Zeke had left the oldest horse he owned, figuring that in an emergency she might carry a rider to town and back. "You rode the mare . . ." he echoed, dumbfounded. Over seventy miles in two days. "All night?"

Jackson hung his head. "Yes, sir. I rode her as hard as she was able that first night."

"She's resting back at camp," Jake said. "Looks none the worse for her exploit."

His assurance seemed to ease Jackson's mind, but the horse was the least of Zeke's worries.

"I checked at the land office on Tuesday, but you weren't there yet, so figured I'd meet you somewhere along the road from Fort Union." Jackson hurried on. "We rode on down slow-like and looked for your camp."

Not too slowly. He'd covered an incredible amount of trail in two days. Zeke had to admit that even in his panic, the boy had thought things through.

When he spoke again, Jackson's voice had taken on a tone of apology. "You left me in charge, Pa, and I tried to think what you would do. I tried real hard. I hope I did right."

The defiant attitude had evaporated, replaced by a boyish tenor of hope and respect that melted his father's mistrust. "You did good, son. You did real good."

Zeke's words of praise seemed to catch the boy off guard—to stun him a little.

"I tried, sir."

Glad they'd finished their talk away from the others, Zeke felt ready to go on now—back to camp where, hopefully, supper waited.

They nudged their horses to a slow walk, and before long the light of a campfire guided them through the darkness, casting flecks of light on the ripples of Wolf Creek.

~~~

After supper, Zeke slipped away from others to check on the faithful mare, picketed just beyond the ring where the firelight danced with shadows in the windblown prairie grasses.

Her head bobbed, and she whinnied in recognition as he drew near then went back to cropping the grass. *Poor ol' stove up critter.* She'd earned a rest.

Zeke stroked her neck and whispered his thanks before running practiced hands along her flanks and legs. She was covered in trail dust and in need of a brushing. Her mane and tail were gnarled with bits of twigs and pine sap, but he needed no light to assure himself that she was sound—no serious scrapes, no swelling. *Good girl.* He straightened and found her staring at him with calm brown eyes that glistened sagely with reflected light. Horses and cattle he understood; women and children, not so much.

When he thought about Millie and the baby, his chest felt cold and hollow. Fear spurred his to act, but it would be foolish to set out tonight. Even with the moon near full the overgrown trail would be difficult to distinguish, and somewhere ahead his adversaries lay in wait. He wasn't fool enough to think they'd just gone home. Their main ambition was to keep him from paying off his land, and they'd not be easily swayed from their purpose. They'd already shown that they were not above endangering his sons to accomplish their ends.

Jackson had passed through more than one kind of peril without knowing it. Only by the grace of God had he come so far unharmed. If Crump's men were hanging around Cimarron, the boy's questions had likely confirmed that Zeke was on his way with his pockets full of cash. If they weren't waiting in town, there were several miles of trail where they might be waiting for him. It would be best not to meet them in the dark.

But losing his land was no longer his foremost fear. What good was the land without the family he worked it for? He'd lost precious time this afternoon, playing the fool. He needed to get home to Millie and the baby . . . if they both yet lived. Whatever had come to pass happened two nights ago. There was nothing he could do about it now. That peril was past, but not knowing the outcome tore at his heart.

The crunch of boots on gravel alerted him to Jake's approach. Zeke watched him, somewhat wary, but his friend—if they were still friends after today—merely plucked a handful of prairie grass and held it beneath the mare's muzzle on the flat of his glove. When her soft lips accepted his offering, Jake moved around to her off side and set himself to stroking her mane, combing the twigs and tangles out with practiced fingers.

Zeke watched as a grateful shiver rippled down the crest of her neck.

Jake continued to work wordlessly.

"You gonna say anything?" Zeke finally asked.

Jake never looked up from his calm, methodical motions. "Thought I'd let you lead off."

Zeke crossed his arms over the horse's withers and dropped his head to rest against her shoulder, kicking at a clump of wild grass with the toe of one boot. "Been trying to figure out how to be in two places at once." He looked up, locking eyes with Jake over the mare's back. "Thoughts?"

Jake snorted a derisive chuckle. "I think you still have trouble asking for help . . . or accepting it."

Zeke inhaled a deep lungful of night air and let his head roll back. He stared up at the benevolent moon and blew his breath out slowly. "You might be right." Asking for help made him feel weak and helpless in the best of times. That went more'n double for tonight. "All right, then, I need help."

Jake grinned a crooked grin. "See there? That didn't quite kill you, did it?"

"Not quite." The tension and irritation, though, were making his eye twitch. "What d'you got to offer?"

Jake patted the mare's neck and rested his hands on her crest. "I say we need to split up. You take your boys, go home, and see to Millie, and I'll head north to Cimarron and pay off your land."

Zeke started to find fault with the suggestions—just out of habit, mostly— but quickly saw that the idea had merit. Still . . . "I'd hate to send you into danger." This was his fight, not Jake's.

"I don't know that you'd be sending me into danger," Jake countered. "Crump's men are looking for you, not for me. There's at least a better than decent chance that they won't put two and two together if they see me ride into town."

Zeke thought on that. "Yes, but they've seen us together."

Jake nodded. "At the shindig in Elizabethtown, but that was almost a month ago, and we were just new faces in a crowd."

That wasn't all. "They saw you with me on the trail when they stampeded my herd."

"Did they?" Jake challenged. "I was riding on the far right flank when they swept in, whooping and shooting, and by the time I circled around to the back to help Adam with the *remuda*, they'd pretty much ridden beyond us." His hands provided a re-enactment in miniature. "Besides, I can tell you from firsthand experience that in the heat of a battle you don't stop to look long at faces. If they took note of me at all, any memory of my face is likely pretty much a blur."

That made sense. "So you'd take the money . . ."

". . . and ride north with Adam. We can take the two old ones . . ." he patted the mare, who huffed her objection to his description. "I'll keep the money hidden on me, just in case, and if we don't encounter anyone by the time we get a ways past Rayado, we'll circle around and enter town as if we're just coming in from the east on the main road."

Zeke was catching on and finished the arrangement. "The boys and I can take the chuck box, and we'll have the spare horses so we can ride hard." Yes, Jake's plan might work. "We'll go home across country—the way we meant to trail down—and we don't really have to split up until we get to Ocate Crossing."

"You should be fine once you reach the cut-off," Jake agreed, "but I'm thinking it would be best to head out separately, just as a precaution."

For the first time, Zeke balked. "I'll have to chew on that thought," he said. "Not sure I want to take the chance of facing two gunmen with just my boys."

A slow grin spread across Jake's face, and he lifted one eyebrow. "I'd say all three of your boys have shown you what they're made of on this trip."

That much was true.

"It'd be two men against four," Jake continued. "I think the 'Pickens Posse' could handle things just fine, but Adam and I will be less than half an hour behind you—likely within sight range and definitely within earshot."

Zeke nodded slowly. This could work. He trusted Jake with his life and with his money, but could he trust him with his secrets? The conversation was about to get awkward, but there was more to say that had to be said. "'Bout that other business . . ." He sidled up to the subject cautiously, like a bronc buster sidling up to a wild mustang.

"What other business?"

There was no way to make this easy, and his friend didn't seem inclined to help. "What happened back there at Loma Parda . . ." He wasn't sure if Jake was playing dumb for the sake of discretion or just giving him enough rope to rig himself a noose.

Jake looked him square in the eye. "You want to talk about it? Or you want me not to talk about it?"

Two minutes ago he'd been sure it was the latter, but the urge to explain—to defend himself—rose up strong. "It was just a drink. Nothing happened."

"All right." Jake held his gaze steady.

Zeke lifted his chin and set his jaw. "I only had one." *That was a lie.* "Maybe two." That was only true if he didn't mention that the second was a double. "I did far less than many men." How in tarnation did Jake manage to make him squirm with guilt just by staring at him?

Jake went back to combing the mare's mane. "If that's what you want, it's your choice to make."

Was that what he wanted? A few hours ago he'd thought so. Now he couldn't remember why the notion had held such fascination.

One question had been niggling at him. "How'd you know to look for me there?"

In the moonlight he saw one corner of Jake's mouth lift in a wry smile. "I served at Fort Union a few months after the war, before I mustered out and went to work on the Big Ditch up on the Red River. The allures of Loma Parda were no secret. To my way of thinking, that place always reminded me of a baited trap, but when we didn't find you in Watrous . . ." He narrowed one eye, like he was considering whether to stop or go on, then he fixed Zeke with a frank stare. "That woman back there . . ."

Zeke started to object. He'd carefully avoided saying anything about a woman—stepped around the subject like it was a fresh cow patty—but he knew it'd be no use to deny what Jake had discerned all too plainly.

The glint of naked truth gave Jake's eyes a hard edge Zeke hadn't seen before. "Unless I'm very much mistaken, she was likely done up like a fine show horse, but, Zeke, that's all that is. Show. Inside that girl feels as worthless and used up as you likely do. What she wants is your money. Nothing more." He caressed the old mare's muzzle. "When you need a partner to get you through a rough spot, stick with a horse you know."

Then he turned the conversation back to the main subject "Look, I don't consider it my place to say anything to anyone . . . anyone who doesn't already know." He'd resumed speaking in a calm and reasonable manner.

Zeke's guilty conscience found it quite irksome. "Jackson, you mean." His son had obviously pieced things together and had likely filled in the blank spots. The whiskey. The woman. He hung his head.

Jake nodded. "Boy that age is sorta between hay and grass—'not a man, nor a boy, but a hobbledehoy.' He'll forgive you. Probably already has. He looks up to you. You're his Pa, and that's a powerful thing to a boy." His tone, which had been surprisingly understanding, considering, now took on a note of caution. "He'll be following your example, is all . . . and that's something you'll want to think on, maybe."

Zeke suddenly felt very tired—like he'd spent the last fifteen years of his life struggling through a blizzard to wrestle the north wind only to discover that his best efforts had all blown south. If only he could work out the tangles in his relationships as easily as Jake loosened the snarls in that old mare's mane, 'cuz it surely seemed he'd made a right mess of things all the way round.

Chapter 25

Fish for supper; fish for breakfast.

At least it wasn't beans and cornbread like at home.

Home.

No matter how hard Zeke tried to guard his mind against worrying over things he couldn't do anything about, fear and guilt pounded in his head like the land agent's henchmen in the dark of night.

He'd been quick to cloud up and rain on Jackson for daring to disobey him, but the boy had been doing his best to help. In truth, he'd been right to do what he did . . . and very brave.

What if Millie, in her own way, had just been trying to help? He hadn't given her much room to do that. Like Jake said, he wasn't much good at asking for help . . . or even accepting it when it was offered.

A solid month of beans and cornbread. From where he sat it had been a daily reminder that his best efforts at providing were barely enough to keep food on the table—nothing anybody'd be proud to have, leastways. Was it possible, though, that Millie was pinching pennies because she understood how much every one of them counted toward paying off the land? That she was working with him?

That maybe she felt it was up to her to replace the money that had gone to pay the doctor when she got sick?

What Jake said about sticking with the horse you know—now *that* he could understand. A cowboy and his horse were partners. *Like Jake and Eliza.* Not like Millie and him. *Not now, anyway. Before, maybe? At the very beginning?* Zeke stretched his mind back. *No, not even then.* Then she'd been more like his pet. He'd adored her. Taken care of her. Worked *for* her . . . but never with her. Somehow over the years, that had changed. The shiny had worn off, and they'd just sort of begun to live separate lives in the same cabin. He was beginning to see the difference, but to be honest, he wasn't sure how to do things any other way.

He really had made a mess of things, but if God gave him another chance with Millie—a few more years in the same cabin—he aimed to try.

The pink glow of sunrise—a faint hue of hope—had just begun to tinge the eastern sky. Zeke was chomping at the bit to be off. He shook his head to clear it, settled his hat to contain unkempt hair and thoughts alike, and went to saddle the horses with Beau.

Forrest was packing up the chuck box by the light of their breakfast fire.

Before the last star faded, they mounted up.

Somber faces told Zeke his boys were as worried as he was, and as anxious to put miles behind them. They gathered the spare horses and fell in with him.

Jake and Adam pulled away, their horses champing.

"Like we said, then—my boys and I will head up toward Ocate, and you'll follow."

Jake nodded. "Yup. 'Bout half an hour behind." He didn't say *Don't worry.* That would have been useless, anyway.

Zeke clasped his friend's hand and let his eyes convey what words could not.

They spurred their horses and set off at a brisk trot here where the way was clear. The little Indian pony jogged to keep up.

No one talked.

Half an hour later they rounded a curve and rode over a rise from which Zeke could see the road behind them.

Jake and Adam had left the campsite and were following in their trail.

This first part of their journey was the tricky part. The Santa Fe Trail was not so much a road as a broad byway cleared of trees in most places, but here and there clumps of cactus, scrub brush, and even a few trees grew tall and dense and close enough to the overgrown road that highwaymen might find cover to hide themselves and lie in wait. If Crump's men had followed Jackson down to spy out their campsite, the jig was already up. They would likely have returned to one of these clumps to hole up and wait for their prey to pass in the morning, but if they laid in wait further up the road or in Cimarron, the plan might yet work.

As they rode up on the first such thicket—the first likely spot where anyone might be hiding, waiting to ambush them—Zeke was careful not to indicate alarm, but moved his hand casually to his thigh, nearer to his pistol in its holster. From the corner of his eye, he saw that Beau did the same. As if on cue, Forrest and Jackson checked their saddle scabbards to make sure their long guns would be easy to draw. All remained calm, though.

They rode on in peace.

Anyone who waited was either further along the road or had guessed that Zeke no longer carried the money. He hated the fact that Jake and Adam had placed themselves in danger in his stead, but a restless night spent casting for alternatives when he should have been sleeping had convinced him that there was no other way.

When they'd ridden a distance of about fifteen miles, they reached Ocate Crossing. Here they turned toward the west and came up on an outcrop that gave them a good overview of the land to the north, east, and south. Reigning their horses in, they watched as Jake and

Adam rode past the first clump of trees.

Zeke's lungs were burning when he finally exhaled several minutes later.

"They made it." Beau voiced his relief.

Zeke nodded. "For now."

Was it his imagination, or did Jake mean to touch his hat brim to message the same sentiment?

༄༅༅

As they passed the shadowed copse of trees in safety, Jake looked toward the western ridge and slid two fingers along the brim of his hat.

Adam squinted and followed his father's gaze. "Is that them, Pa? Up there watching us?" Even as he spoke, four figures on horseback turned and trotted out of sight.

"Yup, I reckon," he answered, suppressing a smile as he made use of one of Eliza's favorite expressions.

They rode on for a few moments in silence before Adam said, "Trail rides and life really are like Mr. Pickens said, huh, Pa?"

"How's that?"

"Mostly routine—even boring, maybe—with surprising parts that flush up when you aren't expecting them and scare the wits out of you!"

Jake chuckled deep in his throat. "I guess that's pretty much true, son."

"Why do you think that is, Pa?"

"What do you mean?"

"Well, if we tend to business and do what we're supposed to, seems like we could manage to stay out of most trouble."

This time Jake laughed out loud. "I remember when I thought that, too, and I was quite earnest in my attempts. But then I encountered a few of those 'surprising parts' for myself—wars and floods and the like—and I realized some things you just can't see coming. They lie in wait."

"You think the devil sends trouble out to hold us up like Mr. Crump sent his men out after us?"

"Something like that, I guess." This was turning into one of those teachable moments—the kind, Jake suddenly realized, that Zeke had not gotten with his father, who'd gone to war and then gone too soon from this world. A boy without a father had to learn some things the hard way. "The trick, son, is to prepare the best way you know how, do what you can to avoid trouble, and keep a watchful eye out . . . but not to forget to enjoy the journey."

Adam straightened and looked around him. "It is pretty out here, isn't it?"

Jake nodded. "It's easy to forget during the boring parts to do the important things and to forget during the frantic parts why you did them."

Chapter 26

By the time the sun slipped behind the Sangre de Cristo ridge, Jake and Adam were well within the foothills. Alternately jogging and walking to rest their horses, they'd put good miles behind them and so far encountered no threat. Adam seemed relaxed, enjoying their adventure.

Even though his days as a sharpshooter were twenty years in his past, Jake's old training had not left him. He'd entrusted his old Sharps rifle to Adam and carried a Winchester repeater, levered and ready, across his own thighs. His manner was casual and discrete, but he kept a vigilant eye on the road ahead and the terrain on either side.

Because he was prepared, he was able to appear unalarmed when, about five miles south of Rayado, two men armed with revolvers stepped into the road. Unmounted, they used their horses to block any possibility of passage without a confrontation. Like young bucks with their first set of real antlers, they were bold, but overconfident.

Jake recognized them easily from the picnic in E-town. Had they recognized him as well? With his hand mostly hidden by the saddle horn, he eased his finger closer to the rifle's trigger. Still he had no desire to initiate trouble if trouble could be avoided. "Evening." He greeted the men calmly.

The darker of the two men grinned, displaying a missing tooth.

The taller, fairer man smiled falsely. "Good evening! You two out for a ride?"

Jake gave no indication of irritation. "We are, indeed."

An glint of evil intent sparked in both men's eyes.

"Mind if I ask where you're heading?" asked the tall, blond one.

Jake schooled his features and replied simply, "North."

Obviously.

The blond man nodded smugly and grinned as if he were enjoying this game. "Would you care to be more specific?"

Adam turned wary eyes toward his father, but Jake did not allow his son's concern to unsettle him. "I would be more specific if I had an answer to give you."

"And how's that?"

"Well, sir, I'm not sure what your interest is in our business, but I'm a trapper by trade. A hunter." *Let that serve as fair warning.* "I aim to find land in the upper reaches where the game is plentiful, but not so remote that I can't pack my furs into some settlement where I might barter them." He purposely told enough truth to dispel any impression that he had something to hide without revealing anything of substance.

"Going to Cimarron, then?"

"Not tonight," Jake said casually. "It's too far, I think."

"But you are headed to Cimarron?"

Jake cast his eyes toward the western ridge. ". . . or Elizabethtown. Maybe even further." He smiled reassurance toward Adam, pleased to see he had the Sharps rifle close to hand. "Got no permanent plans as yet, do we, son?"

"No, sir."

The spokesman raised his eyebrows and cocked his head in mock interest. "So you coming from down around Fort Union?"

The man was definitely fishing for information.

Jake's hope of avoiding a confrontation was fading. "Watrous, yesterday," he supplied. It was a common enough crossroad. Then he said again, "I'm not sure why our travels should be of particular interest to you, but I'd be obliged if you'd let us be on our way. It'll be dark soon, and this boy will be hungry."

There. He'd asked nicely. *If they've got a lick of sense . . .*

"Indeed! Traveling and looking for land. I'd find it most unusual if you weren't carrying a good bit of cash for your journey."

Apparently they have no sense at all.

The spokesman signaled to the dark-haired man, who reached to draw his pistols.

On instinct, Jake swiveled his Winchester and shot from the hip.

A .44 caliber bullet tore through the dark-haired man's right shoulder.

He screamed and dropped his gun, a dark red stain blooming near the sleeve of his ruined shirt.

Jake had another round chambered before the man thought to go for his second gun.

Adam, following his father's lead, had leveled the Sharps at the tall, blond man, who carefully raised his hands so that they were nowhere near his side arms.

Jake sat unmoving in the saddle. Without shifting his aim he said, "Son, please relieve these men of their weapons."

"Yes, sir." Adam slid from his mount and collected the highwaymen's guns and holsters. Rebuckling their gun belts, he hung them over his saddle horn.

"That's good." Jake still covered both men. "Now go get your rope and tie him up." He shifted the business end of the Winchester to indicate the blond man. "That other one's not going anywhere for the moment."

The dark-haired man groped his wounded shoulder, moaning as he tried to stanch the flow of blood.

The blond man placed his hands behind his back and looked wide-eyed at his associate. "You can't just leave him. He'll bleed out."

His voice squeaked.

Some gunslinger. "I have no intention of leaving either of you," Jake informed him.

Adam set to work on the tall blond man, using some of the knots he'd learned when they roped and branded the cattle.

Jake stifled his amusement. "Got him tied up good and tight?"

"Yes, sir."

A long tail of rope remained. Adam still held its end.

"That's good, son. Now get your rifle and cover them while I dress and tie this other rascal."

Jake dismounted and grabbed his lariat. With all eyes on him, he walked past the dark-haired man and began to search through his saddle bag for something he could use as a bandage. Halfway down he found a shirt of unbleached cotton, relatively clean. *That would do.* He ripped off both sleeves and folded them into compresses, which he pressed to the gaping shoulder wound.

The dark-haired man yelped in pain.

"Hold that in place with your good hand," Jake directed matter-of-factly. He ripped the collar off the shirt and, starting each strip with a rip of his teeth, shredded the rest. "Fold your arm and hook your thumb in your collar," he ordered.

The man flinched as he moved, but did as he'd been told.

Knotting the strips of cloth together, Jake bandaged the man's chest. Then he jerked the man's good left arm behind his back and tied him up like Adam had tied his partner.

When he finished, he turned the man back around. "Think you can walk?"

The dark-haired man's skin looked like biscuit gravy gone cold, but he nodded.

"Good, because if you pass out we'll have to tie you onto your horse, and that'll hurt plenty. So don't." He turned abruptly to gather the reins of the men's horses, but not before noting that the dark man's eyes grew round as he gulped back a wave of nausea. He almost felt sorry for him. Almost.

Nah. If he hoped to rob this train, he waked up the wrong passenger.

With Adam holding the rope that tied the blond man and Jake holding the other, they mounted up and headed north, trailing their captives' horses.

It was full dark by now. The moon would not rise for another hour, at least.

"You gonna make us walk all the way to Rayado?" the blond man grumbled.

Jake laughed. "That was your doing, not mine. My original plan was to make camp, build a nice fire, and fix supper."

Chapter 27

The moon was just rising when they rode into Rayado, which was little more these days than a wide spot in the road. Kit Carson was gone, as was Lucien Maxwell—legendary forces of the not-so-distant past. All that remained was a Post Office, closed at this hour, and the hacienda headquarters of Jesus Gil Abreu's sprawling ranch.

Light streamed from the front windows of the hacienda, but Jake dared not barge in on the family's evening, unannounced, with these two troublemakers in tow.

Lamplight also glowed in the windows of the bunkhouse where Abreu's *vaqueros* were housed. This, he figured, was a much more appropriate destination under the circumstances.

They rode up to the long porch and stopped. The sound of laughter and conversation—most of it Spanish—came from within.

Jake dismounted and handed his rope and reins to Adam before knocking gently on the bunkhouse door.

The conversation stopped. Spurred boots jangled, and in short order the door opened to reveal a lean, tanned face. "*Buenos noches, señor. Cómo puedo ayudarse?*" Then taking in Jake's Anglo features the man repeated, "Good evening, sir. How may I help you?"

Good so far. Now to explain. "*Perdóname, por favor.*" He removed his hat and nodded to show deference. "My son and I were traveling on the road about five miles south of here, and these two men attempted to waylay us."

The *vaquero*'s eyes widened. "*Sí?* You did well to take them both, *señor.*" Something about his grin and tone implied that he suspected the ambush might have been the other way around.

"My pa's a real quick shot," Adam interposed.

The man squinted into the darkness then to take a closer look at their captives, and his countenance changed. "*Ah! Sí, señor.* I know these men." He reached behind the door for his hat, then came out onto the porch and closed the door behind him. "You come with me, *por favor.* I take you to *Señor* Abreu."

They tied their horses to a post at the bunkhouse, then crossed the lawn and approached the main house—a long, low dwelling of red adobe—with their prisoners still in tow.

The *vaquero* rapped softly on the door, and a young woman carrying a candlestick appeared. Speaking low, he asked if they might see *Señor* Abreu.

She nodded and stepped aside so they could enter.

Jake quirked an eyebrow at their escort, then at the men he'd brought in. "Them, too?"

"*Sí, señor.* I think *Señor* Abreu will be most interested."

So they all stepped inside the cool walls to a tiled entry, and the *señorita* lighted their way into a well-appointed office. If Jake had not been impressed by Abreu's obvious wealth before, he was now.

An older man with kind, intelligent eyes and a magnificent white beard—trimmed to perfection—looked up, then stood to greet them. "Gentlemen, how may I help you this evening?" he asked in perfect, gracious English, then nodded to indicate that his foreman should provide the explanation.

"*Señor*, this man and his son were accosted as they entered your land five miles south." He stepped aside so that the light fell on the faces of the two men in bonds. "And these are the two who attempted to rob them."

Abreu studied the faces of the four newcomers carefully before saying, "Thank you, Ernesto." Then turning to Jake he asked, "And who are you that these men should desire to lighten the burden of your pockets?"

"Jacob Craig, sir. I . . ."

"Ah!" The aristocratic old face brightened. "I know of you!"

Jake stopped, befuddled. Surely he'd remember if he had ever before encountered Jesus Abreu, but he had no such recollection. "I'm fairly sure we've never met, sir."

Señor Abreu's wrinkles rearranged into a good-humored smile. "No, I've never until now had the pleasure of an introduction . . . but I have heard of you," he said, wagging his index finger in the manner of old men.

If it were possible, Jake was more baffled than before. "I'm just a hunter, sir. A trapper and sometime prospector."

"Yes, but you have lived, I think, in Elizabethtown."

"Now and again, in years past," Jake acknowledged. He did not like to lie, but with Crump's men still present and listening, it did not seem wise to elaborate on the whole truth, either.

The twinkle in Abreu's eye told him he understood. "I remember this now because I was in Cimarron recently and saw there Clay Allison and his wife, great with child."

If he was puzzled before, Jake was flummoxed now. The hair on his neck stood on end at the mention of Allison's name, but he kept his manner calm. "I thought he'd left the territory," he said, his voice indicating only mild interest.

The lines at the corners of Abreu's eyes wrinkled with amusement. "Indeed, sir! Gone to Texas by way of Missouri and Dodge City in Kansas where, I'm told, he was as much a maker of trouble as he was here. But you, sir . . . you may be the one who rid us of his presence."

Jake didn't know what to say, so he said nothing. He simply stared, as did those with him, as the cattle baron, immersed in his story, emerged from behind his desk.

"Come now, you needn't be modest," *Señor* Abreu continued. "I would have forgotten it, myself, had I not seen him just yesterday." Turning to Ernesto, he explained. "This man is one of only three that I know who successfully backed down the gunman Clay Allison. The last man to do it was none other than Wyatt Earp!" He paused for dramatic effect, then to Adam he said, ". . . but your father did it twice and, I believe, pursued him so that he left these regions."

Jake was surprised to feel a flush of embarrassment heating his cheeks, but his son's eyes glowed with pride, and the eyes of the men he'd brought in were wide with fear.

To them *Señor* Abreu said, "Allison was a squatter and a manslayer. Lucien Maxwell, my brother-in-law, lost a great deal of land to men who would not pay—land he had come by fairly." The face that had been wreathed in smiles before now darkened in warning. "I am not so agreeable a man as my dear brother-in-law, especially toward those who bring trouble to my door." With firm steps he returned to his desk like a judge about to pronounce sentence. "Take them, Ernesto, and lock them in the smokehouse for the night. Give them water, but nothing more, and post two guards with orders to shoot them if they attempt to escape."

"*Sí, señor*," the *vaquero* said, and without questions he gathered the men's ropes and led them from the room.

Jake, Adam, and Jesus Abreu watched them go. Abreu signaled to the girl with the candle. When she, too, had left and closed the door behind her, he indicated two comfortable rawhide chairs and waited until Jake and Adam were seated before resuming his chair. Folding his hands upon the desk, he again studied Jake carefully. "I trust my little story will serve you well," he said with a wink.

Jake smiled. "Yes, sir. Though I'm not sure I deserve the credit, I believe it can do me no harm."

"I did not ask, while they were here, but I would very much like to know if there is more to tonight's story. Tomorrow, you see, I shall have my men convey these two to the marshal in Cimarron, and I would like to build a strong case against them." He smiled knowingly. "You were not, I take it, out hunting this evening."

Jake shook his head. "No, sir." He liked to think he was a good judge of character, and Jesus Gil Abreu struck him as a man who could be trusted. "We came from Fort Union where my friend sold his cattle to pay off his land."

Abreu's eyebrows raised.

"This shocks you, sir?"

Abreu nodded. "Frankly, yes. I did not exaggerate. My brother-in law lost much to men who would not pay. Even now the ownership of the land is in dispute." He shrugged. "Where there is not law, disreputable men take advantage."

Jake nodded. "I understand, sir, but I am not a disreputable man . . . and neither is my friend. His wife is suffering a difficult childbirth, though, and he was obliged to make a hard choice. He took his sons with him to be at her bedside, and I volunteered to continue to Cimarron to pay off his land."

Again Abreu's raised eyebrows conveyed surprise. "Your friend trusts you a great deal."

"Yes."

"And you must value him, I think, to volunteer to place yourself and your son in such danger on his behalf."

"Well, we did not think it so dangerous at the time. Like I said, sir, I don't actually live in Elizabethtown. I don't claim land around those parts, so I've got no part in the Colfax County land war. We were fairly certain the men who were after him would not even recognize me." At this he looked down, brushed a fleck of dust from his hat brim, and met Abreu's eyes again with a self-deprecating smirk. "Looks like I guessed wrong on that one."

Jesus Abreu laughed. "You did not know you were so famous, eh?"

"No, sir. I didn't."

The old man steepled his fingers and stroked his beard as he thought. "Your road may still hold dangers, and I have a vested interest in seeing you safely to your destination—because you are a guest on my land and also for the sake of my brother-in-law, whom your friend honors even though he no longer owns the land." Apparently reaching a decision, he placed both palms on the leather writing surface that covered his desk. "Here is what I will do— tonight you and your son will stay here as my special guests."

Jake started to protest, but Abreu stilled him.

"I insist." He continued. "And tomorrow I will send Ernesto with you to Cimarron to make sure that you are not hindered on your mission . . . though you hardly seem to require assistance." He winked again. "Only when he returns will I send these land thieves to the marshal under guard." His face became suddenly serious. "I don't know, you see, which side the marshal is on." He shrugged. "Should he release them, your business will be completed and you and your son will be miles along your way."

"I would be very sorry, sir, to see them released to cause you any more trouble."

Abreu shrugged again. "In a wild territory, *señor*, there may be many paths to justice."

He stood, then, and they did, too. It was late, and their business seemed at an end.

Abreu rang a small bell, and soon the girl with the candle reappeared. "Luz, please show our guests to the best quarters and ask the cook to prepare a light supper." Patting Adam on the shoulder he said, "This one, I am sure, suffers a powerful hunger."

Adam grinned, nodded, and thanked him before following the *señorita* into the tiled hallway.

Jake began to follow, but a hand on his sleeve detained him.

"And as for you, Jacob Craig," *Señor* Abreu said with lowered voice, "choose any unclaimed land you like within my territory, and I will be happy to grant you favorable terms." He smiled. "You are a brave and honest man, I think. This territory could use more men like you."

Chapter 28
Moreno Valley, New Mexico

The **"Pickens Posse" pulled up reins** on the western slope of Cieneguilla Mountain. Zeke rode in the lead position, as he had all the long way from Wolf Creek, with Beau right beside him. Close behind them Forrest and Jackson rode abreast.

Their arrangement wasn't something they'd talked about. They hadn't talked about much of anything, each consumed with his own thoughts, fears, and prayers. Their order was instinctive—willingly following the leader, the way cattle were wont to do.

Zeke recollected the conversation he'd had with Jake about how foolish it would be to wear himself out driving cattle when he could enlist their cooperation and let them think trailing him was their own idea. He wasn't exactly sure where it happened, but somewhere along this trail he'd quit trying to drive his sons and begun to just let them trail along the path with him. The mutual orneriness that always set them at odds seemed to be behind them now, and for this he was grateful.

Across the broad and verdant valley, they caught their first glimpse of the Slim Pickens Ranch, dwarfed by distance.

Normally the first view upon homecoming caused Zeke's chest to swell with pride, and seemed to make his heart beat so high in his throat that he couldn't swallow right . . . but not today. Today he felt an odd mixture of relief and dread—relief, because they were within sight of their destination . . . dread, because with most of his cattle sold and the few that remained off foraging on the lower slopes, he could see no sign of life from this distance. His heart beat like an Indian war drum—a primal pulse preparing him for the unknown. Fear threatened to choke him. He took off his hat and clutched it to his chest.

"The troublesome thing about mountains is that there's times your road takes a turn, and suddenly you can see where you want to go . . . but that don't mean you're close to getting there."

Zeke didn't realize he'd spoken out loud until Jackson added, ". . . or that you know what lies between where you are and where you want to get."

". . . or that it'll be easy," Forrest said, quietly.

When did his boys get so wise? When had they become men . . . and friends?

He set his hat back on his head and noticed that his boys did the same.

He clucked his cheek and gently spurred his horse into motion.

His boys did the same.

How many times had he cautioned them to "watch yourself" when, truth be told, they were watching him all along?

Zeke couldn't decide which of his sons had surprised him more on this journey, but he knew who hadn't. Beau was as steady as ever. He'd always been his right-hand man and likely always would be, but he'd gained a new respect for Forrest. The boy hardly slept. He was industrious in his own quiet way and soaked up learning like the thirsty earth absorbs rain, and from that watering he brought forth a harvest of practical skills that had served them well. Not just cooking, though their stomachs would have been grateful for that talent alone. There were other things—odd bits of knowledge he'd read in books, but it wasn't only books that he read. The boy could read the land and the stars for direction, and he could tell tomorrow's weather by reading the sky and the wind. There was a natural poetry to him, a sort of song without words that kept him in tune with life and nature.

But perhaps the biggest surprise was Jackson. All these years Zeke had thought that Beau was most like him. That wasn't true. Beau was most like what he hoped he was, but Jackson was the summation of who he truly was for better and worse. Passionate. Impetuous. Determined. The sparks between them were caused by iron sharpening iron, as the Good Book says, or, in the common parlance, "filing." There was pain involved as they ground off one another's rough edges, but he had to admit the boy impressed him. He had grit and resilience. He spoke the truth even when the truth was ugly. He'd grown up earlier and faster than his brothers, and for all his hotheaded, impulsive recklessness Zeke would bet money that he'd become a fine man—one he could trust in a rough spot.

It gave him hope for his own future.

He'd created a rough spot for himself with Millie. Maybe, just maybe, he had enough passion and determination to find his way to where he hoped to go with her. He'd had a glimpse of what their life together could be, but he had no idea how to get there or what might lie between. It wasn't likely to be easy, but he vowed he'd never give up trying.

At last they came down into the basin at the headwaters of the Cimarron River. From there they followed Moreno Creek until they came around to the house on the main road.

Home.

They rode along the fence line—more than a mile of split pine rails he'd chopped, split, and stacked himself. Without thinking he reached to rub his shoulder. He'd spent his youth and strength on chores like this, and they'd worn him thin and ragged in spots.

The fence was blooming now, covered in berry brambles Millie had rooted and planted when Beau and Forrest were babies. Bees swarmed and buzzed over the blossoms. He breathed in the earthy scent of them, sour and dusty compared to the sweet berries Millie would make into jam before the bears could get them.

As they rode on the garden came into view, nestled between the house and barn where it would be protected from the harshest winds. He'd cleared the stones and broken the sod, digging the rows and turning the soil and withered stems over every fall at the end of the harvest so the land could rest beneath the winter snow. Millie planted her rows of seeds every spring and tended the plants through the summer, drawing and hauling water from the well, assuring that the short growing season produced enough canned goods to keep the family fed throughout the year. He was relieved to see it well-tended.

Next to the garden Millie's hens, raised from chicks, clucked and scratched in the chicken yard he'd built. He smiled when he thought of her carrying "her girls" out to the garden to eat bugs and posting the children to stand guard against hawks.

Behind the house, near the well and the tripod where she washed clothes, an assortment of quilts Millie pieced during quiet evenings hung from the clothesline he'd strung for her.

In less than a moment Zeke took it all in.

His fence; her berries and jams.

His stone-rimmed garden patch; her canned goods.

His barn and chicken coop; her eggs and fried chicken.

His clothesline; her washing and quilts.

Everywhere he looked, he saw evidence of the life they'd built together. Everything he'd built, she'd made beautiful and fruitful.

They'd been partners for years.

How had he missed that?

Zeke's throat felt thick.

He gulped. Had he lost her? He'd know soon, and the fear of knowing nearly swallowed him.

∂∂∂

Dixie Lee must have been keeping a lookout for them. She appeared on the cabin porch, the front door slamming shut behind her.

From somewhere inside a baby wailed.

This was good news. Half good, anyway. But the way she bounced up and down on her toes and wrung her hands . . . what was he to make of that?

They crossed the bridge, the horses' hooves echoing as loudly as his own heartbeat in his ears.

As they rode through the gate, Zeke was seized by a wild urge to turn around and run—just spur his horse to a frantic gallop and leave everything in a cloud of dust behind him. It made no sense, he knew. It would be irresponsible. It would change nothing. But as long as he did not know the truth, Millie was neither fully alive nor fully dead in his mind. Somehow that seemed preferable.

But he resisted the urge to panic and bolt.

His boys were watching.

He must show them how to be men.

They rode up to the porch and stopped, waiting. None of them wanting to be the first to break the silence.

"Hello, Papa," Dixie Lee said sweetly.

He studied her face, trying to read the news in her emotions, but it was pointless. He might have figured out his sons, but this daughter was still a mystery. "Hello, darlin'. Is your mama . . . ?" He couldn't finish.

"She's asleep." Dixie Lee winked at him and set one finger to her lips to explain her unusually tranquil demeanor.

Zeke felt all the air leave his lungs. He grabbed his hat off his head and slumped forward in the saddle, wrestling with a rush of emotion. Finally, smiling with joy and relief, he turned to signal his boys to dismount and saw that they, too, seemed to have gotten dust in their eyes.

They tied their horses to the porch posts, then Zeke gathered

Dixie Lee up in his arms and gave her a firm squeeze.

"Papa!" She giggled and dodged his whiskery kisses and wriggled to be let down. "I'm too big for that now. I'm not the baby anymore!"

He set her down and took her hand in his. "Well, then, why don't you take us in and introduce us to this new . . ."

"Brother," she said, wrinkling her nose in feigned disgust. "Another one . . . but he's cute. Come see!" Letting her hand slip almost free of his, she dragged him toward the door by two fingers.

Zeke hardly felt his boots touch the pine floor boards as he crossed the porch. As his daughter towed him through the main room of the cabin toward the lean-to bedroom off the kitchen, he glanced over his shoulder long enough to picture a new room against the eastern wall—its door where a window now gave a view of the road coming in from Cimarron. A cradle would fit fine in their bedroom for a few months, but within a year, not only his daughter but also a toddler would be needing a room on the main floor.

He had only a few moments to think of Cimarron and Jake and the final ranch payment as Dixie Lee pulled him through the kitchen, and then they were at the door of the room he shared with Millie, with the boys tiptoeing behind.

Their five faces peering through the doorway must have been comical, but Millie didn't see them. She slept soundly, peacefully, with his newest son cradled in the bend of her arm.

The baby fidgeted a bit, and Zeke hardly dared breathe lest he set the little tyke to wailing again.

On the far side of the bed, Eliza sat in a ladder-backed chair, reading, while Beth arranged wildflowers in a pitcher on the chest of drawers. Both looked up and smiled as they entered. Then Eliza rose and set her book aside, signaling to her daughter. They slipped into the kitchen quietly, and Eliza closed the door behind them.

"How is she?" Zeke asked, flashing her a crooked grin as he became aware that he'd been gripping and rolling the brim of his

Stetson in both hands as he clutched it against his vest.

Eliza's smile reassured him. "She'll be fine, though she had a rough go of it four nights ago." She looked past him at Jackson, fixing the boy with a knowing look from beneath one raised eyebrow.

A shuffling noise let him know Jackson had interpreted the gentle reprimand and squirmed beneath Eliza's chastisement, but he said nothing to excuse his actions. In hindsight, Zeke had to admit that he would have done the same thing, but there would be time to explain later.

For now all Zeke said was, "Jackson tells me she was in a lot of pain." Even now it pained him to think of what Millie had gone through birthing his child.

Eliza nodded. "The babe was breach and would not turn. Charlotte was able to turn him in the end, but the effort wore all three of them out, and Millie suffered the worst of it." Her brows drew together at the memory. "She's a resilient woman, though. Strong." Laying a hand on Zeke's forearm she added, "You should be proud of her."

And he answered earnestly, "I am."

"Zeke? Is that you?" From beyond the door, Millie called. "I'm awake. Come and meet your son."

There was pleasure in her voice—a serene, nurturing he remembered when their other children had arrived. Had their talking waked her? Zeke didn't care if she heard. It was high time she heard him express his pride in her.

He opened the door just a crack and peeked inside, then smiled and let it swing open wide. Up until now Millie had been his main concern, but now he could not wait to meet his son—this new boy-child they'd made. Together.

Millie smiled gently and motioned him closer.

The baby squirmed a bit as she shifted him for a better presentation.

Cute little fella! Zeke took in the downy wisps of thatch-blond hair and the ruddy cheeks—all that kept his face from looking like a little old man, scowling. His lips were pursed and chapped from nursing, and as they watched he smacked them hungrily. *Good. Boy's gonna need a lot of feeding.* How tiny he was, compared to the others!

Millie pulled back the coverlet to reveal ten impossibly tiny toes, and Zeke was struck with how much growing it took a boy to become a man—to be ready to fill the boots of his forefathers. He reached a finger out to touch him, and the baby woke. Red-faced and tight-fisted, he boxed the air. *Ready to take on his siblings.*

"Does he have a name yet?" he asked, his voice husky with emotions he couldn't quite name.

Millie nodded, the gleam of a good joke in her eyes. "I thought we'd call him Stuart Ross."

"Stuart Ross Pickens." Zeke let the name play on his tongue. It took him a moment to realize what she'd done. "I see we didn't run out of Confederate generals to name him after," he admitted, chagrinned. Apparently he was forgiven, but with a lasting reminder.

"Nope." Millie flashed him a victorious smile. "In fact, I think we can lavish him with two generals as namesakes, for surely this child will be our last."

Chapter 29

After they'd had a chance to meet their new brother, Beau and Forrest hitched up the wagon and drove Eliza and Beth back to Rufus and Charlotte's home in Elizabethtown.

Two days later Rufus' delivery wagon rattled over the bridge.

Drying his hands on a dishrag, Zeke stepped out on the porch to greet the visitors.

Jake transferred the driving reins to one hand and waved in greeting, then guided the horses to the side of the house and pulled up on the hand brake. Sliding easily from the seat to the porch, he offered his hand to assist first Eliza and then Aunt Charlotte.

"Thought I'd hitch a ride out to check on our patient." Charlotte said as she retrieved a basket from the wagon bed. "Didn't think you'd mind if I brought supper, too." She winked as she pulled back the blue gingham dishtowel covering the meal. "There's a cherry pie in there, somewhere."

A wonderful aroma of cinnamon, beef stew, snap beans, and biscuits made Zeke's mouth water. "We won't mind a bit, I assure you," he said, holding the front door for them to pass through. "Forrest has volunteered to continue in his role as cook, for which my entire family is most grateful, though I do my best to cauterize a steak from time to time."

They laughed at the jest as he rapped his knuckles softly on the bedroom door.

When Millie responded, Aunt Charlotte and Eliza slipped in to visit with her and baby Stuart.

Zeke shut the door again, then he and Jake walked back to the front porch where a light breeze blew some of the heat off the late summer afternoon.

"Well?" Zeke finally asked.

"Well, what?" Jake responded, then smiled. "Oh! You'll be wanting to know about the mortgage and how that business all worked out," he said, as if the thought had only just occurred to him.

"Yes, if you please." Humor and tolerant patience were the appropriate response, but Zeke had been anxious to hear how things went in Cimarron ever since he settled his mind about Millie and the baby. "Start at the beginning, and don't leave anything out. I owe you more than I can ever repay."

"That's not true," Jake assured him. "In fact, it may be quite the opposite." He told him of the attempted robbery by the two highwaymen, how he and Adam had turned the guns on them and turned the would-be thieves over to *Señor* Abreu in Rayado, and of that gentleman's offer of safe passage into Cimarron and a fair price on any land he might choose. "So you see, it is I who am indebted to you," he said, smiling broadly.

"So you met with no difficulty at the land office?" Zeke pressed.

Jake shook his head. "Nope. Ernesto and another of Abreu's *vaqueros* rode with us and acted as bodyguards to assure that both we and your money made it safely to the offices of the Maxwell Land Grant Company." As he spoke, he puffed out his chest comically and hooked his thumbs beneath his leather suspenders. "Yessiree, we strode right in like we owned the land outright, plunked your money down on that big desk, and the man in charge gave us a memento that might interest you." Jake pulled a neatly folded paper from his shirt pocket and proffered it with a triumphant flourish.

Zeke accepted the document and unfolded it carefully, then he read and reread the lettering at the top.

Deed of Title.

He shook his head in wonder. *All these years* . . . Fifteen long, anxious, back-breaking years he'd labored, but finally this land was his. His beyond question.

Immediately he corrected himself. *Ours.* He'd find a private moment to share the success with Millie this evening.

For now he read the deed slowly, lingering over the permanence implied by each word, then tucked the document into his shirt pocket until he could store it safely in the cash box later. "So you had no trouble from Crump's cadre in Cimarron or on the road after?" Zeke indicated a pair of rockers, silently inviting his friend to sit a spell and spin the yarn as long as he liked.

Jake took him up on the seat, but the story he told was a short one. "Oh, we saw them . . . and they saw us . . . but our two *amigos* stuck close, escorting us all the way to the Cimarron Canyon, and after that we felt safe enough." He pushed back in the rocker and let his gaze drift from the canyon road where it emerged in the east all the way to the place where Elizabethtown lay beyond the horizon to the north. A slow smile spread over his face. "Let's just say our neighbor, Mr. Crump has received a clear message, and I believe he is fully cognizant of its implications."

Again Zeke shook his head in wonder.

"'For the mountains shall depart, and the hills be removed; but my kindness shall not depart from thee, neither shall the covenant of my peace be removed, saith the LORD that hath mercy on thee,'" Jake quoted, still smiling, but with eyes closed in reflection.

"Where's that from?" Zeke asked. It pretty well summed up what he'd seen, though he would never have believed it even two weeks earlier.

"Book of Isaiah," Jake said, lifting his eyes to the mountains—to a notch in the Sangre de Cristo range due north in the far distance. "Don't remember the chapter and verse, exactly, but I think of it every time I'm up there."

"That's where you'll build your cabin, then?"

Jake nodded. "In the Valle Vidal—the 'valley of life.' I feel more alive up there than anywhere I've ever been. The mountains speak to me . . ." He tapped his fist to his chest, over where his heart rested. ". . . in here, telling me that as grand and impressive as they are, the blessing of God is stronger still."

And then they simply rocked for a while, each lost in his own thoughts.

For Zeke's part, he'd miss the Craig family, but he had a hunch their paths would cross again. "When you find the place you want, remember my boys and I will hold to our promise. We'll come and help you build your cabin."

"My family will be much obliged," Jake assured him. "And I think we'll be needing to build a new room onto your cabin, as well. For a man who claims 'slim pickens,' you seem to be bursting with abundance."

"That, my friend, is truth!"

Zeke pushed out of his chair, and Jake rose with him. Together they walked around the side of the cabin and began pacing off dimensions of the new addition.

Chapter 30

Millie nursed her baby by lamplight, aware of her husband's gaze warm upon her. She felt her cheeks flush, but it didn't bother her, particularly. In fact, it didn't bother her at all.

For so long she'd been afraid that he would never look at her again with tenderness or desire, but God had heard her prayers. The baby was safe—small, but lusty—and her sons were home safe, as well. Best of all, Zeke was home and happy—more like himself than she'd seen him in many years.

He'd shown her the title to their land earlier in the evening. "Our land" he'd called it, and then he'd surprised her by thanking her for working and sacrificing alongside him. "We did this," he'd said, ". . . and this," he'd added, caressing little Stuart Ross's downy head with his calloused hand.

Her eyes drifted closed, and she murmured, "Thank you."

"How's that?" Zeke asked sleepily, but she hadn't been talking to him.

Instead of explaining, she changed the subject. "Do you think Jake and Eliza will really move so far away?" It was beyond her understanding how anyone could crave such isolation. She'd been overjoyed this evening when Zeke had promised they could ride in to church in E-town next Sunday if she was feeling up to it.

"That's their plan," Zeke confirmed. "Can't say that I'd enjoy the life of a mountain man, myself, but it suits them." Then, as if he read her thoughts, he added, "They'll still come down to see Eliza's aunt and uncle, I'm sure, and we'll go up before the snow flies to build them a shelter. Might even stay to build a barn if the weather holds."

"How can we leave the ranch for so long?" she fretted. "There's the garden to tend, produce to can, the chickens to feed . . ."

"We'll manage." Zeke laid back on the bedstead and crossed his hands over his chest as if he hadn't a care in the world.

. . . and suddenly, neither did she.

RESEARCH NOTES FROM THE AUTHOR

Though this story is a work of fiction, it is based on historical events.

At the end of the Texas Revolution in 1836, defeated Dictator-General Santa Anna signed not one but *two* Treaties of Velasco (One was a secret.) The Mexican government recognized neither of them, claiming that because their leader was captured while trying to escape the Battle of San Jacinto, the treaties were signed "under coercion."

Mexico never recognized the Republic of Texas, and when the United States annexed Texas as the 28th American state in 1845, Mexico refused to recognize that as well. Though the Rio Grande had always served as Texas' border, President Polk offered to purchase disputed lands between the Nueces River and the Rio Grande to smooth things over. When Mexico rejected his offer, U.S. troops were sent in 1846 to stabilize the area.

Mexico attacked, laying siege to the American fort, killing 12 American soldiers, and capturing 52 others. This started the Mexican-American War. Mexico lost badly. In the Treaty of Guadalupe Hidalgo which officially ended the war in 1848, Mexico gave over to the U.S. all the land which is now California, Nevada, and Utah, most of Arizona, and portions of Wyoming, Colorado, and New Mexico.

The land where this story is set was part of Mexico under the Beaubien-Miranda Land Grant of 1841. When Lucien Maxwell married Charles Beaubien's daughter, Luz, and set up his home in Rayado in 1849, the land was in limbo as the American government hashed out slavery issues. The New Mexico Territory was officially formed in 1850, but legal issues, translation of documents, and under-the-table deals created massive confusion even before the gold rush of 1867 caused chaos. Maxwell could hardly keep up with the squatters on his land. When he sold his grant to an English syndicate in 1870, the new owners resolved to remove the dishonest settlers.

The range war that ensued--the Colfax County Land Wars (1873-1888)--caused no end of risk and danger to ranchers like Zeke.

Jesus Gil Abreu is the only historical figure in this story.

Zeke and Millie Pickens as well as Jacob and Eliza Craig and their families exist only on these pages . . . to the best of my knowledge.

Books in the
SANGRE DE CRISTO SERIES

More Precious Than Gold

Stronger Than Mountains

Flowing Like A River (Coming 2018)

Have you read Book 1 in this series?
MORE PRECIOUS THAN GOLD

Prologue
Waco, Texas—February, 1867

Torches bobbed above the crowd gathered around the jailhouse. The flickering light cast unnatural shadows beneath the oaks on the courthouse lawn, animating the underside of the arching boughs. Like hellish fingers they seemed to hold the mob in their grip.

Eliza Gentry slipped her hand into the crook of her father's arm, her breath forming clouds as they hurried through the starless night. At six foot six, Papa's long legs covered a lot of ground, but she managed to keep up—one of the rare advantages, she supposed, of inheriting her height from him.

With the passing of each city block, the sounds of the uproar grew louder and more distinct, punctuated now and again by angry shouts.

"You got no call to hold those men. Turn 'em loose, you carpetbagger, afore we fetch 'em out ourselves!"

"Go on home, Yanks, while you can still leave standing!"

Judging from the ensuing swells of approval, the threats expressed the general sentiment of those gathered, though only a few were brave or foolish enough to speak out, surrounded as they were by cavalry. Most folks in Waco were good church-going people—the type who disapproved of the use of liquor—but this group was drunk on hate.

Torchlight contorted the features of many familiar faces. The grocer and the proprietors of several shops Eliza frequented. The school's headmaster and a handful of older students. Women who attended the fine ladies' teas and Bible studies at Papa's church. Respectable citizens clamoring alongside the commoner residents— barmen and drunks, drifters and prostitutes—people who pretended not to notice one another by daylight. Tonight rage lent them a grotesque similarity that transcended social status.

Papa quickened his pace, and Eliza tightened her grip on his sleeve. She could see the federal soldiers now, standing at rigid attention, rifles at the ready across their chests. As her foot left the hard-packed street, a shadowed figure broke from the mob and lunged for one of the infantrymen who guarded the barred door.

The soldier's eyes widened in surprise. As if by instinct, he took a step backward before determination hardened his jaw.

A shot rang out as he fired into the air, the report echoing in the cold night air.

Eliza flinched.

For the space of a collective gasp, a shocked silence fell over the scene. The only sound was the startled squawk of thousands of blackbirds rudely awakened from their roosting places in the courthouse trees, then the rush of wings as they flew in search of safer havens.

The crowd seemed to erupt just as the birds had. With cries of protest they surged forward, and skittish horses moved to intervene.

Papa dropped Eliza's hand and broke into a run. Diving into the crowd, the swelling human tide carried him forward even before he began to stroke, swimming through a sea of people, pushing aside anyone who stood in his way.

Eliza hitched up her skirts and ran after him, reaching the fringe of the mob just as Papa reached the jailhouse door. Peering over the heads of the men in front of her, she hugged her arms about her chest and shoved her hands beneath them to stop their shaking. She fixed Papa in her gaze as if she could somehow protect him by doing so.

Taking a position between two soldiers, Papa faced the aggressors and raised both hands as if in benediction. "Brothers!" His voice carried easily from years of practice projecting from the pulpit. "Brothers!" he said again, and this time his booming voice seemed to penetrate the frenzy and turn the tide.

Eliza's heart swelled with pride just like it did every Sunday she could remember.

"This is not the way civilized people handle disagreements."

No one could argue with that. After four years of civil war and two bitter years of occupation, Southerners were acutely aware of the consequences of passionate disagreement. But the passion remained. The government's efforts to enforce restoration had only succeeded in forcing the issues beneath the surface. There they festered like an uncleansed wound. Now and again the abscess of old hatreds ruptured into unimaginable atrocities.

"What's he going on about? Trying to stop a lynching?"

"No. Trying to convince them a fair trial is in order." Intent on watching Papa, Eliza had barely noticed the cowboys who pressed in behind her. "They're holding a landowner and a doctor. These people want them released."

Five pairs of eyebrows sprang up. "The prisoner's a doctor? What'd he do?" The tallest—a handsome fellow despite a layer of trail dust—acted as spokesman.

How could she explain the horrible deed in mixed company? She groped for words before deciding to put the crime in terms cattlemen would understand. "He gelded a boy."

The men gulped in collective sympathy before the spokesman said, "Why?"

Why, indeed. Assumptions. Accusations based on prejudice. She had no wish to rehash the details, but the cowboys stared at her in silent expectation. Outsiders, obviously. Everyone in town knew the ugly facts.

Frustrated, Eliza rattled off the essentials, tossing the words over her shoulder without taking her gaze from Papa. "The Freedmen's Bureau sent Lt. Manning to investigate this incident as well as the murder of a former slave. When the local judge refused to try the murder, he realized this case would never receive a fair hearing, so he made the arrests himself pending further instructions."

"Oh." Heads nodded. "The boy's black."

A furious pulse roared in her ears. "What difference does that make?" she snapped. "The boy had a name. Tony. He had hopes—a future—his whole life before him, and now it's. . ." She started to say "gone," but Tony's future was worse than gone. It was empty.

The men stared, uncomprehending. Without comment they sauntered closer to the commotion.

A sick feeling twisted her stomach. The whole sordid situation should have caused her to weep, and before the war it would have.

When had she stopped crying? Three years ago? Four? The year her own dreams died. When, like this boy, she fell victim to a fight she had no part in. Crying changed nothing. Every day was a struggle to reconcile the faith of her childhood to the empty life that had been thrust upon her. Empathy should have helped her pray for the boy, but her prayers hadn't seemed to change much, either. She'd quit asking God for anything about the same time the tears stopped.

Her loss, like Tony's, was pointless. No one could avenge the wrong. Nothing could repair it. This crowd was not interested in truth or justice, only in defending their own prejudice. How could educated men praise God on Sunday and harbor the potential for such evil in their hearts? What was a shade of skin compared with the blackness of men's souls?

"It ain't right!" One stubborn voice rose from the crowd. "You oughtn't to punish a man for sterilizin' vermin!"

Eliza tasted the bitterness in his words, and bile rose in her throat as she confronted the depth of wickedness surrounding her. These people had been her friends, her fellow church members. Had the whole world gone mad, or just her corner of it?

"Go home." Papa's tone was stern—like a judge pronouncing sentence. His eyes flashed with righteous fury, but the fire was quickly quenched by welling tears. "Y'all go on home, now." Eliza heard the brokenness of his heart in the breaking of his voice.

Though disgruntled murmurs made it clear that their hearts had not changed, the crowd began to dissolve grudgingly back into the shadows of the night. As they passed, no one looked at her. No one spoke. One woman, a deacon's wife, spared her a quick glance and the hint of an awkward smile, but she looked down again when her husband gave her arm a yank and glared his disapproval. In a matter of minutes, Eliza stood alone beneath the towering oaks, dark now that the torches were gone. The taste of coal oil smoke lingered on the night air.

In the light that remained by the jailhouse, Papa spoke with the guards.

Eliza did not approach them. It would be inappropriate to eavesdrop on men's business, but in the still night she couldn't help hearing snatches of conversation.

"I appreciate your cooperation." One sergeant spoke on behalf of the federal soldiers.

What he called cooperation most folks were likely to term

sympathizing with the enemy.

Papa tugged at his stiff collar. "They're good people, mostly. This situation's just got them riled up."

Papa didn't like the Yankee occupation any better than anyone else did—and with good reason—but he was determined to obey the governing authorities. To him it was a matter of religious integrity. God was sovereign, and whomever He set over the affairs of men must be obeyed, even if obedience required sacrifice.

Eliza had always found obedience to be something of a sacrifice. When she was a child, she often exercised an independent spirit, and Mama did not hesitated to swat her backside with a switch whenever she got sassy. "Spare the rod; spoil the child," she'd say, and Eliza's strong will ensured that the fruit trees around the parsonage received regular pruning. But Papa believed that all differences could be settled through cooperation and understanding. He preferred to reason with Eliza, patiently listening to her frustrations and explaining why certain rules were necessary. Many times, she'd wished he would just spank her and get it over with, but he insisted that any lasting change must come from the inside—from the heart.

It was surely the same now. No lasting change could be enforced by government troops until the hearts of men were changed and filled with compassion for one another. From the looks of things lately, they had a long way to go.

At last Papa shook hands with the officer in charge and turned to look for her, squinting as his eyes adjusted to the dark. His face was weary, etched with furrows of unspeakable sorrow, but a smile touched his eyes when he saw Eliza.

Eliza smiled back. "You were wonderful. I'm so proud of you."

"We're a good team," he said. He tucked her hand once again into the crook of his arm, warm and safe, and gave it a pat.

They walked home in silence. How many hours had Eliza spent studying Greek and Latin with him in his pleasant library? Yet the two of them seldom needed words of any language to communicate. Eliza reveled in the feel of his arm beneath her hand. Solid. Unshakeable. That was Papa.

ॐ

An oil lamp on the parlor table cast a welcoming glow across the porch of their modest parsonage. When they rushed out at the first cry of alarm, Eliza had not paused even long enough to retract the wick, but now she was glad of it. The cheerful light promised peace inside.

Papa held the door as she entered. The latch gave a reassuring click as the door closed behind them, and Eliza turned to hang her shawl on its hook. Despite whatever happened outside, all was well within.

The expression on Papa's face made her blood run cold. His eyes were fixed on the stair hall behind her. Turning again, she saw a figure emerge from the shadows and recognized the man whose warped and bitter words had sickened her a quarter hour before. He was a good head shorter than she was and had a dull, weaselly look about him. Papa towered over him, but a six-shooter was a great equalizer of angry little men.

"Put your gun down and be on your way. There's nothing here you want." Papa opened the door and stepped aside so as not to bar the man's escape.

"You got that straight, you miser'ble traitor. There ain't nuthin' here I want." The man lurched a bit, as if inebriated, waving his gun around to indicate the parsonage and everything in it before pointing the muzzle again in their direction. "I don't want you, and don't nobody want her!" He sneered at Eliza, his words piercing as surely as any bullet, causing an explosion of painful memories. How could old wounds still cause such anguish?

Eliza had barely time to register the muzzle flash before the revolver's discharge deafened her. The concussion wave hit like an invisible thrust, turning her insides to quivering jelly. She screamed, but could not hear her own voice—only the ringing echo of the pistol blast. By instinct her hand went to her belly, but she felt no pain. She stared at the gunman who stared back at her, eyes wide, then looked down in disbelief at his shaking hand.

His lips moved. "Oh, Lord! I've shot the preacher!"

He threw the gun to the parlor floor as if it were a snake that bit him. Bolting past her, he jumped the steps and disappeared into the night in the time it took Papa to slide slowly down the wall of the parsonage entry, leaving a red streak on the wallpaper behind him.

Eliza snatched her shawl from the hall tree and pressed it to Papa's wounds, cradling his head in her lap. She felt the door creak open, squeezing them against the wall. Stifling a cry she leaned forward to shield him with her body.

It was only a neighbor. "I heard a shot. Do you . . . oh, Lord! I'll get help." His words seemed to come from a great distance.

An eternity passed before he returned with a doctor in tow, but it was a wonder he found a physician at all, with one in jail and another in hiding as an accomplice. Who knew where the sympathies of the town's other physicians lay? Eliza didn't ask, and she didn't care at that point. Stanching the flow of blood was of paramount importance.

When it seemed safe to lift the bloody compresses, the doctor studied Papa's wounds, his face grave. "The bullet passed through just below the shoulder. It's a wonder it missed the bone."

Or his heart.

"There's still a risk of infection, though. Help me get him upstairs."

Between the three of them and Papa's own feeble efforts, they managed to half carry the patient to his room. Papa groaned considerably as they settled him on his bed, though they made every effort to handle him gently. Eliza fumbled for a match and struck a light while the men pulled off Papa's boots.

The doctor rummaged in his bag. When Eliza saw that he withdrew a vial of laudanum, she nodded to the neighbor. "Thank you for your help. He should rest easier soon."

With promises to check in on them in the morning, the man left.

Eliza's relief was short lived, though. Papa waved the bottle away. Stubborn man. The doctor shrugged and pulled out another vial.

The tang of alcohol burned her nose as liberal amounts splashed over the entry and exit wounds, sterilizing them.

Papa sucked in a sharp breath and moaned. A fine sweat broke out along his upper lip and forehead, and his face turned pale in the lamplight. His eyelids fluttered and drifted shut, and his weight sagged against her.

Eliza looked away, biting her lip, but kept her arms firm about his shoulders, holding him upright while the doctor packed his wounds with bandages and wrapped his ribs in several yards of rolled muslin.

At last he dropped his scissors into the black satchel that lay open on the lamp table. "He should rest more comfortably now, but he'll be weak from the loss of blood," he said, snapping the bag shut. "It's been a long night." He stretched before taking up the medical bag. "I'm going home."

Eliza eased Papa back against the pillows. Was that it then? Was that all that could be done?

Whatever his political leanings, the doctor gave her hand a compassionate pat. "Watch him through the night. I'll be back tomorrow."

Eliza walked with him as far as the door of the bed chamber.

"Stay with him. I'll see myself out."

She heard his weary steps on the stair treads then a creak as the front door opened and closed again. Holding her breath, Eliza listened for the comforting rattle of the latch, but it never came. Pressed small against the door jamb, she listened to the silence as her blood rushed loud in her ears. Every imagined whisper reminded her that the gunman was still at large, still bigoted, still angry—him and a host of others, and now there was no man to protect her. A cold hand of fear lay heavy between her shoulder blades, urging her to bolt down the dark staircase and secure the lock, but a greater fear froze her where she stood.

She mentally cataloged all the small sounds in the shadows below, hardly daring to breathe, then crept to a straight-backed chair beside the bedstead and sank into it. A twist of the lamp stem lowered the wick to a dim glow. With as much composure as she could muster, Eliza watched Papa's chest rise and fall steadily. Solid. Unshakeable.

Her mind rambled as she settled in for the long night watch—back to her coming-out party ten years ago. Papa thought such things were silly, but Mama was the daughter of local aristocrats, and Eliza longed for once not to feel different from the other girls—the ones she towered over, the ones whose papas preached no controversial sermons. And so at sixteen she had her introduction into polite society, though afterwards that society politely ignored her for the most part. Her friends were courted and married in short order, but no one spoke for her.

Until Grayson, a young seminarian who came to apprentice with Papa. The three of them studied scripture together; then the two of them studied alone, first in the pleasant parlor and then on long walks beside the Brazos River. When war broke out between the states, Grayson went with all the other young men. He left Eliza with such sweet words, telling her he cherished their time together—cherished her—and begged her to wait for his return. "Come magnify the Lord with me, and let us exalt His name together." No proposal could have pleased her more. But Grayson never came home. Part of Eliza died, as well, that sad Christmas when she received his commander's letter. She devoted herself to relief work with Mama, burying her pain in the solace of service.

Mama. How she missed her! She was Papa's helpmate in every way, and Eliza found comfort in assisting as she ministered to the sick, both slave and free. But Mama was not like Papa and Eliza. She was tiny and fragile. In the last year of the war, worn and thin from hard work and deprivation, she caught a fever from one of the children and quickly succumbed. Union troops blockaded the harbors, blocking the simple medicines that could have saved her.

Eliza exhaled a ragged breath. The grief of all she'd lost threatened to choke her. *Not Papa, too.* He was all she had left. She pressed a handkerchief to her lips.

Papa stirred slightly, and Eliza jumped to her feet. She grabbed a cloth from the edge of the basin and poured cool water from the pitcher to dampen it, wringing it out before she pressed the compress gently to his brow.

His eyes flickered open. He stared up at her for a moment before he seemed to realize where he was and remember how he came to be there. "Think I'll live?"

"Yes! Oh, yes, you must." Eliza's most desperate hope took the form of an answer before she noticed the smile lines tugging at the corners of his mouth.

He patted her arm, still trying to take care of her even as she cared for him. "There's a letter on the bureau." He gestured weakly.

"Don't worry with it now, Papa. You can read it later."

"I've read it," he said, his voice thin and strained. "I want you to read it."

Eliza fetched the correspondence. Even in the dim light she recognized her aunt's familiar handwriting. She hesitated, but Papa urged her on with a nod. Resuming her seat beside the bed, she pulled the scented paper from the envelope and began to read.

Dear Rutherford, dear Eliza,

I know I need not tell you of our difficulties in the wake of the war. When Earl did not return with his regiment, Rufus was lost in grief. I find that I can no longer bear these familiar surroundings where every room and every scene remind me of our great loss.

After much searching of our souls, Rufus and I feel our best chance to begin a new life lies in a new place. They've discovered gold in New Mexico territory, and we aim to go there. Rufus has no prospects for mining, but the men who do will need food and clothing, lumber and supplies. We will close our store here and set up shop north of Ft. Union and Cimarron.

You have faced losses of your own—first Eliza's intended and then my sister—and I know the carpetbaggers are a burden to you there. Julia misses her brother dearly. She would welcome a cousin, and I'm sure the territory could use a man of God. Won't you consider joining us as soon as you may?

Warmest regards, Charlotte

Eliza dropped the letter into her lap. "Papa, you must be joking. You're in no condition to travel. We have no money, and your people need you. Tonight proved that. They need godly men to lead them back to peace."

Papa's eyes had drifted shut while she read. "Not safe."

Eliza bent close to hear his voice. The lingering scents of gunpowder, alcohol, and blood confirmed his words. "When have you ever cared for your safety? God holds you in the palm of His hand."

"I don't care for my safety. I care for yours."

He would leave his ministry to protect her? She could not ask such a sacrifice. "He holds me, too. Our work is here."

"My work is here, but there is no future here for you."

What was he suggesting? "My future is with you."

"No, Eliza. I am not afraid, but God showed me tonight how fleeting my life is. He could require it of me at any moment, and then who would care for you?" She drew breath to object, but he put up a hand to stay her. "You need a husband, Eliza, and a home of your own. It's God's plan."

"Not always. Look at Anna, the prophetess who saw Christ. She served God in the temple."

". . . after her young husband died."

Eliza turned her face and stared out the window toward the street. She could not tell if the wavy glass or welling tears distorted her reflection in the dark panes. "I've had my love."

She folded the letter and slid it into the envelope once more, then laid it back on the bureau.

Papa watched her return with sadness in his eyes. Sadness was often in his eyes these days, but he always smiled when Eliza smiled at him, as she did now.

She bent to kiss his cheek.

"'Entreat me not to leave you,'" she said and turned out the light.

Chapter 1—February 1870

"Things are looking up." Papa wiped his lips and pushed his chair back.

Eliza scowled as she reached for his plate. "How can you say that?" Receiving no immediate answer, she headed for the warming kitchen, returning directly with pie and coffee. It was good to serve coffee again instead of the bitter chicory they'd made do with for years, and there was sugar now for pie, but those improvements were hardly newsworthy.

Papa picked up his newspaper, scanning the headlines as she set a cup before him. "Business is good with the cattle drives coming through town. The new suspension bridge is 'a bridge into our future' they say." He summarized the editor's opinion before adding his own. "Folks have begun to forget the war and set the past behind them."

"You wouldn't know it to look at your congregation." She smirked, hands on her hips. "When that federal officer came for Easter services, no one would sit within three pews of him."

Papa waved off the incident. "That was last year. The animosities can't last forever. Now that the amendments have passed, Texas will be welcomed into the union again, like all the other states."

He was obviously working up to something—trying to put a bright face on a situation they both knew was far from over. Eliza waited.

Papa tested his coffee and signaled for sugar. "I got another letter from Charlotte."

So that was it. He'd been trying to sweeten her up.

"Mmm?" was the most enthusiastic response she could muster. Every time the subject came up, she hoped it would be the last she heard of it.

Her cool response didn't daunt him. "It's old news by now— mail's slow from the frontier—but she says they're happy in Elizabethtown. Julia is married." Papa paused for her reaction, but she refused to exhibit one. He plunged on with optimism. "Their store is a great success. She asks again if we will come."

His polite prodding left a sour taste in her mouth, since she knew he had no intention of going himself. Eliza squared her chin. Her height wasn't the only thing she'd inherited from her father. She could be stubborn, too. "Papa, we've discussed this before. I am happy with you. Things are safer now. Besides, there's no way to get there from here." She'd memorized a list of objections for these not infrequent occasions and began to tick each one off on her fingers. "The cattle drives come through Waco because the railroads don't, and those trails all head north. The stage routes to California run too far south, and they're too expensive anyway. We don't own a wagon, so unless you plan for us to go on horseback . . ." She paused only when she had to draw breath.

Papa took advantage of the gap. "I talked to the Major yesterday." He plopped two cubes into his cup as he dropped this most recent bit of information. He'd cooperated with the officer in charge of federal forces garrisoned in Waco since the riot three years before, but his tone told her this conversation was different.

Eliza froze with the sugar bowl in her hand.

"Some of the troops are transferring to Fort Union in New Mexico territory. A few of the officers are taking their families. It would be an appropriate travel arrangement for a lady, and you'd be protected." He stirred his drink with casual deliberation.

Eliza scrunched up her face and tried to look implacable. She couldn't help it.

"Don't look at me like that, young lady." For all her stubbornness, Papa had been practicing recalcitrance longer. "There's money enough for a stage from Fort Union to Cimarron, and I can write Uncle Rufus to meet you there. Charlotte says he makes the trip once a month for supplies." He tapped his spoon twice against the rim of the cup and rested it on the saucer as he rested his argument.

Eliza set down the sugar bowl with enough force to jar the lid. "Why must I go if you will not?"

"Because this is the time to travel—after the snows and before the heat. Perhaps I will join you, when the situation here is resolved, but that could be next year or even longer." His expression became tender. "You're twenty-eight, my dear. Time is passing, and your opportunities are passing with it. There are few men of your age left here after the war." Kindness kept him from saying that those who returned whole had married others.

"I won't be any different there than here. I'll still be nearly six feet tall. Men seem to find that intimidating for some reason." She winked. She cared for Papa too much to mention that his outspoken political views were likely more to blame for the wide berth most folks gave her.

"It is entirely my fault, my dear."

Eliza hoped he referred to his own towering height—something that couldn't be construed as anyone's fault but God's. She doggedly continued to play the game, determined to protect him from guilt. "How could I blame you? You cannot change your frame."

"Not that."

Eliza caught her breath and prepared to argue, but his next comment caught her off guard.

"It was the Greek."

"I beg your pardon?"

"It was the Greek. Women who speak three languages are considered formidable intellects. I should have stopped with Latin." He tipped his cup in mock salute then winked back, and she laughed in spite of herself. "So you'll go?"

She acknowledged defeat with a sigh. "I will obey your wishes."

Papa smiled over the rim of his cup, but when he put it down his face was sober. "Now that that's settled, why do you not want to go?"

Had he not heard her at all these three years? "We've been over and over my reasons."

"We've been over and over your list of objections. I would like to understand your true reasons." His eyes were soft, open to see things from her perspective.

"You're all I've got left." . . . in more ways than he knew, but she couldn't tell him that. Papa's faith seemed as solid and unshakeable as he was. She could not bear to disappoint him.

"The whole truth, please, Eliza."

How could he see through her like that? Like she was glass. Most days, nothing was clear to her anymore. Unshed tears choked her. No words came. Eliza shrugged, her hands flopping lamely by her sides.

And then Papa was there, embracing her as if she were a small child—something she hadn't been in a very long time. He stroked her hair with strong hands. "I ask why, too, sometimes." His deep voice rumbled through her.

"It's more than that." Her voice emerged as a hoarse whisper.

He waited as she struggled to find words.

"I know there's a reason. There has to be or 'we are of all men most miserable.'" She searched his face for signs of understanding. "But I was so sure I knew God's will for me. I've studied His Word—in three languages, no less. I prayed. I waited and worked while I waited. All I ever wanted was to serve God with my life. I thought He'd sent the answer to my prayers." Sharp tones of resentment edged into her voice, but she didn't care.

"And it feels unfair."

She nodded. "But more even than that. If serving the church and marrying a godly man isn't in God's will for me, then what is? And if a future with you and Mama and Grayson wasn't His answer after all my praying, how can I know what to do with my life?" A sob shuddered like an echo in her chest though the well of tears had long since run dry. "I don't know what to do. There's no light for my path, Papa. It's all just dark, and when I pray there are no answers."

Papa was silent. No glib advice, at least. Her grief was deep, her faith broken beyond patching. "Eliza, will you trust me?"

A sigh tore through her. "As I told you, Papa, you're all I've got left."

He gripped her hands. "I still want you to go."

As his words stabbed at her hopes, she marveled that they found anything left still capable of feeling pain. But they did. How could he ask this? She stared at him, unbelieving.

Papa caressed her cheek. "Sometimes, Eliza, God gives us a light for our path. Sometimes only a lamp for our feet. I do not know His path for you, but I feel strongly that this is the next right step." He paused, searching her eyes, before he spoke again. "I would see you happy. Will you trust me?"

Her voice was hollow as she answered. "I will obey your wishes."

Made in the USA
Columbia, SC
13 September 2021

44706752R00130